THE BIG TIDE CHRONICLES III

Mangrove Martini

by Jerry Buckley

This book is dedicated to
E. H. Joyce.
My grandfather,
who instilled a love of reading
and story-telling,

&

J. G. Buckley, Sr.
My father, who taught me to
measure twice and cut once.

PROLOGUE

During a six-month period in 2024 the world changed. An aquatic blitzkrieg, slowly building over decades, unleashed itself. From the time of the Industrial Revolution in the mid-19th century, on average, sea level had risen a little over a tenth of an inch each year or about one foot per century. Throughout the 20th century the increasing glacier melt in the Arctic, Antarctic, and Greenland hastened that rise.

The melting ice sheets had not gone unnoticed, at least in the scientific community. As the respected publication "Scientific American" pointed out in its February 2019 issue "the enormous ice sheets of the planet hold more than 200-feet of sea level rise; a small change to them can create big changes to our coastal areas."

In the late 1990s dramatic changes to the Jakobshavn Glacier in Greenland provided a hint of what was to come. Increased water temperatures dismantled the ice shelf in front of the glacier, causing Jakobshavn to advance more rapidly, while at the same time thinning. Through the 2000s this became one of the largest contributors to sea level rise. In 2002 the Larsen B Ice Shelf in the Antarctic disintegrated in five weeks. This event did not immediately raise sea level, but it allowed the ice sheet on land behind it to flow faster to the ocean.

The tipping point was reached in the summer of 2024 when the ice shelf protecting the immense Thwaites Glacier Basin in Antarctica melted. The resulting rapid rise in sea level affected the entire planet with islands and coastal areas hit hardest. This became known as the Trans-antarctic Thwaites Stochastic Event. In the Florida Keys it was known simply as THE BIG TIDE.

The Conch Republic
post-Big Tide

Military
Maintenance
Bridge

Breakwater
North
Perimeter Road

The Breakwater

EDGERS KEY

Fly Navy

Boca Chica
Naval Base

NEW TOWN

Breakwater
Eastern
Maintenance
Bridge

Martello Water Taxi

First St.

Airport

Southern
Perimeter Lock

New
Airport Road

The East
Martello Tower

The Conch Republic
pre-Big Tide,
insert right

CHRONICLE III
MANGROVE MARTINI
CHAPTER 1

The weather never cooperates in September. Those Spanish galleons strewn on the sea floor off the coast of Florida are a testament to that well-worn adage. Finn and Nick labored in thick *humidity on Toby Ireland's houseboat, the Emerald Isle. It was late* September, in the Conch Republic. Summer hung on like a stubborn heat rash. The two men could only spend a few more hours searching, before turning their attention to the Cat 4 hurricane that was due to arrive within days in the Southernmost enclave of misfits. Forecasters predicted a direct hit from the storm within the next seventy-two hours.

Finn was aggravated. This was the third time he and Nick had searched Toby's houseboat since his death in June at the hands of a mad man. Finn was convinced that Toby hid a certain amount of treasure from the Atocha, a gift from Mel Fisher, somewhere on the Emerald Isle.

Much to his chagrin, he had not yet located it.

"Feel how thick the air is?" he asked Nick.

"Yeah, worse than usual."

"This storm is going to be a bad one, the air is nearly saturated, well before this thing is supposed to get here."

"What else do we need to do at the mansion?" Nick said, referring to their shared digs in the abandoned, submerged, northwest end of Big Pine Key.

"I think we're good."

"Are you two about ready for some lunch?" the familiar voice of Dr. Kate Sullivan said from the finger pier to which the houseboat was moored.

She was accompanied by her grad student, Tara O'Hara. They each carried a picnic basket full of assorted sandwiches, homemade coleslaw, and some green tea.

"What's the latest on the storm?" Finn asked as he stopped his inspection of the forward hold.

"We're still in the cone of death," Tara said cheerily.

"It's holding steady, looks to hit us four days from now," Kate said.

"Still haven't found it?" Tara asked.

Finn shook his head, not willing to give up yet, "I'm missing something. Obviously. I'm open to suggestions, but right now, we better eat and get things buttoned up here. Steve Johnson, Toby's neighbor on the boat over there with the "Go Razorbacks" pennant on it will keep an eye on it through the storm."

The wait leading up to a bad storm could work on your nerves. Even in the days before the Big Tide when you could evacuate, the dire consequences of the wrong decision weighed heavy on locals and tourists alike. Since the Big Tide, the only way to access the Conch Republic was by air or by sea via the ferries that regularly ran between Key West and the mainland.

"What's this one's name?" Nick asked as he helped Tara spread the picnic food out on the deck beneath a temporary tarp sunshade Finn rigged up for the work on the Emerald Isle.

"Fiona," Kate answered.

"Uh oh," Finn said, "When they end in an 'A,' they always end up really whacking us. Donna, Wilma, Irma."

"So, tell us what you think is the problem about not finding the treasure?" Kate said to change the subject.

"I'm an idiot, most likely," Finn said with a straight face.

"Stop it," Kate said.

"He's just pissed because he can't figure it out," Nick said.

"Hasn't figured it out yet, would be more accurate," Finn shot back.

"Have you tried the weird, spooky, free association thing you do?" Tara asked.

"Nothing, I tried," Finn answered as he took a bite of a grouper sandwich.

"What are your plans for this storm?" Finn asked the women.

"We're staying with Rick and Sher," she said referring to their friends who ran an inn located in Old Town. By the way Finn, I need you to look at a house I've found. We can do it after the storm, but I want your thoughts on it before I buy it. Mote Marine was happy to know I'd decided to live here full time and they've given me a small bonus to help with the move. At some point I'll have to go to the mainland but not for a couple more months. And this place has plenty of room for my grad assistant too. We still have a couple of years' worth of work to do down here."

"In fact," Tara said, "We'll be collecting data through the storm as best we can."

"I guess this is going to put a damper on the Bartender's Convention," Nick said. "I was looking forward to all the sample drink concoctions that the sponsors will provide."

"Did you hear they have a bottle of the most expensive Irish Whiskey ever made on display. It's called the Emerald Isle Collection and it's made by the Craft Irish Whiskey Company," Tara said.

"Really?" Nick answered.

"Yeah, one bottle of this stuff, it's a triple distilled, single malt whiskey went for two million dollars several years ago."

"Well, that's interesting," Finn said with an odd look on his face. "I mean the Emerald Isle collection. Toby's houseboat, the Emerald Isle. I wonder if this is a case of 'spooky action at a distance' or have I read too many Phillip K. Dick books lately. Man, this humidity must be affecting me."

"Well, there's going to be some spooky action right here, up close and personal in four days," Nick said.

"What are you two going to do?"

"Kate, we were discussing that when you arrived with lunch, which is delicious, thank you," Finn said.

"Are the bed races still on for this afternoon?" Nick asked.

"Last I heard, yes," Tara answered.

"To answer your question, we're playing it by ear. Norm always needs a couple extra hands when a storm like this is coming at us.

We don't have to be out there, the Mansion will weather whatever this thing has, we left it buttoned up for the worst when we came to town yesterday. We're staying at Rick and Sher's place ourselves."

"Sher has pressed us into helping the Bees, which we are glad to do anyway," Kate said.

The Conch Bees or CBees, as they were known on the island, were a volunteer group that helped first responders with chores like manning the "hot line" at the Emergency Ops Center or going door to door to warn people of possible flooding. Rick and Sher coordinated the group from their Bed and Breakfast Inn on Whitehead Street.

"I think this will be our worst one since the Big Tide," Finn said.

"Two million bucks for a bottle of booze," Nick said shaking his head.

"Well after all, it was triple distilled," Finn said with a passable Irish accent.

The pre-storm drill was already underway at the small marina where Toby's houseboat was berthed. The Margaritaville Marina was a legacy of Buffet, who along with others, financed and helped build a marina for local musicians and artists. Fifty houseboats of various sizes, colors, and reputations were berthed at the marina located at one end of Key West Bight.

Terry Graham, the marina operator strode by and waved as he walked to the far end of the central pier. Several men carried sheets of plywood to board up the marina office. The hardened shoreline around Key West reduced the potential for storm surge flooding, but rain and wind held the potential to cause damage if not mitigated.

"We can help with whatever needs to be done here," Kate said.

"Offer accepted. As soon as we finish eating, we'll get to it. I'm obviously not going to find Toby's treasure today," Finn said with mock indignation.

"I think the Sandbox has an entrant in the bed race," Nick said.

"Is Angel participating?" Kate asked.

"No, they disqualified him because he isn't a bartender, but they've got a pretty solid crew without him," Nick said.

"Sooey," rippled through the air as a stout man approached the Emerald Isle. He was wearing an Arkansas Razorback jersey and carried several bags of groceries.

"Finn, Nick, how goes it?"

"Good Steve, how 'bout you?" Finn answered.

"Hangin' in there," he told them as he boarded the houseboat next to the Emerald Isle.

"We are getting ready to batten down the hatches here. Steve, if anything comes up call me or Nick and we'll get over here ASAP. We'll most likely stay in town through the storm."

"This looks to be a bad one," Steve said. "Terry is coordinating the marina prep. Boats too. We're all pitching in, it's the Margaritaville Marina way. By the way, did y'all get rid of all those things from Monkey Island?"

"Yes," Finn said succinctly not wanting to talk too much about it.

"I better get these groceries put up, catch y'all later."

"See ya," Finn said with a wave.

"We better get busy if we're going to make the Bed Races," Nick said.

CHAPTER 2

A man checked into his suite at one of the upscale establishments in Old Town. He walked out on the second-story balcony to view Mallory Square and the outer mole where two cruise ships were berthed. He lit a Dunhill cigarette and tried to collect his thoughts.

The early afternoon sunlight had an intangible quality to it. It reminded the man of Provence, in the south of France. The expatriate Brit watched the curling tendrils of smoke from his cigarette play in the cascade of sunlight that streamed down onto the balcony.

He was nervous. This hurricane was damn inconvenient with its timing. The entire plan was a rush job, in his estimation. Opportunities to make a dent in the world of international art forgery did not come along often. Interpol had been lucky and picked up some low-level soldiers in one of the Eurogangs. One of them was overheard discussing a major museum heist that occurred several months earlier. It was part of a series of art thefts that occurred across Europe in the past year. The conversation revealed that the fence responsible for moving the art work was in Key West.

He had been dispatched to lure the fence out and if possible, retrieve the paintings that had been stolen. He glanced at the rectangular object wrapped in sturdy construction paper and bound with heavy duty twine. It was a forgery of one of the stolen painting, a lesser known, early work by American artist Edward Hopper.

The man responsible for the fake was an accomplished painter who from time to time worked with Interpol to stymy the thriving criminal activity of art forgery and illegal acquisitions of stolen art. His specialty was twentieth century American artists such as Hopper. His knowledge was encyclopedic, and his skill was exceptional.

His attention to detail separated him from lesser competitors. Details that derailed many would-be forgers, details like using pigments not discovered until after a painter's death that identified the painting as a fake. Details such as maintaining the exact ratios of different components in a pigment mix used by a certain artist. The list of pitfalls that would reveal a piece as a fake was lengthy, but the man was good. The Brit hoped he would be good enough to fool the fence. An expert in his own right.

The problem was that the real painting and the real thief were unaccounted for, he could be in Key West right now. The man took a deep drag off the cigarette, then slowly exhaled it. He didn't like hastily thrown together operations such as this one. His superiors, pummeled by political pressure, were forced to act. The result, a poorly organized effort that put his life in danger.

He had informed the local constabulary that he was here and, the nature of his visit. The acting chief seemed very capable. In fact, the man offered him what support he could. They were scheduled to meet briefly in the morning. He did not look forward to telling this man the details of a scheme he himself thought was sadly lacking.

This ceaseless sun was another thing. God, to be in England on a blustery, rainy day. How did these, what did they call themselves, Conchs, stand it. He walked back into the air-conditioned coolness of his suite, shut the faux French grille door, and drew the curtains behind him.

He turned on the flat screen, wall-mounted hi-def TV, checked the menu, and brought up the Weather Channel. This was not his first trip to the Caribbean, and he knew the storm headed toward Key West could pose significant problems for not only his operation but life and limb as well.

Weather was big business in America, or so he thought. His Anglican sensibilities were offended by the non-stop hype of threatening weather. Although he grudgingly admitted that the improved ability to predict and track tornados and hurricanes saved lives, he did not like the sensationalized coverage of those events. Life-altering events that were pushed aside and forgotten as quickly as they occurred by the media. A group driven by what kind of ratings would the "Next Big One" generate.

He tried to relax; it was not his best characteristic. He preferred action to sitting around. An enthusiastic weatherman, on the telly, listed the many ill effects of sustained 130-mph winds. It was hard to ignore that his temporary home was square in the center of the "cone of death," as these Americans called it.

The policeman he met earlier, Lieutenant James, seemed like a competent chap. He would meet with him again tomorrow morning. The focus of the operation was not the stolen painting, but rather the fence, and the man the fence worked with most consistently. A man that Interpol had chased for several years and one that was at the hub of the illegal art trade worldwide. A multi-billion dollar a year enterprise.

The extent of forgery in the art community was shocking, and its economic effects were disastrous. One of the ironic responses to the numerous art thefts was for reputable museums such as the Prado in Spain, the Rijksmuseum in Amsterdam, and even the Louvre to commission fakes of well-known works of art to display while keeping the originals in a vault.

He lit another cigarette as he smugly wondered how many fakes were in the Tate Gallery in London. "Surely less than the bloody French place with the pyramid outside," he thought.

CHAPTER 3

Bed races were a crowd favorite in Key West. The southernmost answer to the Soap Box Derby. Beds, mounted on wheels, were pushed by a four-man team of runners and one coxswain who remained firmly on the bed, along the streets of Old Town. Teams representing various bars and eateries vied for the prize at this year's Bartender's Convention.

Nick and Tara found Angel among the spectators lining Olivia Street near the start line. The week was comparatively subdued when measured against the assault on the boundaries of good taste that was Fantasy Fest. The naked truth is that public nudity should come with a disclaimer that prepares the unsuspecting eyewitness for the effects of gravity on the bare revelers. Sag and gag, as some locals refer to it.

The team from the Sandbox was going over last-minute strategies prior to the start of their heat. Their opponents in this prelim race were from the venerable Bottle Cap, a long-time locals' bar preferred by professional drinkers. The kind of place that even if everybody does know your name, they aren't going to say it out of respect for the solitary imbiber that simply wants to drink alone. As George Thorogood reminds us, when "I drink alone, I prefer to be by myself."

The mood was festive despite the killer storm four days away. It was always difficult to judge exactly what state of consciousness the participants might be experiencing. The spectators too, for that matter.

"Can the Sandbox team win this one?" Nick asked.

"If Ricky hasn't had too many Bloody Mary's and Sandy's on her meds, then yeah, we should take it."

"Is Sandy the girl on the bed?" Tara wanted to know.

"She weighs the least, so she got the sitter's job."

"I remember a couple of years ago, a sitter got slung off the bed into a banyan tree."

"Thrills and spills, man," Angel answered.

"Have you seen the most expensive bottle of Irish whiskey in the world?"

"Not yet, I heard they've got some private security around it."

"It looks like the race is starting," Tara announced.

A curvaceous young woman, ala the Fast and the Furious flicks, shimmied out to the middle of the street. She waved a brightly colored scarf to signal "on your mark" followed by the dramatic drop of the scarf to start the race.

The team from the Bottle Cap jumped out to a quick lead, nearly knocking down the scarf dropper. Ironically, twenty yards into the race and in the lead, one of the bed's attached coaster wheels jammed on a discarded pop top and abruptly stopped almost dislodging the sitter as the other wheels swung the bed around in a tight circle. The crew from the Sand Box lumbered by the disabled bed, steadily picking up speed as they rounded the corner and out of sight.

The Bottle Cap team worked like a pit crew from the Willie Nelson racing team. They finally dislodged the pop top and unjammed the wheel. They gamely started rolling again as the crowd cheered encouragement.

Two more beds were rolled to the start line for the next heat. One team represented La Te Da, with a crew of divas led by Nick's friend and fellow rugby player Marilyn. The six-foot-three inch drag queen was well accessorized for the race with Nike running shoes, a white sailor's suit, and fuchsia fingernail polish. He waved when he saw Nick but continued to coordinate the team, composed of The Divine Ms. M, Ellen, RuPaul, and himself as runners, with Cher taking the position of sitter.

"They look pretty brawny," Tara said.

"Well, Marilyn is a rugby mate," Nick said, then added, "I think Ellen was a Golden Gloves champ when he was young, and RuPaul was on the Jamaican track team years ago before he came to the Conch Republic. So, yeah, they got some athletes."

"They don't have to spend so much on bouncers either," Angel quipped.

"Who are the other team?"

"Tara, I think they're from Shanna Key," Angel replied.

In contrast to the bed festooned with purple satin sheets and pink ribbons on the bedsteads, the Irish bar's bed was bedecked with huge four-leaf clovers and Kelly-Green sheets and pillows.

Some of the Irish carpenters in town doubled as bar tenders at night. Shanna Key had a stout compliment of lads from across the Irish Republic that slung suds in the evening hours. They looked ready to go as they each finished off a pre-race glass of Arthur Guinness.

"This one should be competitive, by the looks of things," Nick said.

The starter again sashayed to the middle of the street and conversation died. Her a-size-too-small party dress received whistles from the La Te Da crew and proved to be a slight advantage for the drag queens. The Irish, somewhat distracted by the figure in the skimpy dress, got off to a slow start as Marilyn and the girls surged ahead as the scarf floated to the pavement.

"Only in Key West," Tara said.

Two more teams prepared for the next heat. The pre-storm humidity would have wrung perspiration from a corpse. Fashion, in the Conch Republic, was always about how to stay cool but keep enough of your body covered to stay out of jail. The geriatric thong wearers usually waited for the insanity of Fantasy Fest to unleash themselves. The abundance of free booze coupled with cloying heat led to creative modes of fashion not for those easily offended by semi-nudity.

Angel's height advantage paid off as he admired several coeds dressed for the heat. The crowd constantly turned over as some moved on to other stations along the course and others took their place as different teams lined up for their race.

"Why don't we go over to the home stretch and watch from there," Nick said.

"If you can tear yourself away from the fashion show, Angel," Tara said with a grin.

They slowly sidled their way through the thickest part of the crowd until they reached the outer fringe. They started to cross the intersection when on the far side of the street four men jostled their way past a knot of people leaving a lot of cursing in their wake. Nick watched them as they moved rapidly down the street. He thought they looked like Euro-toughs and wondered what they were doing in town.

"Ever see those guys before?"

"No, not that I recall, Nick but I don't think they're here for the bed races."

"Or the fashion," Tara added picking up the same vibes as Nick.

CHAPTER 4

The mood was somber as Finn, Kate, Rick, and Sharon, watched the latest update on Hurricane Fiona. The storm would approach from the south, skirting the west coast of Cuba before crossing through the Conch Republic on her way into the Gulf of Mexico.

"At least it's not a voodoo army or genetically engineered hybrids. It's a hurricane, we've seen them before," Rick said to lighten the conversation.

"When Padraig Kennedy hardened the shoreline and built the locks, causeways, and bridges we have today, he also added some storm mitigation features," Finn told them.

"He must have anticipated the increase in hurricanes and their strength."

"He did, Kate. He is that one-in-a-million guy who despite a military career, maintained his individualism and creativity. If not, there would be no Conch Republic. The Big Tide would have taken care of that," Finn answered.

"I saw him the other day at Fausto's," Sher remarked.

"I think Norm is recruiting him to help out at the Emergency Ops Center when the storm gets closer."

"I'm sure they will bring George Kenny in on this too," Rick said referring to the current commander of Naval Air Base, Key West. "There's another guy you wouldn't think would get to that rank."

"You're right about that. Kenny is the Pentagon's worst nightmare; a free thinker with a lot of brass, some below the waist."

"You get the feeling that Naval Air Station Key West is not on the aspiring admirals' list of stops on their way up the command ladder," Rick said.

"I imagine some would see this command as a detour or worse, a dead end," Finn said, "But we've been lucky to have had nonconformists like Padraig and George Kenny who recognize the symbiotic relationship between the naval air station and the Conch Republic."

"Especially since the Big Tide," Rick said, "I hate to think how it would be if we had to deal with some hard-ass, by the book, pinhead."

"It would make life a lot harder for Norm," Kate said.

"When do you want to start boarding up?" Finn asked.

"I thought we'd do that tomorrow," Rick answered, then he added, "I've put new hurricane shutters on the first and second floor windows, so we shouldn't have as much boarding up to do.

"Kate and I are going shopping in a bit before everything is picked clean," Sher told them.

"We keep a good supply of necessities for storms like this one, but you always need some last-minute items," Rick added, "Finn I was hoping you would help me take a look at the roof. See if there are any spots we need to reinforce."

"Sure. I've got to meet with Norm and some guy from Interpol tomorrow at nine o'clock in the morning, but other than that I'm good to help you with whatever needs to be done."

"Interpol?"

"Yeah, something about a stolen painting."

"No kidding?" Kate said.

"Have we become a hub of stolen art trafficking?" Sher asked.

"I'll know more after the meeting," Finn said in a tone that discouraged further questions.

"We need to get going," Kate said, "Sher, I need to go by El Patio and get a few things, if that's OK?"

"No problem," Sher answered.

"We are going to look over the storm system specs for Norm while you two are shopping," Finn said.

"I didn't realize you were qualified ..." Kate said and paused.

"Oh, we're not," Rick answered, "Think of us as a poor man's hydraulic engineers. We're just identifying the areas that will receive the worst of the storm surge and wind. Then we will ground truth things and evaluate whether additional strengthening is needed."

Finn added, "When Padraig built the original hardened shoreline to neutralize the Big Tide, he designed it to be adjustable for added storm protection. He also realized that hurricanes would probably be worse after the Big Tide so he built much of the array with the capability of adding internal extensions that could be raised or lowered as needed."

"Once again faced with leaving you two unsupervised we will just trust to blind luck that you won't hurt yourselves," Sher said with a grin as they departed.

"You see the trust and confidence that marriage builds," Rick replied with a sad-eyed cocker spaniel look.

"Heartwarming," Finn deadpanned.

Rick inserted a flash drive into his laptop that was connected to the hi-def television monitor in the sunroom. A plan-view map of Key West appeared on the screen. Rick selected a file from the menu and several segments of drone produced video appeared. They began the tedious task of examining the structures for faults or weaknesses that might be visible on the drone footage. A crew of engineers from the city's public works department was working on the problem also, but Norm wanted Finn and Rick to act as a backup. He trusted their skills when it came to "attention to detail."

"Let's start on the segments facing to the southeast from the West Martello around to Key West bight. They will probably catch the brunt of the tidal surge," Finn said.

"Yeah, that makes sense."

"I think the cruise ships are heading out tonight, so at least we won't have to worry about one of them getting loose."

"Can't you picture that, a cruise ship floating down Duval Street."

"I'd rather not."

"Do you think this will be worse than Irma?"

"Maybe, but we are better prepared than we were for Irma."

They scrutinized the segments of breakwater for any defects or weathering that might have occurred since the last storm. Any spots that were flagged from the video examination would be ground truth and repaired if needed.

"So, my friend, what's the scoop with you and Kate?"

Finn responded with a thumbs up but remained silent.

"Sher tells me she's buying a house down here."

Again, Finn gave a thumbs up."

"Okay, okay," Rick said with a smile, "I'll change the subject, how's the hunt for Toby's treasure?"

Finn quickly turned the thumbs up into an index finger barrel and a thumb for a trigger and pointed it at Rick and said, "Bang."

"That bad?"

"Something came up earlier today that gave me a different perspective on it," Finn said.

"Oh yeah, how so?"

"Well, I was convinced that the Emerald Isle was the key. But, maybe, it's another Emerald Isle, not Toby's boat. But so far, I can't come up with anything else."

"You'll figure it out."

"For Moira's sake, I hope I do," Finn answered referring to Toby Ireland's daughter. "She could use a windfall like that."

"What kind of windfall?" Nick asked from the doorway.

"How were the bed races?" Rick asked.

"The Sandbox team moved to the loser's bracket, but they've still got a chance," Angel answered.

"Nick we were talking about Moira with respect to Toby's treasure," Finn said.

"Where's Kate and Sher?" Tara asked.

"They've gone shopping. You just missed them."

"What are you two doing?"

"We're taking a look at the breakwater segments."

"No offense, but shouldn't an engineer be doing that?" Tara asked.

"Appearances can be deceiving, you know," Finn said.

"Finn, you are not an engineer," Tara declared, "you're a, a, I don't know what you are, but you're not an engineer."

"Right you are," Finn said with a grin, then looked pointedly at Rick.

"I'm guilty," Rick said with a grin.

"I thought your field was electronics?" Nick said.

"It is, but I'm really an electrical engineer, which also includes electronics. I have an undergrad degree in Civil Engineering. So that's why Norm trusts us to do this along with the engineers who are employed in Public Works."

"Wow. Have you spotted anything yet?" Tara said.

"Usual wear and tear but nothing that looks like a major problem. But we haven't reviewed even half of what Norm asked us to check out," Finn said.

"Anything we can do to help?" Angel asked.

"You know, I think we'll take you up on that," Rick said, "How 'bout I give you a couple of flash drives with footage of segments we've yet to look at. Focus on any cracks or unusual weathering, you might see and make a note of them for us. That will save some time. We'll set you up with another large monitor, give me a few minutes."

"Nick, could you and Tara rustle up some Joe," Finn asked.

"Sure thing," Tara answered, "I know where Sher keeps all the fixings."

"Thanks," Finn said as he continued to look at the breakwater.

"I need to tell Finn about those guys we saw earlier," Nick said to Tara, "I'll be there in a minute."

Tara headed for the kitchen and Finn asked, "What's up?"

"Maybe nothing. But, when we were at the bed races, we saw some guys that just didn't fit. And before you say anything, I know, how can you tell in the Conch Republic? But it was a gut feeling."

"Yeah, something wasn't right with those guys," Angel added.

"I trust your gut, Nick. Tell me more."

"Not much more to tell but I'd bet they were not there for the bed races or bartender's week either."

"I wonder if they have any connection to what Norm wanted to see me about in the morning?"

"What's up with that, you haven't said too much about it?"

"Something to do with a stolen work of art, that's about all I know."

"I'll keep my ears open, I better get to the kitchen and help Tara," Nick said and walked away.

Rick and Angel returned with the second monitor and placed it at the end of the long table, away from where Finn and Rick worked. When Nick and Tara returned with the coffee, the monitor was connected and ready to go.

Armed with a mug of Sumatran Gold from Baby's coffee shop, each person focused on the breakwater segments that appeared on the screens.

"Man, we've had a helluva summer and now this," Angel said.

"Icing on the cake," Finn deadpanned.

"No rest for the wicked," Nick said.

"Rick, take a look at this," Tara said as she pointed to a place on the monitor she shared with Nick.

"Good eye, Tara, make a note of that, it needs to be looked at closer."

"So, what do you figure our biggest threat will be with Fiona?" Angel asked, "I'm not as used to hurricanes as you guys are, so hang with me."

"If any of the breakwater segments fail it could lead to extensive flooding. Wind can do unbelievable damage depending on how long it lasts. Angel, it's not so much that the wind blows 110 miles an hour, but that the wind blows 110 for sixteen straight hours."

"We could be without water and electricity for weeks," Rick added.

"You should get a job with the Chamber of Commerce," Tara ribbed.

"Honestly, the aftermath is the worst. Irma was almost unbelievable, and I've been through some bad storms," Rick said.

"And now, since the Big Tide, we can't depend on much help from the state. But, the relationship that Norm has cultivated with the Navy through Padraig and George Kenny at Boca Chica has paid dividends. We actually get more help from the feds funneled through the Navy than we do from the very soggy state of Florida.

And that," Finn paused a moment, then went on, "rankles the hell out of the assholes in Tallahassee. Since we don't rely on state funds, they can't hold us under their thumb like they did for years."

"I feel like I'm back in my Political Science class," Tara said.

"In a way, we are the modern version of a 'City-State,'" Finn told her.

"The Southernmost city that could," Rick cracked.

"Sadly politicians have given politics a bad name," Finn said, "If you think about it, the word 'political' has a broader meaning than that of the 'science of governance.' We use negotiation and political maneuvering in our everyday life, with our friends and family. We just don't think of it as such."

"Hadn't ever thought about it like that," Angel said, "But, I see what you're saying."

"I'm not good at that game, but Norm knows the ropes and has played the political game to the huge benefit of the Conch Republic," Finn admitted.

Conversation waned as the five focused on the breakwater videos. Finn looked at the videos in a systematic manner, hoping to reduce the chance of missing something. To his surprise he found himself thinking about Kate and her comments earlier about buying a house in Key West. A small grin appeared as he remembered her exploits on Monkey Island. Exploits that led to a team of Navy Seals writing a drinking song about her.

A woman who did not miss a beat when a corpse's arm pulled free of its decomposing body in her grip as she tried to extract a notebook from the grasp of the dead man's hand. A woman who saved his life after he was stabbed by a syringe containing arsenic. Not a woman to let slip through his hands.

Finn's professional career kept him on the move for twenty years. There had not been time for serious relationships. There had been casual affairs, but nothing that would last under the demanding conditions of Finn's job. He knew that a committed relationship would have to wait.

He broke his reverie to back up and check out a segment a second time. He made a reference on his note pad, then continued his search.

Finn was comfortable in his own skin. He enjoyed Nick's company and they made a good team. When he met Kate Sullivan last summer he had no idea they would be thrown together into a life or death situation that would test them to the limit. Kate proved herself up to the challenge, Tara also.

Finn was not a dummy, he knew Kate cared for him. His lack of experience with relationships with women was evident, he was certain.

"Finn," Rick's voiced broke the reverie, "I just received an update on my phone. Fiona is edging up toward becoming a Cat 5."

"It doesn't surprise me, all the ingredients are there. Warmer than average water temps, no significant land mass in its way to knock it down, no high pressure ridges to mitigate development before it reaches us. What's its speed, Rick?"

"Looks like ten or eleven miles an hour right now, but the update says that is expected to increase."

"Better it come through fast, than crawl along or become stationary," Nick said, "I've learned that much since I've been down here."

"Norm told me they were diverting two additional ferry boats from their normal runs to help evacuate anyone that wants to leave. With the Bartenders Convention, there are more people than usual on the island," Finn told them.

"When's the last boat scheduled to leave?" Angel asked.

"Friday afternoon. If they don't move it up."

Once again, conversation lulled as they scrutinized the breakwater segments. It was the next-gen breakwater array with its hydraulic extenders that protected the Conch Republic from the risen waters of the Big Tide and from the increasingly violent storms that plagued the Caribbean. Finn was not surprised that the array was in good maintenance for the most part. Norm knew how reliant they were on the breakwater and he made sure it was kept in good condition.

Somewhere from the front of the house Sher's voice declared, "We're back."

"I better go help out," Rick said.

"I'll go with you," Tara said, "I need to talk to Kate."

The four men took a break and Angel topped off everyone's mug of coffee from an urn on the sideboard.

"Are they doing anything tonight at the Bartenders Convention?" Nick asked.

"I've got a schedule of events on my phone," Angel replied, "Let me take a look."

While Angel looked for the schedule, Finn sipped coffee then said, "I hope the tourists understand what's coming our way."

"Finn, you know they don't give a rat's ass. They're on vacation, and that's that," Nick said.

"It looks like tonight they're having a wet T-shirt contest at the Parrot. All tops will be soaked in spirits provided by the sponsors."

"T-shirts drenched in booze," Nick said with a smile.

"Remember your slingshot toting girlfriend," Angel admonished with a grin.

"I doubt they will continue on with events after tomorrow. If Fiona gains much more speed it could get here by late Friday. We'll be feeling gale-force winds by tomorrow night," Finn said.

"I'd still like to see the million dollar bottle of whiskey," Nick said."

"Where is it on display," Finn asked.

Angel spoke up, "They've been moving it around. Tonight it's at one of John's restaurants, Pasta Heaven. We can go check it out later, won't be a problem getting in."

"Thanks."

"Let's finish up our inspection, I want to get the notes to Norm ASAP," Finn declared.

———

Later, they were seated in the B and B's dining room at one of the large round tables. Two smaller tables were taken by two vacationing couples in town for the Bartender's Convention. The meal featured a shrimp and lobster lasagna, with a salad of mixed greens, tomatoes, and cucumbers. For those with room for dessert, a key lime pie.

Conversation was congenial so as not to alarm the paying guests.

"Angel said we can see the million dollar whiskey at Pasta Heaven tonight," Nick told Tara.

"Cool, I'd like to go. Can we make it to the wet jockstrap contest too?"

"The what?" Nick said.

"The wet jockstrap contest, they're holding it along with the wet T-shirt contest that I know you guys have been talking about."

"First I've heard," Nick said in a tone as convincing as a kid smeared with chocolate denying any knowledge of the cookie jar theft.

"Tell us more about the jockstrap contest, Tara," Sher said with evil intent.

Finn wore an expression of mild amusement as Nick and Angel seemed totally unprepared for the conversation.

"Is there a wet T-shirt contest?" Angel asked with a choir-boy look on his face.

"Men," Tara said and rolled her eyes.

"Sounds like tit for tat, to me," Sher said, "Rick looks great in his, don't you honey buns?"

Rick turned fifty shades of red and kept eating.

Nick realized they were in a "can't win" situation, and tried to reverse the momentum, "Hey, I'm always up for something new, let's go. But can we go look at the million-dollar whiskey first."

"Sure," Tara responded.

"We can go to Pasta Heaven first, then over to the Parrot," Angel said.

"Sounds like a plan," Nick said.

"By the way," Tara said with a grin, "There is no wet jockstrap contest."

"Well there should be," Sher said with a grin."

Nick and Angel looked vastly relieved, and both seemed to regain their appetites. Finn decided to help them out further by changing the subject.

"I have to meet with Norm in the morning but I think we should get as much weatherproofing finished as possible by tomorrow night. The storm is moving faster and may reach us sooner than expected."

"How long will you be tied up with Norm?" Rick asked.

"Not sure."

"What's it about?" Kate asked.

22

Finn glanced at the two tables that were occupied, then lowered his voice before he answered.

"There is a man here from Interpol trying to find a notorious fence. Apparently the fence is here in Key West and they are planning to lure him out and make an arrest. That needs to stay here at the table."

Everyone nodded in agreement and Finn added, "I'm not sure what my involvement with it will be, I guess I'll find out tomorrow."

"Intrigue," Sher stage whispered.

"International intrigue," Kate said.

The conversation turned to storm preparations as they polished off the food on the table. They drank coffee with their key lime pie and contemplated the worst-case scenario but hoped for the best.

There was a line outside Pasta Heaven waiting to see the famous bottle of Irish whiskey. Foot traffic was heavy for a Wednesday night. People acted as if there was not a Cat 4 storm approaching the Conch Republic. Angel led Nick and Tara down a side alley and into the restaurant through a side door used for deliveries.

"There's no need to piss folks off by cutting the line," Angel said. "Bad for business. We are less noticeable this way and won't cause any bad feelings with the paying customers."

Several of the bar staff fist bumped Angel as they walked through the restaurant toward the lobby where the bottle of whiskey was on display.

As they approached the display area, Angel said, "That doesn't look very secure to me."

"Aren't you in charge of security for John's businesses?" Nick asked in a low voice.

"Normally, yes. But they brought their own security for the million dollar whiskey."

"Who is it?" Tara asked.

"Don't know, the brewery handled that," Angel said.

The display sat on a round dinner table under an accent light that shown on the bottle of single malt, triple distilled Emerald Isle from the Craft Irish Whiskey, Co. It sat in a wooden case with two glasses and a decanter. There appeared to be nothing to prevent a grab and run.

"Maybe it's a fake, something they dummied up to pass as the real thing," Nick said.

"Maybe."

"Hey, look who is in line," Tara said.

Nick casually looked around and he scanned the crowd to see who Tara was talking about. He caught sight of three of the men they say earlier at the bed races. Nick gave no sign he recognized them but nudged Angel to get his attention. They pretended to look at the display but quietly discussed the presence of the three who did not come across like tourists.

"I wonder if they're casing the place," Nick mused.

"Maybe, but the display will be moved to another location after closing for tomorrow."

"But they could be scoping out the display itself, I mean if it's going to stay the same."

"It has so far," Angel answered, "It's the same set up they had a couple of nights ago at Mangia Mangia."

"I'm surprised somebody hasn't already grabbed it," Nick observed.

As the line moved along and the three men drew closer, Nick could see they looked Slavic. The line of people who were there only to view the whiskey and not to eat were cordoned off so that passed by the display then were routed back out the front doors of the restaurant.

Angel picked out the security detail for the whiskey as the two guys who looked like retired NFL linemen standing inside the cordon-off area. They were menacingly big, but Angel wondered if it was all size and no substance. He'd seen ex-pros from several sports hire on as body guards or special security details like this one without the skills and experience needed if the shit hit the fan.

There was one couple ahead of the three Slavs before reaching the display. Nick caught Angel's eye, at the same time he grabbed Tara by the wrist and casually moved back into the restaurant.

The couple moved directly in front of the display, eyed the bottle, then continued on past. The three men paused in front of the bottle display but Nick could see they were not looking at the bottle, but seemed edgy as if waiting for something to happen.

The plate glass window to the right of the door several feet away from the line funneling people back outside exploded inward. A large SUV rolled into the lobby as people screamed and tried to retreat outside or into the restaurant proper.

A smoke bomb went off enveloping the lobby in a thick, dark, cloud of fog. Alarm bells sounded as the sprinkler system kicked in with a torrent of cascading water.

The precautionary move to back away from the display saved Nick, Tara, and Angel from the flying glass. They were crouched beside a waist-high faux brick wall. Nick peeked over the top and saw that both of the security guards were down. He saw through the rapidly dissipating smoke that the three slavs were nowhere in sight. The display table was covered with shards of plate glass but there was no sign of the bottle or its carrying case. The SUV had also disappeared.

Angel was on his phone talking to John Rocco. Restaurant staff was tending to any patrons that needed attention while the waited for EMTs to arrive.

"You really know how to show a girl a good time," Tara quipped.

"Marines try harder."

"John told me he was worried about this happening. He didn't think their security was worth a crap either," Angel said as he pocketed his phone.

"I got a picture on my phone of the SUV before the smoke got thick," Nick said.

"Good instincts, Nick. We might be picking glass out of our hides if you hadn't pulled us back when you did," Angel said.

"Honestly, I did not see the smash and grab. Just the grab. I knew something was breaking, and thought we needed to move."

"I'm going to be tied up here for a while," Angel told them.

"We've got a long day tomorrow," Nick said, "Are you ready to head back to Rick and Sher's?"

"Sounds good to me."

"Could you send me that photo of the vehicle?" Angel asked, "It may help Norm."

"Sure."

"Let me go try to rally the troops," Angel said as he broke away and walked toward the central dining room.

Nick and Tara walked along the well-lit sidewalk of Whitehead Street. They skirted around a large banyan tree whose roots had pushed the broken concrete up into a small hillock. Many businesses were boarded up in readiness for the storm. The restaurants and bars would stay open as long as possible. Always looking for an easy tourist dollar to add to the collection.

"So what would you think if I moved down here permanently too. Kate's house, the one she's looking at, has a separate mother-in-law cottage that she wants me to take."

"I think I would like that. I wouldn't have to travel as far to rescue you."

She eyed him with a smirk and said, "Cool."

They walked on past T-shirt shops, sandal boutiques, tattoo parlors, clip joints, and leather dens. A few revelers, their senses sharpened by Mojitos, boisterously defied the hurricane to dampen their vacation. The hardcore flaunters of reality, the party 'til you die crew, were annoying fixtures in the Conch Republic. Testicular-driven bravado was not an even match with a Cat 5. Nick and Tara walked on, somewhat saddened at the possible fate that awaited some of these Darwin Award finalists.

The air had the saturated feel that Finn pointed out earlier. A reminder that a beast of a storm was on a direct path toward them. Clouds scudded silently across a moon-drenched night sky. Palms rattled in the steady breeze blowing across the island as feral chickens scurried to roost.

CHAPTER 5

Thursday morning dawned and by mid-morning the Conch Republic knew things were bad. Jim Cantore was spotted on Duval Street with a crew from the Weather Channel. The "kiss of death" as one old Conch muttered as he nailed plywood up on his storefront.

Rick and Sher's place was busy as a bee on a hot brick. Several of the guests opted to ride it out at the B and B rather than take a ferry after their flights were canceled. Sher was explaining to them what they could expect and trying her best to reassure them that the B and B would withstand the storm.

Finn arrived at Norman James' office right on time. Cheryl McIntosh, Norm's second in command greeted him when he entered the lobby of the cop shop.

"Hey, Finn. Norm's expecting you, go on back," she said as she held open a short swinging gate that allowed access to the area behind her desk. Finn walked through a door and down the hall toward Norm's office.

The door was partially open, he knocked and entered. Norm and another man were discussing something but stopped when Finn crossed the threshold.

"Finn, come on in. I'd like you to meet Nigel Fairchild."

Finn nodded to the man as he rose from his seat to shake Finn's hand.

"Lieutenant James," Nigel said but it sounded like *'leftenant'* to Finn's ear, "speaks highly of you, Mr. Finn."

"Good to meet you, just Finn."

"Finn, Nigel is a Detective Inspector, formerly of Scotland Yard currently working with Interpol on a special detail."

Fairchild was about six foot three and Finn guessed somewhere between thirty-five and forty-five. The aroma of tobacco smoke clung to him but most ironic, at least to Finn, was that the man in front of him looked enough like Sean Connery to be his brother.

Finn must have betrayed some recognition because Fairchild smiled, then said, "Bloody inconvenient looking like that bloke."

"There must be some advantages," Finn replied.

"Possibly," the man said.

"Finn, DI Fairchild is in town to put the kibosh on a very elusive character in the counterfeit art world," Norm explained.

The two men resumed their seats and Finn quietly waited to hear the reason for his presence.

"I'm afraid this hurricane of yours is playing havoc with our schedule." Finn heard *"sheddule,"* but remained quiet.

"The original plan, which I must say I was not in favor of, gave us a few more days to set things up. Now, we've had to push forward. If it was my decision, I would wait. But, there is immense pressure from above to carry on, so there you have it."

"Finn I know that look," Norm spoke, "We're getting to the good part. Nigel's partner will not be able to get down here in time under the new time clock. I explained to Nigel your past experience in ops like this, and told him you wouldn't mind helping out."

Finn remained silent as he studied the men in front of him. He knew Norm wouldn't throw this at him cold without good reason. He also felt the tingle of adrenaline at the thought of getting to use some old skills. He decided he would hear them out before he made a decision.

"Go on I'm listening."

They explained the proposed plan to Finn. He understood why Nigel would prefer to wait, under the circumstances. He also understood the type of "pressure" Nigel referred to, he had felt it himself, more than once.

"So, it is flawed, at least in my opinion, but it's what I've got to deal with and hope the real thief doesn't show up. The storm might help us out with that," Nigel concluded.

"I'm in," Finn said, "Besides, how often do you get to work with James Bond."

The hint of a smile appeared briefly on Nigel's face, then he said, "Jolly good."

"Norm, any luck on the million dollar bottle?"

"Not yet, Finn."

"Nick and Tara were there, with Angel when it occurred."

"I told John that I did not think the sponsor had enough security, he agreed but told me his hands were tied."

"Seems to be going around," Nigel adroitly observed.

Finn was warming up to the Brit. The man was self-disciplined and cautious, two of Finn's favorite traits.

"Nick told me the three Slavic men were observed earlier yesterday at the bed races."

"Angel briefed me after I arrived at Pasta Heaven last night. We've got BOLOs out on them. Angel also got a decent photo of the SUV, that may help."

"Norm, you know I hate coincidences. Any chance the whiskey heist and the reason Nigel is in town could be connected."

There was complete silence as each man contemplated Finn's statement. Finn added, "Maybe somebody who thought 'two birds with one stone' might work."

"The bottle grab seemed heavy-handed," Norm said.

"If I may say, the Russian mob is known for tactics like that," Nigel offered.

"Could have been on purpose to shift focus away from the true culprit toward the Russians," Finn said.

"I think Whoever grabbed the booze will be staying on the island until the storm passes. I've already instructed the airport to contact me if any private planes attempt to file a flight plan in the next forty-eight hours."

"Nigel, this storm is probably going to get here late tomorrow night or early Saturday morning. Are you ready to put your plan in action tomorrow morning?" Finn asked.

"Yes, I would like to go over a few things with you later today. If you wouldn't mind?"

"Not at all. Why don't you meet me at my friend's B and B. Nick and I are staying there through the storm. I'll give you directions."

Nigel departed after putting the address in his phone. Finn knew Norm would not have thrown something like this his way unless there were extenuating circumstances.

"Finn, I owe you big time for helping Nigel out. The guy is solid, or I've lost my ability to read people. And, he's in a bind. The kind of snafu you and I have witnessed up close and personal in the past."

Finn knew he referred to their past lives in counterintelligence, Norm in Army Intelligence and Finn, part of an elite group of in-country operatives that worked against terrorists in the Caribbean and Central America.

Finn's group, simply did not exist. On any books, at least. Their work made plausible deniability a must for any sitting president.

"No worries. Norm I owe you to the point I've lost count, glad to help."

"Given the fact that all three of us hate the plan, be careful."

"You know, I can't shake the feeling that the whiskey heist and Nigel's stolen art fence are somehow connected."

"This is Key West, I wouldn't rule out anything," Norm said solemnly.

"As this past summer has clearly reminded us."

"Yeah, I have to admit that on New Year's Day I really did not see fighting a voodoo army and eight weeks later taking on a bunch of psychopathic hybrids that wanted to poison the water. And we've got three and a half more months to go this year."

"Would you mind bringing up a weather update on your wall monitor?" Finn asked.

A moment later the sixty-inch smart TV on Norm's wall silently burst to life. Finn noted it was on the Weather Channel, so Norm was monitoring closely. An energetic weather girl with sweeping arm motions indicated the predicted path of Fiona. From where Finn sat, it looked like the eye was headed straight down Duval Street.

During the night, Fiona had strengthened and now threatened to become a Cat 5. Her sustained wind speed was at one hundred-fifty miles per hour. The minimum speed for a Cat 5 was one fifty-seven.

"Fiona is starting to look like a bitch," Finn said, then added, "I brought the vids of the breakwaters back with our notations on a flash drive. I gave them to Cheryl. They looked pretty good, overall."

"This will be the most severe test they've had."

"It would be catastrophic if they failed during an event like Fiona."

"That's what I like about you, a cup half-full kinda guy."

"Let's hope the water in the cup isn't salty by the end of next week."

"There are at least three crews out now checking them in person."

"She will be here by tomorrow night, no doubt," Finn said as he pointed to the screen where the storm's speed was shown on a diagram."

"I'm guessing that by early afternoon we'll have feeder bands," Norm said, "Do you think there will be enough time to implement Nigel's plan?"

"It'll be close, but given his situation I think we should do what we can to help. I don't mind."

"I think our Anglican friend will be weathering the storm with us because I think the last ferry out will be the seven a.m. departure. You might want to mention that to him," Norm said.

"Will do. If you need me I'll be at Rick and Sher's."

CHAPTER 6

There was not much in the way of hurricanes that the Conch Republic had not experienced. In the years since the Big Tide, hurricanes had increased in intensity. Warmer waters, planetwide, had contributed to this phenomena. There was a push to add a Category 6 label to the Saffir-Simpson scale.

As Finn drove back to the B and B he noticed a lot less loudmouthed partiers mocking the storm and a whole lot more people battening down than usual. He remembered the aftermath of Irma and the resilience of islanders to come back from that devastation. Then, the cruel irony of the Big Tide, engulfing much of the island chain, leaving small pockets of habitation spread throughout the islands in addition to the Conch Republic and Boca Chica, saved by the heroic efforts of Padraig Kennedy.

It was the price you paid for living in Hurricane Alley. But like everything else, the cost of living seemed to be rising at an alarming rate. No matter the risk, he would rather be here than on the mainland. Apparently Kate felt the same way, and that caused him to smile.

Finn's former professional life prevented him from having a family or even a committed relationship. It would not have been fair to a wife or children. His old job carried a high degree of risk and long periods of in-country surveillance and operations.

These days, Finn had a family. At least he thought of the tight circle of friends that had been through so much in the past six months as family. He would jump a high fence for any of them.

He braked the Jeep at the intersection of Whitehead and Fleming Streets for a red light. A conch tour train went by with advertising that touted the Mangrove Martini as the official cocktail of the Bartender's Convention. Finn preferred a good gin and tonic on a hot day but a martini would do in a pinch. He fondly remembered a Rudy Krause Christmas party that featured Key Lime martinis that were delicious.

The light changed and Finn rolled on toward Rick and Sher's. Traffic was heavier in the direction of the ferry terminal. Finn wondered if the "Peter Matthiessen" was the last ferry out. If so, the passengers would have the best pilot they could hope for in Boatdock Bill Davis. Boatdock had been piloting boats of all shapes and sizes along the Ten Thousand Islands and the Keys for over fifty years.

They would need his skill and experience. The ocean had a sullen look to it, as chop gave way to sustained turbulence. Finn knew Nigel would have to hunker down with the rest of them because no ferry would run tomorrow after the early departure at seven.

He found the half-hidden parking spot beside the dumpster empty and pulled the Jeep to a stop. The dumpster was located to serve not only the B and B but several other businesses and sat next to the picket fence that ran on three sides of Rick and Sher's property. The short wheel based Jeep fit snugly into the space most vehicles could not fit. To say, "parking was a problem" in Key West was an understatement of massive proportions.

The hurricane preparation was ongoing when Finn walked into the lobby. He saw several of the volunteers known as ConchBees or CBees as they were called. They were manning the crisis hot line to answer questions and keep folks off the panic button.

There was always a flurry of rumors prior to a hurricane; everything from who was cheating on who due to storm stress to free beer at the Parrot. Most were harmless but one time Conch Radio aired a rebroadcast of the vintage Orson Welles' version of War of the Worlds prior to a storm. The idea was to get everyone's mind off the storm. The combination of alcohol-drenched brains with the sheer realism of the show and the aforementioned "storm stress" produced several broken arms and legs when people went into full panic mode.

Sher breezed through the lobby and said to Finn as she passed, "We'll have a buffet lunch in an hour, Rick's up on the third floor, Kate's in the kitchen."

———————

Nigel arrived at three on the dot. Finn had warned his friends of Nigel's resemblance to Connery so they would not stare. They all stared liked the great Scot himself had entered. Nigel exhibited composure under duress and managed a riposte that earned Finn's respect. He turned to the group, smiled and said, "Shaken, not stirred."

The ice broken, Finn ushered Nigel out of the lobby and back to the sunroom with Rick in tow.

"Nigel, this is Rick, the man I referred to at our meeting with Lieutenant James."

Nigel extended his right hand and said, "Nice to meet you."

"How about some coffee?" Finn asked.

"Would it be possible to get a cup of tea and to push my luck, would you have some Twinings?"

"I think we do," Rick said, "We have quite a few guests from the U.K. and Sher keeps a good stock of tea."

Finn thought he saw a look of relief on Nigel's face at the prospect of a good cup of tea.

"I'll be right back," Rick said as he departed.

"I thought it would be good to have a drone in the air recording whatever happens at the art gallery. At least from the outside," Finn explained.

"Yes, I agree. Finn, I've got to say that I don't give a damn for this plan."

"I understand your concern, hopefully we can work on some details while you're here that will minimize some of the risk."

Rick returned with a small tray with a cup of tea and assorted dispensers for cream and sugar. He placed it on the table in front of Nigel.

"I haven't had a cuppa since I arrived in your fair town."

"Rick, I explained to Nigel about the drone, that's all we've covered so far," Finn said.

"Why don't we start at the beginning for Rick's sake," Nigel said.

"Go ahead."

"I work with a special task force within Interpol concerned with stolen art, art forgery, and recovery of items lost during conflicts like WWII or more recently the attempted take over of Ukraine by that bugger Putin."

Rick had pulled up a street map that showed the art gallery and the adjacent streets. It appeared on the large flat screen TV on the wall of the sunroom.

Nigel looked at it for a moment, then continued, "The person we are after is not only a fence but a skilled broker of deals also. Notice that I'm not assigning a gender because we do not know if this person is a man or a woman."

"What about the fact that the real thief is out there. That is the kind of wild card factor that is a real pain in the ass."

"Finn, I received word last night that Interpol has the man for whom he works under surveillance in Spain."

"That may well be true, but it's a loose end. We should be aware of it, that's all I'm saying."

"Agreed."

"Rick, show Nigel the photo Angel took last night at Pasta Heaven."

Rick typed a command into his laptop and the map on the TV screen was replaced by a blurry shot of the three Slavic-looking men as they stood in front of the Irish whiskey display.

"Do you recognize any of them?" Finn asked.

Nigel arose from his chair, walked closer and peered at the screen. He carefully looked at each man before he said, "Unfortunately, I do."

"The plot thickens," Rick intoned.

"We pegged them as Slavs," Finn said.

"Bulgarians, to be exact. Would these be the chaps who made off with the whiskey?

"Yes."

"Well that is interesting."

"How so, Nigel?"

"These three are midlevel members of a large crime syndicate in Europe. They are more than, what's the term you Americans use, 'muscle,' I would describe them as 'soldiers,' they're on the pension plan."

"Who do they work for?" Rick asked.

"That's the interesting part, it's the man I referred to a moment ago. His name is Eduardo Santos, he's Spanish, from Barcelona"

"Glad we showed you the photo," Finn said.

"I don't believe in coincidences," Nigel said softly.

"Hey, Finn, he doesn't believe in *coinkydence*," Rick said with a grin, then added, "Welcome to the club, Nigel."

"Good, then I won't have to waste time convincing you that this affects our plans quite significantly."

"Why are the Bulgars here?" Finn asked.

"To ensure the switch goes off smoothly?"

"Maybe," Nigel responded.

"Would they recognize you if they saw you?"

"Quite possibly."

"We could tell folks they're filming a new Bond movie in Key West."

"Very funny, Rick."

"This changes things," Nigel said. "I need to smoke, would it be alright if I step outside?"

"Sure, we'll come with you," Finn said.

Nigel paced on the porch while he smoked. His cup of tea sat on a small table. Finn and Rick sat patiently, they realized the man was under pressure. The steady breeze wafted the cigarette smoke in every direction. Finn could see Nigel was mentally reviewing the options open to them. He stopped and sipped his tea.

Sher's head poked out from the door, "Rick, are you smoking again?"

"Not me, honey buns. If that stuff on Monkey Island didn't cause me to start, I doubt there's much that would make me."

"I'm sorry, madame," Nigel said, "I was under the impression I could smoke out here."

"You're fine, Nigel. Just didn't want my baby cakes to backslide. And Nigel, I've got plenty of food for supper and I hope you will join us."

"Certainly, madam."

"Call me Sher, please."

"Alright Sher, I would be honored."

"Finn, when you are finished out here, there is someone in the kitchen who needs to talk to you."

Without further explanation, Sher disappeared back inside. Nigel sat down in the empty wicker chair next to Finn and Rick.

"I wonder what that's about?" Finn mused aloud.

"Finn, if you need to attend to something else, this can wait a few minutes," Nigel offered.

"No, go ahead. Have you come up with something different?"

"Yes, given this storm. You've convinced me this is a far different beast than what hit the UK in '87"

"I'm glad you understand," Finn answered.

"I think tomorrow, instead of apprehending anyone, we simply identify the fence. If you are right, and I certainly yield to your experience with these storms, then no-one is leaving the island until after this thing blows by us."

"I agree with you so far," Finn said.

"If we're lucky, we might get two birds with the proverbial one stone."

"Santos and the fence," Finn remarked.

"Will your higher ups go for it?" Rick asked.

"This is my call, our call, now; the hell with the politics. I won't risk other people's lives to make some politicians happy."

"Sounds like high jingo," Finn said.

"I'm not familiar with that term."

"Read a Michael Connelly book."

"Here me out, then tell me what's wrong," Nigel said, "We stay on schedule tomorrow morning. I go to the gallery with the fake but I'll just try to gain access, see who meets me. Have the drone in the air and Finn, cover my back. I'll use the fake as leverage, and come up with some excuse to delay one more day. Which should shut everything down and give us some time."

Finn slowly nodded his head, "The time you are inside, what stops them from killing you and taking the painting, fake or not?"

"We'll figure something out, cause that's the best I've got," Nigel answered.

"You fit right in with us," Rick said, "We generally play it by ear. It's worked against a voodoo army and a bunch of bloodthirsty hybrids."

Nigel looked perplexed but got the gist of Rick's statement. He gave a sardonic grin, and said, "Bloody ell."

The men returned to the sunroom and Rick pulled up the map of the blocks surrounding the gallery. They studied it silently for several minutes.

"I'm going to see what is up in the kitchen," Finn said. "Rick, familiarize Nigel with the layout around the gallery, if you would. I'll be back in a few minutes."

CHAPTER 7

Finn found Kate and Sher sitting with a worried-looking Madame Fontaine, the Conch Republic's only voodoo priestess. He had not seen her in more than a month. Today, Camille Garnier wore a long, flowing multi-color caftan with a ball cap that read "LSU Baseball" in purple and gold.

"Finn, thank you for sparing me some time."

"Camille, you look rattled. That's not like you, what's the matter?"

"Give her a moment, Finn. She's had a fright," Kate said.

Camille Garnier, aka Madame Fontaine, ran a holistic health store in Bahama Village. She read Tarot for those that asked, and provided spiritual guidance for the many believers on the island.

Her assistance during the investigation into who killed Toby Ireland had been critical. Her chemistry degree from LSU and her knowledge of voodoo came in handy as she and Kate raced against time to find an antidote for the "zombie juice" that infected a rabble of men being used by a madman.

Finn was shocked. The Camille Garnier he knew, like Kate, was intelligent and poised in the face of danger. The woman in front of him seemed shaken and uncertain. He looked at Kate with concern, then said, "Take your time, Camille. There's no hurry."

Sher handed her a tumbler half full of brandy. She sipped it and slowly regained her composure. Her almond eyes gazed straight ahead with a look of uncertainty. She struggled to control her breathing, finally taking deep, steady inhalations, until she seemed satisfied.

"Finn, I know you don't put much stock into some of what I do. But I didn't want to go to Lieutenant James before I talked to y'all."

"I have an open mind," Finn said to encourage her.

"Well, I'm not sure I believe this myself, but here goes. This afternoon I was doing a reading for Miss Hattie, she's one of my regulars. When I turned up the High Priestess Card, something odd happened."

She paused and took a sip of the brandy, then continued, "I looked down at the card and the face of my ancestress Marie LaVeau stared back at me."

"Has this ever happened before now?" Kate asked.

"Nothing like this, it scared poor Miss Hattie so bad she had to take a sip of her medicine, which I'm pretty sure is a flask full of Southern Comfort. I was performing a standard read of the cards, nothing spooky. When I turned over the next card it was the High Priestess, and as I placed it on the table it morphed into a picture of Marie. I gasped and that's when Miss Hattie went for the flask."

"Oh my God," Sher exclaimed.

"Then the voice of Marie said in French, 'Death rides on the storm.' Miss Hattie heard it too. And that freaked me out because right before Katrina slammed into the bayou, those same words appeared to me in a dream. A very vivid dream."

Finn remained silent. He knew Camille Garnier was not prone to flights of fancy. He waited for her to continue.

"The card stayed transfigured for maybe two minutes. It repeated the message several times. Then it morphed back to the High Priestess. I was so shook, I didn't even finish the reading. I urged Miss Hattie to go home and focus on being ready for the storm with her family. Then, I had a shot of rum, myself."

"This happened earlier this afternoon?" Finn asked.

"Yes, about an hour ago. After I calmed down, I decided to come talk with you and Kate. Do you think we should let Lt. James know?"

"Yes, I do. But, can you tell us anything else," Finn answered.

"For a few moments, I had a vision. Water engulfing the island, coming from a breach in the breakwater. Then it dissipated, as quickly as it had formed."

She took another sip from the tumbler.

"Maybe we better alert Norm to give the breakwater another look," Sher suggested.

"Well, this is definitely 'spooky action at a distance,' but not the way Einstein meant," Kate said as she squeezed her friend's ebony hand.

"Why don't I call Norm and have him come over here," Finn said.

"Thank you, Finn. I wasn't looking forward to making a public appearance at the police station."

"Is there anything else you can tell us," Kate asked.

"I'm trying to remember. It's like seeing ball lightning and then later, you're not really sure if you saw it."

Finn sent a text to Norm, waited for a reply then stepped back over to where the women sat on kitchen stools.

"He'll be here in fifteen minutes."

Nick and Tara tagged along with Angel as he made the rounds of John Rocco's properties to check on the hurricane prep. Most of the buildings were equipped with modern hurricane shutters that reduced the risk of wind damage to doors and windows. Rocco also replaced older roofs on his buildings with new ones that exceeded the stringent Florida Building Code specs.

They were in Finn's Jeep Wrangler with Nick at the wheel and Angel, due to his size, riding shot gun. Tara occupied the back seat and was checking something on a page of paper that she held.

"OK, next stop The Sand Box," she said.

"How many after it?" Nick asked.

"Should be three," Angel answered.

"Correcto mundo, three it is," Tara said.

Nick made a left turn at the next intersection onto a narrow side street that ran perpendicular to Duval Street. Traffic was sparse as the neighborhood became more residential than commercial.

Some nice examples of the maritime themed architecture of Key West lined either side of the street. Ornately carved woodwork on porches harkened back to the late eighteen hundreds when seafaring captains made their home on the island.

"Don't slow down Nick, but I think I saw one of the whiskey thieves on the porch of the house with the gabled windows, painted blue," Tara said from the back seat.

Nick kept the Wrangler on course and continued down the street. He went two more blocks then pulled into a residential parking space and stuck the permit for the Jeep on the inside windshield.

"Let's go take a look," Nick said, "Tara would you hand me the lock box, please."

Nick placed the metal box on the Jeep's hood and opened it. He pulled out a Ruger .357, then closed and replaced the box on the floorboard of the Jeep.

"This is strictly recon, but no reason to be underdressed," Nick said. Tara had her sling shot assembled and ready. Angel sported his dive knife but no side arm.

They casually ambled down the narrow sidewalk back toward the house where Tara saw the man. Frangipani trees formed a tangled fence of foliage along the sidewalk to their right. Up and down the street people secured yard furniture, nailed plywood over bare windows, and placed sandbags around doors.

Trying to reason with hurricane season, as Buffet pointed out, was a way of life in the Conch Republic. As the house came into clearer view, it stood out that no one was in sight, much less taking precautionary measures.

"That's odd. None of the those windows have shutters and I don't see any ply wood," Angel said.

"You'd think somebody would be doing some prep work," Nick remarked.

"Unless they're not planning to be here," Angel answered.

They walked on and Tara covertly took some pictures on her phone. No one appeared on the porch. The yard remained empty as they passed.

"Look, in the back," Nick said in a forced whisper, and motioned his head toward the long side yard that ran to the rear of the property.

A metallic silver SUV pulled away from the back of the house and turned into an alley. They lost sight of it but Nick was sending a text to Norm, then to Finn.

"Norm says stay put," Nick told them. They walked up the pea rock path to the porch and sat on the steps.

"Hope it's not rigged to go," Angel said.

"Thanks for putting us all at ease," Nick smirked.

Five minutes later a squad car pulled up with Big Dog driving and Joey riding shotgun. Norm arrived before the two uniforms could start toward the porch. They huddled for a moment then walked toward the threesome on the porch steps.

"I think we missed them," Nick said when they were in earshot. He explained about the vehicle they witnessed. Tara brought a blurred photo of the vehicle up on her phone and showed it to them.

"Sorry, that's a terrible picture," Tara said, "maybe it will help."

"You are sure it was one of the men from Pasta Heaven?" Norm asked.

"Yes, I'm sure."

"I've got all the possible egress points on the island covered. There aren't many left at this point."

"They may not be trying to get off before the storm. Maybe they figure to split in the aftermath when no one is paying attention. You could steal a boat and be gone," Nick offered.

"Tara, thanks for the ID. Good eye," Norm told her.

"I've got a forensics team, such as it is, on the way."

"Would you mind if we look around, under your supervision, of course," Angel said, "If I can pick up any clues as to where the whiskey is, I know John would appreciate it."

"I don't think the tax payers will mind," Norm said, "Let's go take a look. Big Dog, you and Joey take a look in back, we'll meet you there."

"On it, LT."

The house was similar to many in Old Town, two-story with column-supported porches, painted a bright Caribbean blue. There were no yard ornaments, toys, or tools to indicate the house was inhabited.

Norm led the others up the porch steps to the door. He knocked, then tried to open it. It swung open at a push.

"Hello, Key West police. Health and safety check, is anyone here?"

Nick had his Ruger in hand as they followed Norm into the house. Angel unsheathed his knife and fanned out in the opposite direction Nick had taken.

"Anybody see any trip wires," Norm asked as Tara stepped stealthily over a crumpled paper bag from a well-known fast food chain.

"There's not much furniture," Nick said.

"No trip wires that I can see, LT" Angel told Norm.

"If anyone was staying here, it wasn't for long," Tara said.

The bottom floor was musty, curtains were pulled tight adding to the murkiness of no lights.

Nick tried a wall switch and two overhead lights came on shedding pale luminescence across the room. The floor plan was a central hallway with three rooms to the left and two on the right. The kitchen was on the right at the rear.

There were sparse furnishings throughout. There were sleeping bags and mats scattered in one of the larger rooms.

"Somebody was here," Nick said.

The kitchen showed signs of use, but there was little in the way of provisions in the pantry and the fridge was almost empty. Then they walked onto the small back porch.

"LT," Joey's voice was charged with adrenaline, "You better take a look at this." He stood just outside the small garage area and pointed to something inside.

Joey and Big Dog stood by a freezer with the top open when the others arrived. Inside the freezer a blond woman lay in the fetal position. A name tag on her navy blue blazer identified her as Cassie Massey.

"She's a realtor," Norm said, "I've seen her around. Not many stayed after the Big Tide."

"Do you think she was lured here on the pretense of showing the house?" Big Dog asked.

"That would be my guess," Norm answered.

"But why?" Nick asked, "Why kill her?"

"Maybe it wasn't suppose to happen but something went wrong," Norm answered.

"Joey, get an ambulance over here."

"On it, LT."

"I wish we knew exactly who we are dealing with here," Norm said with a sigh.

"Well, they're not getting off the island before Fiona hits us," Angel said.

Norm glanced at his phone then said, "I need to look upstairs, Joey, stay with the body. Big Dog come with us, I've got a meeting with the mayor and some business men, including John Rocco, in an hour. Let's go."

The second floor of the house was strewn with litter, mostly fast food bags. Empty plastic water bottles were scattered on the floor and erupted from a large trash can that overflowed with garbage.

"Looks to me like at least five or six people were here," Nick said.

"But, where are they now?" Angel asked.

"Look for any notes or paperwork that might be laying around," Norm said.

They split up and worked their way through the rooms on the second floor. The wind scrubbed palm fronds against the side of the house, a reminder of Fiona's imminent arrival. It appeared that nothing of value remained that might afford a clue as to who these people were.

"Big Dog, I need you to finish up here. I've got to go but I will contact Cheryl so she can notify the woman's business and her family if she has any on the island."

"We'll stay and help Big Dog," Nick said.

"Thank you. I'll be in touch," Norm said as he walked toward the staircase.

"They didn't leave much," Nick said.

"There's only a couple more rooms, let's do it," Tara said.

"They built this place solid," Nick said.

"Yeah, these old houses made from Dade pine are sturdy. The workmanship is top notch too. Mostly tongue-and-groove work where it's needed," Big Dog answered.

Tara opened a closet door and used her phone to illuminate the space. On the floor, pushed to the side was a small duffle bag.

"Hey, over here. Got something."

The three men crowded around and peered into the shadowy space.

"At least it's too small for a body," Nick said.

"Hang on," Big Dog said, "I've got a pair of gloves here somewhere. Just a sec."

Hands gloved, Big Dog zippered open the duffle bag. Inside sat a laptop with several flash drives next to it. Some small notebooks and several art books completed the contents.

"We need to get this to the LT pronto," Big Dog said.

"Yeah, I don't think they meant to leave this," Nick said.

"Good eye, Tara," Angel said.

They met Joey downstairs who reported that the body was on its way to the city morgue.

As they dispersed, the skies grew darker and brought a somber feel to the murder scene. The empty feeling of a senseless death laced the air with sudden sadness.

CHAPTER 8

The Bartenders Convention stubbornly refused to quit like the dance band on the Titanic. Old conchs were taking Fiona seriously. Even the Cubans had abandoned their domino games outside 5 Brothers to help with the storm prep. Norm's mind raced as he drove toward Rick and Sher's. He wondered what had spooked Camille Garnier.

As he drove, he saw encouraging signs that the populace was aware of the threat level they faced. Most people who stayed after the Big Tide were individualist, non-conformers, who were self-reliant and pragmatic. Island living post-Big Tide was less charming than Conde' Nast would have liked. The locals knew when to sober up and deal with reality. Unfortunately, most tourists did not.

The love/hate relationship between "locals" and "tourists" was strange. The lifeblood of the economy in the Conch Republic was the "tourist dollar" but along with the economic benefits came the irresponsible behavior; "Hey, we're on vacation," was the justifying mantra for many jailable acts. Worse than that was the idea that they had come to a quaint theme park, where nothing could seriously go wrong. Norm almost chuckled at the thought given recent events.

There would be more than the usual amount of tourons, as he thought of them, on the island for this catastrophic storm because of the Bartenders Convention. Along with some very bad guys. Just another day in Paradise.

He found his friends in the kitchen of the B and B. Wafting aromas briefly distracted Norm from the business at hand but he put on his game face and said, "Camille, are you OK?"

"Better now, Lieutenant, thank you for coming. I feel a bit silly."

"You did the right thing," Kate said, "Norm you need to listen to Camille's story."

"Would you like some coffee?" Sher asked.

"Um, I think I'd rather have a shot of the brandy," Norm said as he eyed the bottle on the counter.

"That kind of day?" Finn said.

"That kind of day."

Camille repeated her story, slowly this time, as she tried to remember more details. They listened riveted to her tale.

"I can see why that would upset you," Norm told her when she finished.

"Beyond that, lieutenant, I think something bad is going to happen.

"You say that in your vision it appeared that one of the breakwater segments was breached?" Norm gently asked.

"Yes, that's what it looked like."

"Well, that's a start. I've got several repair teams from Public Works examining every square foot of the system. Finn and Rick have been reviewing video of the breakwater looking for any signs of trouble also. But, we'll renew our efforts. We are running out of time and if there is a faulty section, we need to find it."

"Camille, I believe you," Kate told her friend, "Do you think you could contact her, Marie, I mean?"

"Are you suggesting a seance?" Finn asked.

"Maybe we can get more information," Kate answered.

"What happened to the Ph.d who deals in facts?" Finn said with a quizzical look on his face.

"We don't have all the answers. 'Spooky action at a distance' clearly demonstrates that there are phenomena that don't fit our description of the world. I'm willing to give it a try in an effort to minimize the danger from the hurricane."

Finn smiled at Kate's poise.

"Let me brief Cheryl at the EOC, go to another meeting, grab a bite, then I'll come back for our little seance," Norm said.

"You're welcome to stay," Sher said.

"I've got to meet with John Rocco, the mayor, and some other businessmen, take care of a few things."

"Camille, what do you need?"

"Just a few things. Kate if you'll go with me to my shop we could be back in less than an hour."

"OK."

"We'll eat when you two get back," Sher said.

The private dining room was crowded with nine people sitting at a long ranch-style table with bench seats. Conversation was animated in the face of the approaching storm.

"We heard you found a body earlier today," Sher said, "Tara are you OK?"

"I'm good. Joey actually found the body, but it was still gross. Poor woman."

"Nigel has identified your whiskey thieves as Bulgarians in the employ of one Eduardo Santos," Finn said.

"But we think they are here in conjunction with Nigel's mission," Rick said, then looked at Nigel and said, "Everybody here has clearance, believe me."

"I see things are a bit unorthodox here, but carry on," Nigel responded. The Brit found himself warming to this unusual mix of Americans. He sensed a high degree of competence behind the banter. They reminded him of his grandfather and his RAF mates.

"Camille, will the sunroom be adequate for the seance?" Sher asked.

"Yes, it will be fine."

"Better enjoy the food, we could be eating MREs for a while after this thing comes through," Rick said.

The conversation had a relaxed cadence typical of close friends sharing a meal. The stone crab cakes and mangrove snapper nuggets were disappearing rapidly. Cole slaw and cheese grits completed the menu.

"We will need six people to participate in addition to me," Camille said, "However, I think it would be a good idea to have someone record the event on video and someone to merely observe."

"I can record it," Rick said.

"Kate, would you be an official observer?" Camille asked.

"Certainly."

"What about the six who will sit at the table?" Finn wanted to know.

"Inquiring minds want to know," Norm said as he entered the dining room with John Rocco behind him.

"Any luck on finding the Bulgarians?" Finn asked.

"Not yet."

"Have some food," Rick said and pointed to the end of the table where there were extra plates and silverware.

"Camille, or should I say, Madame Fontaine was about to tell us the skinny on the six participants of the seance," Finn explained.

"Please continue," Norm answered.

"It would be optimal to have six people who are reasonably open-minded and in touch with their inner energy. Any volunteers?"

"I'm open-minded, not sure about how in touch with my inner energy I am but I'm curious so I'll volunteer," Tara said.

"Count me in," Sher said.

"Finn, I would like you to be at the table," Garnier said, "You're ability to sort through things while you're in a dreamtime-like state makes you a winner."

"I have a feeling Rick will need Angel's help with the electronics so I'll volunteer," Nick said.

"Red," Norm said using Rocco's nickname, "Would you care to accompany me to a seance?"

"It beats watching the Godfather III."

"After our meal I will explain the ritual to you and answer any questions," Camille told them.

"Any update on Fiona?"

"We're still in the cone of death."

"I say, how accurate is that designation?" Nigel asked.

"In terms of the storm's track, it is reasonably accurate," Finn said, "As far as the 'cone of death' being a predictable factor, hurricanes have a way of highlighting wannabe Darwin Award nominees."

"Darwin Awards?

"Yes, handed out to people who have died due to their own stupidity," Rick explained.

"Yes, I know what you mean."

"Normally, I would say we have nothing to worry about, but I'll wait until this seance is finished before I comment," Norm said.

CHAPTER 9

The sunroom seemed somber with all the curtains drawn and only two candles burning to provide light. Two video cameras would record the event, one operated by Angel, the other by Rick. Kate sat in a corner with her notebook ready to write down what she would witness.

Camille Garnier was now dressed in apparel that seemed reminiscent of the nineteenth century, looking every bit the part of Madame Fontaine. Her Tarot deck sat before her on the table. Next to the deck of cards sat a small tea pot and a demitasse of fine porcelain.

"I will ask you to join hands in a moment but first are there any questions?"

Garnier had previously explained to the others what they might expect and how they should behave during the seance. None of the six seated people raised their hand.

"Then let's proceed. I will now take this herbal tea and we'll wait. Please join hands and remain silent."

The two video cameras quietly recorded as Kate observed with her trained eye. Suddenly a clattering sound beat against the outside wall of the building. No one at the table moved. Rick stepped over to the curtains and peeked out, then mouthed "tree limb" to the others.

Garnier finished the herbal tea and gazed steadily into the dim, flickering light of the candles. The others tried to remain calm but several fidgeted in their seats. Time crept by like an iguana on a cold morning.

Suddenly, Garnier sat upright and began to speak French.

Kate quietly moved several steps closer and strained to hear what her friend said.

"Danger dans la tempête, danger dans la tempête."

No one else spoke, they were riveted to their chairs. Norm usually implacable, wore a look of concern and confusion. Rocco made the sign of the cross as sweat beaded on his brow.

Tara gasped as she looked behind Camille Garnier where a smoky mist formed. She squeezed Nick's hand at the same time Sher squeezed hers.

"Mother of God," Rocco muttered.

The mist slowly revealed a figure behind Garnier's chair, it was Marie LeVeau.

"My daughter," she said in English with a strong Creole inflection. Then she said in French, "Dix-sept trente-trois." She repeated it, then uttered, Dieu, ait pitie."

Camille Garnier sat rigid in her chair staring at something only she could see. The figure behind her faded, slowly dissipating into the mist from which it came. Finally, the mist itself evaporated and the room was again empty of all but mortals. Mortals who were shocked and speechless.

Madame Fontaine regained consciousness but it was definitely Camille Garnier who said, "Just tell me what the hell happened here."

"What did she say?" Sher asked.

"Who?" Camille answered.

"Your gran, Marie Leveau," Kate said in an even tone of voice.

"You aren't kidding?"

"Not kidding, girlfriend," Tara said.

"Rick, were you recording sound too?" Kate asked.

"Yes."

"Good then we can check this out but I believe she said '1733,' and 'May God have mercy,'" Kate told them.

"Is that a historical reference, a date that something occurred?" Norm said.

Camille Garnier was slowly regaining her wits. She tried to make sense of the conversation around her but everything was still a blur.

"I don't know, Norm, we'll have to check," Kate answered.

Sher drew back the curtains to let the fading evening light into the room.

"That's much less creepy, thank you babe," Rick said.

Garnier sipped water from a tumbler as her hands still trembled. The others were stunned, even Finn was perplexed at what he witnessed.

"I've seen some unusual things, but that moved to the top of the list," Rocco said.

"What do you remember, Camille?" Kate asked.

"I remember drinking the tea," she paused for a few moments, then added, "and honestly, that's about all. Did I say something in French?"

"Yes, you did. And so did Marie."

"Marie? You act like she was here."

"She was, Camille, she stood right behind you."

"My God."

"We all saw her," Sher said.

"That has never happened before. There must be some compelling reason to expend all that energy to reach me."

"For some reason I find this much easier to believe than I would have a year ago," Norm said.

"We are the home of Robert the Doll, after all," Finn said.

"For now, why don't we accept the fact that we are being warned about something possibly linked to the date 1733 and focus on that," Kate suggested. "How and why, we can sort out later."

"So, you are taking this seriously?" Norm asked.

"We'd be foolish not to."

"I don't need anymore convincing," Finn said.

"Let's talk this out," Kate said.

"What is 1733?" Nick asked.

"I don't know about anybody else but I could use some coffee," Finn said with an expectant look toward Sher.

"Put some Bailey's in mine," Rick said.

"Second that," Rocco intoned.

"Coming right up," Sher said, "could use a hand, cutie pie," she said to Rick.

"Right behind you. Angel, can you cue up the vids from the time Camille begins to drink her tea. We'll be back in a moment."

"It will be easier to show you what happened, Camille, rather than tell you," Kate said.

Finn was not easily fooled, and he didn't think he had been just now. There was no motive for Camille Garnier to stage something as elaborate as this, and Finn knew fear when he saw it. The Conch Republic's only voodoo priestess was scared shitless.

Sher and Rick returned and placed two trays on the table. One held a large urn, the other mugs, cream and sugar, and other appurtenances.

"Rick can you play that footage back on the big TV?" Finn said.

"Working on it," he answered as he sipped black coffee from a blue mug with a dolphin on it.

"Camille, do you feel like looking at this yet?" Kate asked as Sher handed Garnier a steaming mug.

"There's some brandy in with the coffee," Sher told her.

"Let me drink some of this, give me a few more minutes."

"Take your time," Norm said.

"You're the scientist," Nick told Tara, "What's your take on what just happened?"

"Honestly, don't have a clue."

"How 'bout a theory?" Angel chirped.

"We just saw something that's not suppose to happen?"

"No one would disagree with that," Nick grinned.

"Was that a ghost?"

"Well, it wasn't the Coral Reef Monthly centerfold," Nick replied.

"Angel, could you lend a hand here?" Rick asked.

Conversation was desultory as each person mulled over what had occurred. Finn, Norm and Rocco conferred quietly together as they waited for Garnier to feel better.

"I wonder how I'll explain this to the mayor?" Norm said quietly.

"We're ready, whenever you want to proceed," Rick announced.

Camille, nodding her head, said, "I'm ready. Let's see the video."

Again, the lights were dimmed but the drapes remained open as evening had turned to twilight outside. They grouped themselves around one end of the table and looked up to the smart TV on the other wall.

"We will see the footage from camera one first, that was the one directly in front of Camille, then we will look at number two, which was the one Angel set up for a side view," Rick said.

The screen jerked to life with the view of everyone sitting around the table. A moment later the sound kicked in and they could hear Camille asking if there were any questions.

She drank the tea, at which point, Finn said, "Freeze it there, Rick."

The screen froze as Camille sat the cup back down on the table.

"Camille, what was in the tea? If you don't mind me asking."

"If you are concerned that the vapor of the tea somehow caused a mass hallucination, I don't see how that could be. It's a mix of saffron, cannabis, ginger, mixed with some Sleepy Times Celestial Seasonings tea."

"No eye of newt?" Norm asked.

Camille grinned and seemed to regain more energy, "No Lieutenant, no eye of newt, tongue of toad, or wing of bat."

"And that tea is what you usually use when you conduct a," Norm paused for a moment then finished, "seance?"

"Yes. Keep in mind I've only performed nine or ten of these, but none of them featured a special appearance by my kinswoman."

"Alright, Rick if you will," Finn spoke.

The TV screen unfroze and the recording continued. There was eerie silence as Camille responded to the herbal tea and stared into the candle-lit dimness as a child awaiting a butterfly to land.

Suddenly, Camille stiffened slightly, sat up straighter, and said in French, "There is danger with the storm." She paused, still seemingly controlled by an invisible hand.

"Look, low on the screen behind where Camille was sitting," Finn said.

A grayish-white mist was forming, Camille sat staring into the candle light. The mist curled and swayed and grew taller, hovering over the back of her chair. Out of the mist, a shape slowly formed. The shape and likeness of Marie Leveau. She uttered "1733" and

"May God have mercy," then repeated it in a voice that echoed of the dark shadows in a cemetery at midnight.

"Freeze it, Rick," Finn said.

The misty, milky image of a woman dead for more than a hundred years filled the big screen. Her large almond eyes gazed out as if searching in the distance for something.

"My God, that's her," Camille said in a gasp.

"Does anybody have anything on 1733?" Norm asked.

"I haven't found anything that would relate to our situation," Tara said, "But I'll keep trying.

"That's just impossible," Rocco said.

"I'll play the nerdy scientist," Kate said, then continued to speak, "If we accept that energy can't be created or destroyed, but that it can exist in different forms, then the concept of ghosts has some traction."

"Given the circumstances, I don't have much trouble with that theory," Norm said.

"Do we all agree that this warning is real?" Finn asked the group.

There were no dissenters. Even Nigel seemed convinced that the threat was real.

"Bloody unsettling. But, I agree, it can't be ignored."

"Angel and I think we can perform a deep search on '1733' by using one of the algorithms that he has developed," Rick told them.

"But, we need some time, at least twenty-four hours," Angel said.

"Thanks, guys, if you need anything from the department contact Cheryl," Norm said.

"Will do."

"Camille, why don't you stay here tonight, we've got room," Sher said.

"You know, normally I like to be in my own space. But after what just happened, I'd feel a lot better here with y'all."

"Good, I'll put you next to the room Kate and Tara are sharing."

"Thank you, I really would rather not be alone tonight."

"Nigel, we better get you back to your lodging," Finn said.

"No worries, I can call for an Uber, mate."

"I'll run you over in one of Rick's beaters. I know just the one," Finn said, "We can discuss any loose ends on the way."

"Yes, I see your point."

"Norm, I'm headed out to take Nigel back. As of now, we are "go" with the plan. We'll touch base in the morning."

"Alright Finn. Nigel, we'll see you tomorrow," Norm answered.

"John are you riding with Norm?"

"I came over from the local business owner's briefing that Norm held at the EOC with him. If he's headed back there, I can go with him."

"I am, Red."

"I think us girls will hang out and discuss the evening's events," Kate said.

"Nick want to tag along?" Finn asked.

"Sure, let me get a couple of things from the room."

"I think I'll step outside for a smoke," Nigel said already reaching for the hard pack of Dunhills.

Finn followed Nigel to the porch after securing a digital key from Rick that would open one of the several garage spaces Rick maintained.

The steady breeze made it tricky to light a cigarette, but Finn could see that the Brit was battle tested. The air was oppressive even with the wind. Fast moving thick clouds obscured most star light, the neon lights reflected eerily off the cloud layer above, casting a mirror image down the length of the street.

"Finn, that was remarkable. What we just witnessed, I mean."

"Wonder what Conan Doyle would have said about that?" Finn said.

"Ah, I see you know British history."

"Doyle's interest in the supernatural is well known," Finn replied modestly.

"I'll wager a week's pay he never saw anything like that," Nigel said.

Nick joined them on the porch wearing his bush hat with his .22 in its holster clipped on his belt.

"Ready to go?"

"We'll walk to the garage, it's about three blocks from here," Finn explained to Nigel.

Old Town was alive with activity but most of it was with a purpose. Finn did not see the irresponsible, mindless behavior that had accompanied hurricanes in the past. But after Irma, and then the Big Tide, the folks who remained in the Keys tended to know when to sober up and fly right. This was one of those times. You still had tourists doing stupid tourist things but you also had the stupid money they contributed to the Conch Republic coffers.

But that was nothing new as locals had endured the intrusion for decades. Finn noticed Nick had dropped a few steps behind them and was keeping an eye on things. Nigel picked up on it also.

"Are we expecting trouble?"

"Nick's got good instincts, let's keep walking."

They turned down one of the narrow alleys that ran through parts of Old Town. It was darker here and no one else was visible.

"It's right up here," Finn said. The walked another ten yards and stopped in front of a sturdy one-story building with metal doors. Finn unlocked the garage and they walked inside. When Finn turned on the lights, Nigel gasped.

On the left side of the garage sat a 1958 MG Roadster with a rumble seat.

"Brilliant."

"I thought you would like this," Finn told the Brit.

"I didn't know they made one with a rumble seat."

"It wasn't a production model, apparently a member of the Royal Family engaged British Leyland to make one for him."

"How did it come to be on your interesting little island?"

"It is an interesting story, but I'll let Rick tell you. It's really his story. We best get you to your hotel. We have a long day tomorrow."

CHAPTER 10

The morning dawned but with no glimpse of the sun. Night turned to a lighter shade of dark, then to a somber gray. Finn was on the porch with his first cup of Joe. He rocked slowly in a hand-crafted chair as his coffee cooled.

"I thought you might be out here," Kate said as she opened the screen door and walked onto the porch.

"Rick and I need to get Nigel by eight o'clock."

"I'm surprised we aren't seeing any feeder bands," Kate said as she peered out into the dimly lit neighborhood.

"I think they will be here soon."

"Should you call it off?"

"I think we can get this phase of the operation completed before conditions deteriorate too much. If Nigel can get an I.D. on the fence, we can call it a day and focus on Fiona."

"You make it sound so, so normal, so everyday."

"No need to overcomplicate things."

"I think I'm still trying to wrap my head around what we experienced last night."

"For the record, there was nothing normal or everyday about that."

"Poor Camille, she was shook."

"Any more ideas about 1733?"

"Not yet. I know Norm's got Cheryl working on it because she called me late last night."

"As soon as I wrap things up with Nigel, I'll give it my full attention."

"Be careful, Finn. Try not to come back injected with some poison or something."

Finn showed the ghost of a smile, then said, "It's not like I impaled myself on the needle during a drunken binge, you know."

"I know. Just be careful."

Breakfast was a light variety of fruit and a help-yourself-omelet with juice and savory coffee. Finn and Rick ate quickly and departed to collect their gear. The others braced for a long day of last-minute storm preparations. In everyone's mind the cryptic 1733 pulsed like a neon sign outside a strip joint.

The streets were empty at such an early hour. They were in Rick's 1948 Plymouth woodie headed to pick up Nigel. Finn wanted to scope out the location prior to Nigel's operation.

He waited for them outside the hotel, dressed in casual clothes. He carried a rectangular package in his left hand, he held a lit cigarette in his other hand.

"Good morning, chaps."

"Morning," Finn answered from the passenger seat.

He snubbed the cigarette and discarded it in a trash bin, then got in the back seat.

Sprinkles appeared on the Plymouth's windshield as Rick pulled away from the hotel. The breeze was steady out of the south. The sprinkles turned into a hard, wind-whipped downpour that lasted about five minutes then stopped.

"That was a feeder band, Nigel," Finn explained, "We may have to work in between them."

"I see."

"It's going to be tricky getting the drone up in this weather," Rick said.

"That's why I thought it would be a good idea to scout out the location first."

"I'm glad you suggested that, Finn. "I don't have a good feeling about this whole thing."

"Look, Nigel, we can scrap this and we'll back you that it was too risky with the weather," Finn said.

"Let's proceed as planned, see if we can get something accomplished, at least get an I.D. on this person."

The gallery was in a high-end row of boutiques close to Mallory Square. The last of the cruise ships departed in the early morning hours leaving the Outer Mole empty. Two hearty joggers loped along the winding path that ran along the edge of the docks. Some workers wearing Public Works jumpsuits searched for items that needed to be secured from the increasing winds. They loaded trash cans into a truck and moved on past the row of shops.

They slowly rode by the gallery, sandwiched between a day spa and a designer fashion boutique. The gallery's front windows were boarded up as were most of the others shops on the narrow street. Finn took pictures with his phone, as Rick drove on past and turned on the first street that would take them back to Front Street.

Rick parked in a small lot about two blocks from the gallery. Another pelting rain lashed the woodie as Rick said, "When this rain stops, I'll try and get the drone in the air, but I can't promise anything."

"Rick, if you can't, you can't. Don't sweat it."

"Thanks, Finn. But, I'll see what I can do."

The plan was for Nigel to approach the gallery and gain entrance. Finn would tail him timing it so he arrived in front of the gallery when Nigel entered. He would wait five minutes, then knock on the door with an excuse about hurricane safety and help Nigel get out of the gallery.

"It looks like we'll get a break from the weather for about thirty minutes during the time you are going to try to access the gallery," Rick said, as he looked up from his phone.

The rain slackened as quickly as it started. Rick opened the back hatch of the woodie and removed the drone and its control panel. They had ample time before Nigel was due to enter the gallery so they helped Rick prep the drone.

"I feel like we are making a training film for everything not to do," Nigel said tersely.

"My idea is to have the drone record whatever happens, assuming I can keep it in the air long enough to do that," Rick said.

"I'll go for a stroll and time how long it takes to get to the gallery on foot from here," Finn said as he donned a heavy-weather slicker that he pulled from the back of the Plymouth.

"Nigel, help Rick, I'll be back shortly."

Finn checked his dive watch then sauntered off toward the gallery. The morning was dim, some street lamps still glowed unsure if the night was ended.

"Have you used a drone?" Rick asked.

"A few times," Nigel answered.

"This one is pretty basic, it takes a video record of its flight along with stills if needed. I control it with this hand-held gizmo."

"One of these feeder bands could knock it down, I should think?"

"Yes, I need to have it high enough not to be noticed, but the less altitude, the better with this weather. So, hopefully I'll find the sweet spot."

"I see."

Rick went through some preliminary calibrations on the drone, then seemed satisfied that it was ready. The wind had diminished but the sky roiled with fast moving thick, dark clouds. Traffic increased as people made last-minute trips for supplies.

Finn returned and said, "It should take six minutes to reach the gallery, Nigel."

"Should we synchronize now?" Rick asked.

"Might as well. I've got eight ten," Finn answered.

Rick and Nigel verified with a nod. Timing would be critical if things were to go smoothly.

"By the way, Nigel, Rick is a former Seabee and I trust him with my life."

"You have quite the circle of friends," Nigel said as he lit a cigarette. "I noticed they've got the front windows boarded up so I won't be able to use one for a quick exit. Looks like it's the door or nothing."

"Duly noted."

They had thirty minutes to kill and Finn tried to keep them loose.

"Either of you have an idea what 1733 could mean?"

"What if it's not a year?" Nigel asked.

"It could be an address," Rick suggested, then added, "Although I'm not sure how that would fit?"

"We need to stay open-minded about it, not get zoned in on it being a year," Finn said.

"As if we could be anything but 'open-minded' after last night," Rick said.

"Hear, hear to that," Nigel said.

"At least, it looks like the weather is going to give us a small window," Finn noted.

"I'm going to put the drone up and see how it does," Rick told them.

They backed away from the unit and Rick adjusted the controls. The small parking lot was deserted as the drone slowly rose in the air. Rick took it up to fifteen feet avoiding overhead wires and let it hover. He then took it up another ten feet, but brought it back down quickly as the wind buffeted the drone heavily at the increased height.

"I think it'll be okay if I keep it below twenty-five feet," Rick said.

"Nigel, you'll need to start walking in ten minutes," Finn said, "Rick, get the drone in place so it will record Nigel's approach."

"Will do. I'll send it off in eight minutes.."

Nigel smoked another cigarette while they waited.

"You know those things aren't good for you?" Rick said with a grin.

"Not much in my line of work is," Nigel replied.

"I see your point. I miss a good smoke every now and then," Rick said with nostalgia in his voice.

"Are you armed, Nigel?" Finn asked.

"Indeed. A Walther in a shoulder holster under my jacket. I have a knife used by the SAS chaps strapped to my left lower leg."

"I like you better every minute," Finn said, "Let's get this pig to the beauty pageant."

Nigel took a final drag on his Dunhill. He nodded to his companions, "Cheers for now." Then took off at a casual pace with the package under his right arm.

Rick started the drone and sent it on its way through the dull, grey morning light. He concentrated on the control panel as clearance was tight and there were overhead lines everywhere.

Finn remained silent. No need for nervous chatter, just focus on the task. Fragments of past assignments drifted through his thoughts. He looked for any similarities that would help with the current one.

"Alright, Finn, I've got the drone in place. Nigel's got about three minutes before he gets to the gallery."

"On my way."

The street in front of the gallery was empty except for a man in a jump suit at the far end picking up some trash. Nigel walked slowly toward the gallery and stopped a few yards from its entrance. He lit a Dunhill and casually surveyed the immediate vicinity. Only the man who now seemed to be checking shutters along the row of shops.

Finn should be coming into sight in a couple more minutes. Nigel saw no evidence of security cameras on the gallery facade. The man walking toward him, was making a notation in a small notebook and seemed oblivious to Nigel as he approached. He carried a slender pole made to pick up trash in his right hand.

The man continued walking but Nigel felt a sudden sting on his neck as the man passed by and kept going. There was no sign of Finn. Nigel dropped his cigarette and fell to the ground losing his grip on the package. The man turned sharply and walked back toward Nigel. He grabbed the package, stuffed it in a sack-like container that was slung over his shoulder and quickly walked around the corner and out of sight.

Finn picked up his pace but as he walked by a stack of plywood a rogue gust of wind blew the top piece of wood off the pile into Finn's head. He went down to one knee, then slumped to the ground.

He regained his senses, but was unsure of how long he was out. He stood and began to jog toward his meeting with Nigel. As he neared the intersection of Front Street, Rick swung around the corner in the Plymouth, threw the door open, and said, "C'mon, Nigel's in trouble."

Finn explained what happened as Rick roared down the street toward Nigel's body.

"It's a good thing we had the drone up, I saw what happened and headed this way."

"Good work, Rick."

"You better have Kate take a look at you too. That's an ugly looking bruise on the side of your face."

Rick pulled to a stop next to Nigel's prostrate form. Finn assessed the situation and told Rick, "We need to get him to Kate, I think he's been poisoned."

They placed him in the rear seat of the woodie as the street remained deserted. There was no sign of life in the gallery. As if to punctuate the moment another feeder band unleashed a torrent of wind and rain at them as Rick drove away with purpose.

CHAPTER 11

Nigel lay unmoving on a table in the kitchen as Kate and Camille worked on him. They had quickly turned the large, commercial-style kitchen into a makeshift emergency room.

"Rick, can you play the drone footage for us," Kate said.

"Will a tablet be a large enough screen?"

"Yes."

"Give me a minute."

Nigel was alive but his respirations were shallow and labored. He remained unconscious. His arms and legs were exhibiting signs of contractions, random spasms that shook his entire body.

"OK, I've got it," Rick said as he held a tablet up so Kate and Camille could see what happened. They watched the man approach, then the quick movement with the slender rod that flicked out, then seem to deflect off something in Nigels shirt pocket, before striking Nigel in the neck.

"Look, it struck his Dunhill box and only caught him a glancing blow on the neck," Kate said as she peered at the tablet.

"We need to know exactly what the rod contained," Camille said.

"My guess would be strychnine," Finn offered.

"Why do you say that?" Sher asked.

"The method of delivery, the fact that the Bulgars have been cozy with the KGB for years, and Nigel's reaction indicates some type of respiratory distress and muscular spasms."

"I'm impressed Finn," Kate said, "Tara have you found anything?"

"I think Finn is right. According to what I've been reading strychnine is a leading candidate for our unknown toxin."

"Camille, let's prevent him from going into anaphylactic shock," Kate told her friend.

"Sher don't you keep some IV fluids for emergencies?"

"Yes, on my way."

"Bring Ringer's lactate times two, please," Kate added.

"It looks like he didn't get a direct hit from the tip of the rod," Rick said.

"What rod," Norm's voice said from the doorway. John Rocco stood next to him as they surveyed the scene in front of them.

"It looks like Nigel was poisoned with an injection of strychnine, or something similar," Kate said.

"I think if we took some skin scrapings from the penetration area it would help narrow things down," Camille said.

"Let's do it," Kate answered.

"Norm, somebody knew what we were doing," Finn said.

"Looks like it, doesn't it?"

"Is our Brit friend going to make it?" Rocco asked.

"Too early to tell," Kate said.

"We can't perform Marchand's test to determine if it is strychnine unless you have a gas chromatograph," Camille said.

"That, we don't have," Sher answered.

"Well then, we'll make an educated guess; based on the symptoms he exhibits he's been administered something that is causing muscle spasms and respiratory distress. Two main symptoms of strychnine poisoning. If we treat the symptoms as we would any unknown substance, then whether it's strychnine or not we will be addressing the the effects until we can identify it."

"I yield to your knowledge, Kate," Norm told her.

"His breathing is getting better," Camille said.

"If there is nothing we can do here, why don't we focus on the storm. And if anyone has any ideas on 1733, let me know ASAP," Norm said.

"Yes, it probably would be better to give Camille and I room to work. Tara could you and Nick drive to the Mote Marine lab and pick up a few things for me? I'll make a list."

"Sure, Kate."

"Do you think we should move him to the hospital?" Finn asked.

"Honestly, I think we can do as much for him right here under the circumstances."

"I suspect he would prefer not to go to the hospital," Finn said.

"Then that's settled," Norm said, "Could we review the video again?"

"Let's go to the sunroom," Rick said.

Finn tossed the Jeep keys to Nick as he walked by and out the kitchen door. Kate handed Tara a list of items to retrieve from the lab and she and Nick departed. Sher returned with an armful of medical supplies that she spread out on one of the kitchen work stations.

The drone footage played on the large wall-mounted television screen in the sunroom. They silently watched the attack, then the Plymouth arrived and Rick and Finn got out and retrieved Nigel. The video ended at that point.

"What happened to you?" Norm asked just noticing the abrasion and bruising on Finn's face and head.

"Got whacked by a piece of plywood. Knocked me out for a second or two and when I was just getting back up, Rick came round the corner with the woodie."

"There was no sign of the attacker?"

"He did a good job of disappearing," Rick said, "He couldn't have got very far, but we were focused on Nigel and he might have been hiding."

"Is this the Bulgarian bunch?" Rocco asked.

"That would be my guess," Finn said.

"Should we contact Nigel's handlers?" Rick asked.

"Interpol is headquartered in Lyon, France," Norm said, "I have their contact information. Nigel gave it to me the other day."

"Norm, if there is a mole involved let's hold off on any communication. Let's see if Nigel pulls through and ask him how he wants to handle it," Finn suggested.

"Yes, I see your point. We can use the storm as leverage to stone wall them for a short time," Norm said.

"I wonder when he might regain consciousness?" Rocco asked.

"I'm sure they will keep us apprised of his condition," Norm answered, "I have to keep moving, we're still checking the breakwater segments, and I've got a conference call with Commander Kenny to coordinate the Navy's help with this storm and the aftermath."

"Keep working on 1733. I'll be at the EOC if you need me."

"It's almost ten o'clock," Rocco said, "Angel and I need to check several businesses I own and see if they are ready for this storm. We have a good staff but I want to personally check things given the strength of Fiona. We should be able to make it back here by mid-afternoon to help you."

"I understand. Nick and Tara will be returning shortly and we'll continue to run down 1733."

"Ciao."

"Later," Angel said with a nod.

"I need to check on a few things myself," Rick said.

Finn welcomed the solitude, at least briefly. The morning had been a cluster from start to finish. If he'd been on time, Nigel wouldn't be fighting for his life now. He knew there was nothing he could have done to prevent it, still it rankled him.

What the hell was 1733? If not a date, then what? He tried to empty his mind, as they do in Siddha Yoga. Finn found the exercise difficult with all that had transpired during the last forty-eight hours. He finally gave up and decided to poke his head in the kitchen and check on Nigel.

He met Nick and Tara as they came in carrying several large duffle bags full of equipment and supplies.

"Here, let me help you," Finn said, extending his hand.

They stopped outside the kitchen door that remained closed.

"Tara why don't you go in, let them know you are back," Finn suggested, "We'll stay out here."

"Sure."

"How's it doing outside?" Finn asked after Tara entered the kitchen.

"The rain is steady, wind is holding at about twenty-five to thirty."

"It probably won't get better from here on," Finn said.

The kitchen door cracked open and Tara said, "He's still alive, they are trying to reduce the muscle spasms right now. If you would set the stuff inside the door, we'll take it from there."

"No worries," Finn said. He knew when they were nicely being asked to go away.

"Gotcha," Nick added.

"We'll be in the sunroom."

"Let's take a look at the latest radar," Nick said.

They pulled up the Weather Channel's projected path for Fiona. It was headed directly for the Conch Republic. It was still holding as a Cat 4 but was predicted to increase its intensity later in the day. The projected speed of the storm had it battering the Conch Republic for more than sixteen hours before moving on out into the Gulf of Mexico.

"One thing I don't get," Finn told Nick, "How do these guys think they're going to get off the island?"

"Yeah, I've wondered why they didn't wait until after the storm to grab the whiskey and the fake painting."

"Another mystery," Finn said.

"Let's find Rick and see if we can help him."

———

In the kitchen, Nigel remained unconscious. His breathing was not so labored, and his pulse was steady and regular. Two IVs kept him hydrated and one was administering an atropine drip to counter the toxin.

"It's a good thing he did not get a full dose," Kate said.

"Getting him here so fast will help his odds immensely," Camille added.

"What's next?" Tara asked.

"We'll have to wait, keep monitoring him. Keep flushing his system and make sure the muscular contractions don't recur," Kate said.

"Any thoughts on '1733' at all?" Sher asked.

"I'm beginning to think it's not a date," Kate told them.

"If not a date, then what?" Tara asked.

Silence hung in the air. No one ventured any suggestions as to what the numbers might signify or why a spectral spirit dead for over a hundred years chose to appear and speak.

"Why don't we take a break. If one of us could stay with Nigel, I'd feel a lot better. But, I think we need to regroup and focus on this storm," Kate said.

"I'll volunteer," Tara said, "You've all been in here for a while, take a break."

Fiona continued to strengthen as it churned toward the Conch Republic. The storm was compact with a tight eye that showed no signs of weakening. Living in Hurricane Alley meant six months of idyllic winter climate, but another six months of constant threat from the cyclones that the Taino people called "hurucan" or "evil spirit of the winds."

The Taino, an indigenous culture that was spread across the Lesser Antilles at the time of the Spanish incursion into the Caribbean, probably never experienced an evil spirit such as Fiona would prove to be.

Hurricanes were more frequent and intense in the years since the Big Tide. Padraig Kennedy foresaw this occurring and designed the breakwater system with hydraulic extensions that if needed could be adjusted to divert the force of any tidal surge accompanying a storm. They could also be raised to give an additional thirty feet of height to selected segments of the breakwater.

The existence of the Conch Republic depended on Kennedy's breakwater system and everyone knew it. Norman James knew this, in spades. As the de facto Chief of Police and Public Servant No. 1, his job was to ensure the safety of the island and its inhabitants.

The EOC was humming with a controlled energy of pros working during a crisis. Several CBees manned the crisis hotline as Norm conferred with his second-in-command, Cheryl McIntosh.

"I would have given a month's pay to have been there last night," Cheryl said.

"I was there, and I wish I hadn't been. Cheryl, this was so far beyond Robert the Doll I don't think he'll ever bother me again. I could tell even Finn was shook."

"So, what do you think the '1733' is?"

"I don't have any theories right now. But, we've got to figure that out, because I think our island depends on it."

"Oh my God, Norm, you're serious."

"As an effing heart attack," Norm replied with a rare lapse of the tongue.

"Are there any crews still out checking the breakwater?"

"Yes, two."

"Let me know if they have anything to report."

"Copy that. How's Sean Connery's lookalike?"

"He was hanging on when I left. Strychnine is a nasty poison but he couldn't be in better hands."

"That's for sure."

"I need to meet with the mayor and a couple of council members, will you be good here?"

"Yes, Tina is coming in soon to help coordinate things, so I think we'll be OK. I've had our generators checked and they are good to go."

"Good work, Cheryl."

"Thanks, LT."

CHAPTER 12

The rain was intermittent, gusty winds swirled through the narrow streets of Old Town. They threatened to reach tropical-storm force within the next few hours. The streets were almost empty as Norm drove his "company car," a modified SUV equipped with a winch and heavy-duty cast iron bumpers, slowly along Duval Street toward his meeting with the mayor.

The man everyone called "LT" was feeling the weight of his job. He had witnessed something counter to all his education and training. Yet he had seen it, of that he was convinced. He considered the group of de facto public officials, and the mayor that he worked with to provide a cohesive form of local government. They were solid enough in the public duties they preformed, but during a crisis they relied on his judgement and experience to lead the way. They managed to keep the framework of local government together. An unorthodox version of local government to be sure, but one that worked for the days of the Big Tide.

How they would respond to his story of an impromptu seance and a dire threat, he could only shake his head. Ultimately, they would follow his plan, trusting his judgement, if the past was any indication. He felt that weight. Heavy is the head responsible for the island's safety in the face of a Cat 5.

Throw in Nigel's attempted murder, and the possibility of some very bad Eastern European hired muscle in town and it didn't get much better. Norm's gut told him the honest truth was not going to work in this situation. He remembered Father Tony, the old Irish Catholic priest on Big Pine Key. He had harbored more than a few Cuban refugees over the years, saving them from cruel deportation after risking their lives to reach America.

The Irish priest was a legend, known as much for his malarkey as his soul saving abilities. The feds were never able to pin him down, as they could never get a straight answer out of him. Norm decided the Father Tony strategy would be his best bet. Feeling a certain sense of relief Norm drove on, noticing the water that was beginning to pond in some places.

Across town, Finn and Nick helped Rick with securing the garages that housed his "beater" collection of restored vintage automobiles.

"Man, I'd hate to lose any of these babies," Rick said as they checked on the small building that housed a pair of beauties. A 1965 GTO and a '64 Chevelle sat side by side on the concrete floor. Both from the "hey day" of muscle cars, one of Rick's favorite eras.

"It would be a shame," Finn answered.

"I tell you that damn seance rattled my ass," Rick admitted.

"I think it did everyone's," Nick said.

"Finn, do you have any clue about 1733?" Rick asked.

"Nothing."

"Nothing more we can do here, let's go on. We've got three more to check," Rick said.

Finn wheeled the Jeep through increasingly sparse traffic as water ran in rivulets across the pavement. Street lights were on responding to the lack of sunlight.

"I wonder where our whiskey thieves are holed up?" Finn said.

"My guess would be the same place the painting is that was lifted from Nigel," Nick said.

"There's something we're missing," Finn said, then went on, "Why would you do something and risk getting stuck on the island for days, if not weeks, with the incriminating evidence."

"Unless, you thought you had a way of the island," Rick postulated.

"In this weather?" Nick said playing devil's advocate.

"Exactly, so what are we missing?"

The Wrangler was quiet as all three friends mulled over the conundrum. Air and sea travel were out of the question. The only two means of accessing or leaving the island.

"Well, that's a puzzle worthy of a Death in Paradise script."

"Finn, I didn't know you watched it."

"Rick, it's one of the very few I do watch."

"Clue in the heathen marine," Nick said with a grin.

"It's a British detective show filmed on Guadeloupe, passing as the fictional island of St. Marie. Each episode features an 'impossible murder' that the team, led by a quirky, fish-out-of-water detective from London, must solve," Finn explained.

"So, are you thinking we should apply some of the same upside down logic to our problem here?" Rick asked.

"Usually the answer revolves around a single, small detail seemingly out of context at the start. But through logical examination of the situation, it is determined how that small detail is the solution to the murder."

"Or maybe they just fucked up, underestimated the storm and what would happen," Nick said.

"That's a very real possibility," Finn said.

"I've been in enough FUBAR situations to strongly consider that option," Nick said.

They tightened a loose shutter on one of the remaining garage's door. The final stop proved uneventful and they returned to the B and B.

Sher met them in the small cloakroom where they were hanging their wet clothes to dry. She had a tray loaded with mugs of coffee that the men gratefully accepted.

"How's Nigel?" Finn asked as he tested the coffee.

"Still unconscious, not out of the woods."

"Have you heard from Norm?"

"Yes, about fifteen minutes ago. He'll be here in thirty minutes to discuss our problem."

"Good."

"Everyone needs to eat something. I've got a late lunch ready, so meet us in the big dining room as soon as you change clothes."

"Thanks, baby cakes. Don't know what we'd do without you," Rick told his wife.

"You'd be a lot hungrier, that's for sure."

Thirty minutes later, everyone but Kate sat at the long ranch-style table eating hog fish nuggets, fish dip, grits, and coleslaw. Two large pitchers of iced tea sat between the plates of food.

"Don't be shy," Finn said, "Who knows what 1733 means?"

"Please, speak up," Norm said from the entrance to the dining room.

"Norm, come in and grab a plate," Rick said.

"Thanks, haven't eaten since breakfast. How's Nigel?"

"Hangin' in there, Kate's with him now," Finn told his friend.

"Camille, have you had any more thoughts on what your kinswoman was trying to communicate to you? I realize you've been busy with Nigel but sometimes things come to us when we are engaged in stressful activity."

"Honestly, Lieutenant I thought something would come to me. Something from the past, but so far, nothing."

"I can tell you that Kate is exploring the possibility that it is not a date," Tara interjected.

"Yes, we discussed that while we were checking the car garages," Finn replied.

"An address, maybe?" Sher said.

"Norm what's the latest on Fiona?" Nick asked.

"Commander Kenny informed me that it is officially a Cat 5 now, and unfortunately she has slowed down."

"That's not good," Finn said, "It will prolong the exposure to the worst conditions."

"Norm, what's the word on the breakwater inspection?"

"The crews have completed a second inspection and found nothing that appeared to be in jeopardy of failing. All the extension mechanisms are working. But, I plan to keep a continual watch on them through the observation cameras set up around the perimeter of the structure."

"How many men do you think are involved in the attack on Nigel and the whiskey?" Finn asked.

"Hard to say," Norm replied.

"We counted at least five the other night at Pasta Heaven," Nick said.

"And it looked like at least that many were staying in that house where we found the dead woman," Tara said.

"So, let's say there are ten to fifteen men involved with this Santos guy. Where would that many men be able to hide out?"

"We had trouble finding two hundred Haitians not too long ago," Norm reminded the group.

"Well, it seems to me that finding them isn't a high priority, at least right now. Our focus should be on 1733," Finn said.

"Finn, I agree. I didn't mean to insinuate that we should try to locate then prior to the storm. Just wondering where the hell they might be."

"The latest track information has Fiona's eye passing directly over the Conch Republic in the late-afternoon on Saturday," Rick said.

"That's only twenty-four hours or so," Finn said.

"What about the control center for the breakwater system?" Rick asked.

"Commander Kenny will send a detachment of Navy Seals. We don't know when they will arrive," Norm said.

"Good to know," Finn said.

"I'm going to spell Kate," Camille told them as she rose from her seat at the table.

A few minutes later Kate appeared looking haggard, but she gave a thumbs up as she entered the dining room.

"Is he going to make it?" Finn asked.

"I think so. For a man who smokes like a chimney, he's in remarkably good shape."

"Any guesstimate as to when he may regain consciousness?"

"Within the next few hours but he won't feel like a game of rugby. But, we may be able to ask him some questions."

"Any thoughts on 1733?"

"I don't think it's a date."

"Let her eat," Sher admonished Finn.

"I could use some food," Kate said with a nod.

"I'll fix you a plate, just sit down and relax," Sher told her friend.

Kate found room next to Finn and sat down. He gently squeezed her arm, and she leaned against him.

"Norm, have you heard from Nigel's people?" Rick asked.

"Nothing yet. I want them to make the first move, since it's obvious that they have a mole."

"How was your meeting with the mayor?" Finn asked.

"It could have been worse. I hate lying to politicians, because they can spot a lie in the dark. They're the best liars in the world. I stuck with the tack that we had reliable info there might be a threat to the island's safety. I avoided any references to voodoo priestesses, apparitions, or mysterious messages from the grave."

"Probably just as well," Finn said.

"Bob picked up that something was wrong, but he knows when to go with the flow. That's one of the reasons he's a good mayor, plus, he trusts my judgement"

"As do we," Rick said.

"I'm open for suggestions."

"Why don't we take another on-the-ground look at the breakwater before the weather deteriorates and it's dark," Finn said.

"It would be good if we could muster two teams and split the work in half," Norm said.

"I'm in," Nick said.

"Me too," Rick added.

"I wonder if we can get Rocco and Angel to help," Norm questioned.

"If they're finished with their preparations, I don't see why they wouldn't."

"Nick, see if you can reach Angel. Ask him if they'd like to participate in a sunset tour of the breakwater," Finn said.

"Will do."

"Norm, do you have another heavy-duty vehicle we can use besides the one you are driving?"

"Yes, at HQ."

"We better get moving, then. We are running out of time," Finn said.

CHAPTER 13

Hurricanes fascinated Finn, as did most natural phenomena. He'd spent most of his youth living on the coast of north Florida and Southeast Georgia. The Spartina marsh held many memories for him with its fishing, crabbing, and oysters. Mangroves had replaced the sedges and saw grass of the Georgia marsh in the Keys. They served as natural breakwaters, helping to mitigate wave energy and tidal surges. When sea levels stabilized after the Big Tide, mangroves proved their resilience and continued to flourish providing a safe habitat for many marine creatures.

Fiona worried Finn. It was no coincidence that he had witnessed the most convincing argument for the existence of ghosts he was likely to see. The "ghost" had specifically called out this storm and left no doubt as to the hurricane's threat to the island. Finn had compartmentalized the question of *"was it really a ghost?"* He would delve into that later. Now, he focused on 1733 and its role in the situation they faced.

Finn, Nick, Tara, and Rick were in one of Norm's heavy-duty SUVs, equipped for search and rescue, with Finn at the wheel. Norm was with Rocco and Angel in a similar vehicle as they inspected the breakwater in the wind-whipped weather. There was a vehicle path that ran at the base of the breakwater its entire perimeter around the island. They started at the point where the breakwater intersected the causeway to the naval base at Boca Chica. Norm took the Northside route, while Finn went Southward with a plan to meet near Fort Zach at the west end of the island.

Finn drove slowly as they looked for anything suspicious. The breakwater was built in modular segments of twenty-foot long, steel walls anchored deep in the rocky substrata. They displayed a slight outward curve designed to lessen the impact of sustained storm waves. But, the critical component of the breakwater was hidden from sight. Each segment rose twenty-five feet above the surface of the water. If needed, an additional fifteen feet of height could be achieved by the hydraulic-driven extension sheets in each segment.

"Finn, have the extensions ever been used?" Tara asked.

"No, so far they have repelled each storm without using them."

"This may be the first time," Rick said, "I hope they've checked the hydraulics in each one."

"I'm sure Norm didn't overlook that," Finn said.

"Could any of this have a connection to basketball?" Rick asked.

"I don't think so, why do you ask?"

"Well, I didn't say anything before because I don't think it's relevant but 17 and 33 are John Havlicek's and Larry Bird's numbers. Seventeen for Hondo and thirty-three for the Birdman."

"We'll keep it in mind," Finn replied.

The rain slacked off and the wind subsided as a break in the feeder bands caused conditions to temporarily improve. Finn kept the Jeep moving slowly along the breakwater's vehicle path.

"Another weekend, another life-threatening event for the ol' Conch Republic," Nick said with a smirk.

"Lately, it seems that way," Rick commented.

"I hope Nigel pulls through. I feel responsible. I should have been there."

"Finn, most guys wouldn't have been getting up off the ground like you were when I came 'round the corner, they would have been out for the count."

Finn's right eye was swollen and a nasty bluish bruise mushroomed along his cheek and ear. Kate had dressed the wound the best she could, but he looked like he'd gone three rounds with Mike Tyson.

"Thanks for being there, so quick, Rick."

"I'm still trying to process the whole 'ghost thing' from last night," Nick said.

"Even for Key West, that was totally off the wall," Rick stated.

"Totally agree with that," Tara said.

"What's that ahead?" Finn said.

"Where?"

"To the left, along the edge of the path."

Finn pulled to a stop next to a tool belt and several tools lying scattered on the pavement. Nick pulled his rain gear hood over his head and stepped out of the SUV. He walked along the length of the segment nearest to the tools. Tara followed Nick out of the Jeep and began to collect the tools that were scattered on the ground. Rick took pictures, while Nick walked back toward the SUV. He picked up the belt, conferred briefly with Tara, then they both jumped back in the SUV's rear seat.

"These must belong to public works, right?" Nick asked.

"I'll text Norm and see if he can confirm that, Rick send me the pictures you took and I'll forward them to Norm."

"On their way now, Finn.

"I didn't see any problem with that segment," Nick added.

"Why don't we mark it on the GPS system in the vehicle, and one of you put it on your phone, just in case?" Finn said.

Finn finished his text to Norm, then they drove on through the darkening evening. The clouds, large and ponderous were swept along like Lego blocks by the swirling, gusting wind.

Three miles farther they found one of the hydraulic station's doors open and banging in the wind. Nick again jumped out to inspect the door. He walked inside the twelve by twelve compartment that housed the hydraulic controls for several segments on either side of it.

Rick joined him a moment later. They carefully went over the controls, but seemingly nothing was out of order.

"Rick, you're the expert here, do you see anything out of whack?"

"Not that's obvious, but I'd need to run a diagnostic on these control terminals to see if anything at that level was tampered with."

"I'll text Finn and let him know to tell Norm ASAP. I wonder if they've found any oddities along their route?"

"Yes, that would be interesting to know."

They secured the open door and returned to the Jeep.

"How'd it look?" Finn asked.

"Tell Norm to send a tech over to run a diagnostic on the controls," Rick answered.

They marked the spot on GPS then moved on down the breakwater. The rain picked up again as another broad feeder band whipped through the island. A loose trash can lid blew across the expanse and slammed into the window next to Tara.

"Whoa," she said as she moved closer to Nick, away from the window.

"These windows are bullet proof, Tara," Finn told her.

"Would have been nice to know two minutes ago," she said with faked aggravation.

"You know, one of these days, a guy like Cantore is going to be out there, right in the middle of things, and something's going to fly by and take his head off, live."

"Film at eleven," Nick joined in.

"If anybody gets out again, use one of the helmets in the back," Finn said, "we don't need anymore head injuries."

They skirted the West Martello and knew they were close to the rendezvous spot where they would meet the others. The rain pelted down as the daylight faded to a wet gray.

It was almost dark when they meet up with Norm and his passengers. They parked in a covered municipal lot used by first responders.

"Thanks for catching that hydraulic station," Norm said as they stood in a circle between their vehicles. "I've got a crew headed over there now."

"Do you think it was an accident, somebody just forgot to secure the door?" Rocco asked.

"We'll know more when they run a diagnostic," Norm answered.

"Did you find anything suspicious?" Finn asked.

"Nothing that screamed "a catastrophe is about to happen.""

"Is there anything else you want us to do?" Rocco asked.

"I think at this point we've done all we can out here. It's time to hunker down for the night. I'll be at the EOC for the duration. And would somebody please come up with what 1733 means." Norm said in mock desperation.

"I need a jolt of Sher's coffee," Nick said.

"Me too," Tara agreed.

"Seriously, any leads on 1733, let me know immediately. Why don't you keep the SUV, we have several at headquarters. Our cooperative agreement with the Navy with regard to smugglers and human traffickers has paid off nicely. We've been able to purchase quite a bit of equipment and vehicles we would not have been able to without the cash from impounded boats and airplanes."

"Thanks, Norm. We may have need for it before the night is over," Finn said.

"I'll take Red and Angel with me back to the EOC. Angel's truck is there."

"Angel and I will be in my office monitoring our restaurants and hotels. If anything new comes up, please text us ASAP."

"Will do," Finn answered.

"Keep me in the loop regarding Nigel."

Wind pounded against the SUV as Finn drove along Duval Street. The gaudy neon lights were subdued and smeared by the rain, the street had the forlorn look of a Scorsese movie. Most businesses were boarded up and closed. The few that remained open, would have to have some hale and hearty patrons. The folks at the leather emporium "Whips-R-Us" waved to the Jeep as it rolled past.

"Ever since you mentioned coffee, I can't quit thinking about a hot mug full," Rick said.

"I think we could all stand a shot of caffeine," Finn said.

What's that?" Nick said as he pointed to a car halfway up on the curb.

"Is it abandoned?" Tara asked.

"Can't tell from here," Nick said.

Finn slowed the Jeep and pulled over next to the car, it appeared to be a rental by the plates.

"I'll check it out," Nick said, "I'm already soaked."

"Be careful," Tara said, "Here, put the helmet on."

Nick jumped out between gusts of wind and walked toward the rental that looked to be an EV. As he approached the car some signage from a store several buildings down tore loose and came tumbling down the street directly toward Nick. Finn blew the horn but Nick had already seen what was coming and smoothly ducked beneath the car roof as the tangle of metal, lights, and wood slammed into the opposite side of the car, then blew over the roof and on down the street.

Nick cautiously peered over the roof, then gave a thumbs-up toward the Jeep.

He could see the figure of a person through the rain-streaked window. He tried the door and it came open, as he slowly brought the door farther out, the body inside fell out and sprawled on the wet pavement.

Nick stepped back, looked at the SUV, raised both arms and mouthed WTF. Finn emerged from the SUV, with a helmet on and joined Nick.

"Looks like another European, but he's not one of the men we saw at Pasta Heaven," Nick told Finn.

"I'll text Norm, let me get in the car for a minute."

"Do we have unknown players here?" Nick mused out loud.

"Could be," Finn answered as he wrote a text for Norm.

"Looks like a single bullet wound on the side of his head. Must have been a small calibre weapon, there's not much mess."

"Norm's on his way with Big Dog and Joey," Finn said as he put his phone away.

"How do you read this?" Nick asked as they crouched low behind the shelter of the car.

"The bad guy got whacked by a badder guy? Maybe?" Finn said.

"How many bad guys do we have running around?" Rick said.

"We may need a list to keep up," Finn answered.

Rick found a tarp in the back of the SUV and they covered the body with it. They heard the sirens before the SUV appeared with Big Dog at the wheel and Norm riding shotgun.

Joey emerged from the back seat with a crime-scene kit in hand and walked to the tarp. A large palm frond torn loose from a tree and whipped toward him but his athletic skills kicked in as he dodged the potential deadly weapon with a juke to his right.

"Careful, Joey," Norm said as he approached with a helmet in his hand that Joey gratefully accepted.

"Thanks, LT."

Finn and Nick joined them. Joey pulled the tarp back to assess the body.

"Any reason to chalk out the body, LT?"

"Under the circumstances, no. I doubt chalk would even stick."

"Nick thought it looked like a single-bullet, small caliber," Finn said and then explained how the body fell out of the car. Joey took photos and some measurements. He searched for identification but found nothing.

"LT, something here in his shirt pocket," Joey said. He handed Norm a piece of paper torn from a spiral notebook. Norm carefully unfolded the paper that was wet and flimsy to reveal in ink that began to run, 1733 in large numerals.

"It just gets better and better," Norm said.

The silence was punctuated by the rain that was pushed by increasing winds as another feeder band made its presence felt.

"I've got an ambulance on the way," Norm said. "There's no reason for everyone to get soaked, why don't you head on back to Rick's and I'll meet you there when we get this wrapped up. Maybe an hour or so."

Finn shook his head in approval. He and Nick jogged to the waiting SUV where Rick and Tara bombarded them with questions.

"No way, 1733. In his pocket?" Tara exclaimed as Rick just stared at Finn but said nothing.

CHAPTER 14

The B and B looked formidable with all the hurricane shutters in place and storm doors placed over the main entrances around the building. Finn drove the SUV over the curb and as close to the porch as he could get it without ruining Sher's flower beds.

Rick led the way, and walked around the porch toward the rear where they entered a small utility room. They discarded their wet gear and hung items up to dry on the hooks spaced around the room.

When they reached the alcove that led to the kitchen, Finn slowly cracked the door and saw with alarm that Nigel was no longer there. Kate, Sher, and Camille sat at one of the counters with steaming mugs in hand.

"We moved Nigel to one of the first-floor rooms. I think he's going to make it," Kate said, as the others followed Finn into the kitchen.

"The man's got the constitution of a horse," Camille said.

"We had to reclaim the kitchen. I'll have something ready to eat in an hour. Sorry to be so late," Sher said.

Finn brought the women up to speed on what had transpired during their perimeter search of the breakwater.

"Merde," Camille uttered, "I wish I could think of what those numbers mean."

"How is it out there?" Kate asked.

"Bad, and getting worse," Finn said.

"The old glass-half-empty weather report," Rick said with a grin.

"I really need to ask Nigel some questions," Finn said.

"Give him a little more time and I'll try to rouse him. He may not be cognizant even if he is awake," Kate told him, she looked at her watch, then said, "I better check on him, I'll be back in a minute."

"Once again the lady scientist and the voodoo priestess shock and amaze," Rick said.

The lights flickered, went out, then came back. Sher began to light candles that were spread around on the kitchen counters.

"Finn, would you give me a hand with the generator?" Rick asked, "Looks like we'll need it sooner than later."

"Sure."

The B and B's generator was industrial strength and was housed in a separate enclosure adjacent to the structure. A breezeway did little to protect them from the slanting rain as they walked toward it. Once inside, Rick made sure the generator was in working order.

"Why don't we take one more look at the breakwater. I'd like to look at some older drone footage that will show the water-side in more detail," Finn told his friend.

"What are you thinking?"

"Nothing specific, trying to cover all the bases. It's probably not going to help us. But, I'd rather be doing something than just sitting around listening to the wind howl."

"Agreed."

"I think these guys will make a play to get off the island as soon as this storm blows past. We need to be ready. I'm guessing that Norm thinks the same."

"I'll dig up that footage when we get back inside."

Kate was waiting to talk to Finn when they came back inside, "Give him about thirty minutes and I'll let you talk to him for ten minutes, no longer."

"Yes, ma'am," Finn said with a grin.

"Any luck with 1733?"

"Not yet," Finn said as the grin disappeared.

"I'll admit it's a puzzler. Camille is convinced it holds the key to stopping a real threat."

"I don't think we've got any doubters in the congregation at this point, I'm going with "there are more things in heaven and earth, Horatio, than are dreamt of in your philosophy."

"Shakespeare, in a time of crisis and I thought you were just a thug with a shady past," Kate said with a twinkle in her eye.

"A well-rounded thug."

"Well-read, I'd say."

"Yeah, that too."

"How's your head? Do you want me to change the dressing for you?"

"Maybe later, I want to look at the breakwater vids with Rick again. See if we can get something we missed. I'll go check with him now, would you mind getting me when you think Nigel is ready? I'll leave it to you to decide, if you don't think he is up to it, we'll wait. It's your call."

"Thanks, Finn. And I will come get you if he's able. You and Rick will be in the sunroom?"

"Yes."

When Finn found his friend, he had set the equipment up and was waiting to start. Rick had placed twin monitors on the table that were synched to the large, wall-mounted TV.

"How do you want to do this?" He asked Finn.

"Why don't we start down at the fort," Finn said referring to Fort Zachary Taylor, "and work back up the south side first, then do the north side. I may have to stop if for a while, if Kate gives the go-ahead to talk with Nigel."

"Sounds good, I'll get us cued up, give me a few seconds."

Rain slammed against the outside of the structure as wind drove it almost horizontal. The B and B stood resolute against the elements, offering shelter from the storm. Both men knew they were in for a long twenty-four hours.

Tara's head appeared in the doorway, "Can we come in?"

"Sure."

"Nick's got a weather update."

"Whatcha got?" Rick asked.

"Fiona's speed has increased. The eye will cross us before dawn."

"Exposing us for a longer time to hurricane winds," Finn said.

"Oh yeah, she's officially a Cat 5 now."

"The good news just keeps on coming," Rick said.

"Sher said supper will be ready in about thirty minutes. She's getting the paying guests squared away first," Tara said.

"Anything we can do in here?"

"Yeah, the more eyes, the better," Finn said, "Plus, if Kate gives the green light, I need to talk to Nigel."

"So, what's the plan here?" Nick asked.

"We are going to review drone footage that was taken of the exterior sides of the breakwater system. See if we get any clues to 1733," Rick told them.

"We're starting at Fort Zach and working up the south side of the structure," Finn added.

"Pull up a couple of chairs," Rick said.

Kate stared down at the British agent in the bed. He was pale, but his breathing was steady. Two IVs provided fluids to him. He opened eyes that were bloodshot and resembled a red circuit board. It was a struggle to focus but he was finally able to see the woman standing next to the bed.

"Dr. Sullivan, I presume."

"How are you feeling, Nigel?"

"Like I've been bolloxed by a lorry," he said.

"Do you think you can speak with Finn now?"

"Yes, and could I get a cup of tea, please."

"Alright, I'll be back in a few minutes."

Nigel tried to remember the events of the morning, but it was a hazy blur. *What the bloody hell had happened?* His mind was not working well, he finally closed his eyes and envisioned a hot cup of tea. It was this image that Finn disturbed when he came in the room and said, "Nigel, thought we'd lost you, friend."

"What happened?"

"Someone tried to kill you with an injection of strychnine."

"The man walking down the street?" Nigel asked, then noticed Finn's head wound, "Finn, what happened to you?"

Finn gave the Brit a detailed summary of all that transpired earlier that morning. When he finished he told Nigel, "Had I not been knocked out by the plywood I would have been able to stop the attempt."

"No worries, my friend. You saved my life, nonetheless, according to Dr. Sullivan."

Kate walked in at that moment with Nigel's tea, "According to me what?"

"That we got Nigel back here to you and Camille in time for you to save his life."

"I see," Kate said, then added "You don't need to do much Nigel. Finn, don't tire him out. I'll bring you some food in a bit and you can try to get something solid in you," Kate said, then left.

"I say Finn, I think this is conclusive we have a mole in my agency."

"That was our thought too."

"If we assume the Bulgars are working with Santos, then why hit me to steal a fake?"

"They didn't know it was a fake?"

"I suppose it's possible."

"What if this Santos decided to cut the fence out of the picture. Just grab the painting and haul ass?"

"Maybe. And don't forget that the real thief with the real painting is knocking around somewhere," Finn said, "Could he be on the island too?"

"I wouldn't bet against it," Nigel said as Kate came back with a bowl of hot food.

While Kate checked Nigel's vital signs, Finn quickly explained their plan with regard to 1733.

"Let me know if you figure out what it means," Nigel said.

"OK, Nigel I want you to try and eat as much of this as you can. Finn, if you need to ask him anything else, do it now," Kate said.

"Nigel, try to come up with how they are planning to leave the island. That would be a help. Talk to you later."

Finn met Rick, Tara, and Nick on his way to the sunroom.

"C'mon, soups on," Rick told him.

The buffet-style spread in the big dining room was a Mediterranean feast featuring fish, pasta, and fruits, with several types of bread and cheeses.

"Sher, thanks for feeding us," Finn said.

"We need to keep are strength up for the next two days. This will help," she answered.

"No tryptophan there," Kate said, "We don't need any soporifics."

"Sop or what?" Nick said with a confused look on his face.

"Things that make you drowsy, sleepy," Tara answered.

"Oh, like Thanksgiving turkey?"

"Just."

"I was hoping for Sher's special coffee, some of that stuff we took up to Flamingo when you were kidnapped," Nick said.

"We've got plenty of the special coffee," Sher said with a reassuring nod of her head.

Conversation waned as they ate, outside the wind and rain became a constant background noise. The sturdy Dade pine beams and trusses anchored the old structure against the onslaught of elements. Fiona would be the harshest test they had faced.

Empty platters and baskets littered the table along with silverware and glasses. A few pieces of fruit remained untouched. Sher stood and said, "I'll be right back. Rick, hon, lend a hand."

The others began to clear the table, putting plates and glasses on a trolley that was kept in the corner. The table was cleared when they returned with a tray of coffee mugs and a large urn. Rick placed the urn in the middle of the long picnic-style table.

The tantalizing aroma of Jamaican green mountain coffee filled the room. Mugs were filled, then slowly sipped to savor the rich, strong coffee.

Camille arose, "I'll check on the Englishman."

"What's the plan," Sher asked.

"Rick and I are going to review the breakwater vids, Nick, are you and Tara still on board to help?"

"Absolutely."

"Kate, Camille, and I will monitor communications with the EOC and get things cleaned up and put away."

"We'll need to monitor Nigel through the night," Kate added.

Camille returned and gave a thumb's up, "He's sleeping again. Vital signs are stable."

"Good to hear," Finn said.

"I need to check on the guests," Sher told them.

"We better get started," Finn said.

A silent intensity coursed through the sunroom as the four friends scrutinized the drone footage. The breakwater segments were composed of a non-corrosive alloy that withstood the constant exposure to sun, salt, and sea. They were designed with an extension plate that could be used to give an additional ten feet of height, if needed.

The plates were hydraulic and computer-operated by the equipment found in the substations that were visited earlier. Drones were used every three months to perform a perimeter check of the entire structure. The Conch Republic depended on the breakwater for its existence.

"Rick, freeze it," Finn suddenly said.

"What is it, Finn?" Nick asked.

"Rick, back it up about ten seconds, please."

"Ten four."

"There, hold it there," Finn said as he stood and walked nearer to the big screen on the wall. He perused the frozen shot on the screen, then added, "What is that in the lower right hand of the segment?"

The others crowded around Finn and peered at the screen.

"See the white, is that lettering?"

"No," Tara said, "It's a four digit number."

"Good eyes, girl," Nick said.

"Rick, can you do some magic and get that clearer?" Finn asked.

"Give me a couple of minutes."

"A four digit number? Isn't that what we're looking for?" Nick said with a hopeful look.

"It's exactly what we're looking for," Finn said.

"Here we go," Rick said as a new screen grab appeared on the big monitor.

They stared at the monitor in rapt amazement until Nick broke the spell with a statement that spoke for everyone, "Holy shit."

"Indeed," Finn said.

On the monitor a stenciled set of numbers reading 1245 was clearly seen on the lower portion of the breakwater segment.

"Where is 1733?" Tara asked.

"We need to get Norm immediately," Finn said as he pulled his phone from his pants' pocket.

"We need blueprints or whatever schematics there are for the breakwater," Nick added.

"I'll tell Kate and Camille, and Sher if she's not with any of the guests," Tara said and walked out.

"We can only hope these segments are in some kind of orderly arrangement," Rick said.

Finn ended his call and told them, "Norm's on the way. In the meantime, we need to think about what our ghostly friend's reference means in light of this revelation."

"I'll go ask them to join us," Nick said.

Finn nodded in agreement, then said, "Rick, while we're waiting for them let's identify some possible threats, if we can."

"The first thing that comes to mind is sabotage, but why would anyone do that if you're on the island?"

"Maybe you're not planning to be here after you commit the sabotage?"

"But we've gone over that, there's no getting off this rock until after the storm."

"It would seem so," Finn acknowledged.

"Maybe it's not sabotage but some type of catastrophic failure of the system."

"Did you find out something?" Kate asked as she, Camille, and Sher hurried into the room.

"We think so, look at the big monitor, do you see the numbers in the lower left?"

"Yes, and four digits at that," Kate noted.

"So you think there is a segment numbered 1733?" Camille adroitly asked.

"I'd bet my bead collection on it," Finn answered.

Tara came in, "Nick's waiting to let Norm in the storm door, he was pulling up when I came in here."

Then everyone was talking, letting some of the built up tension and uncertainty dissipate through conversation. A few moments later a dripping-wet Norman James walked in with Nick trailing him.

"So, we're looking for a certain segment of the breakwater?" Norm asked, "By the way, good work."

"Who would know if they were assembled sequentially according to the numbers or if it was random?"

"I better put Cheryl on that," Norm said referring to his second-in-command. He quickly sent a text then said, "Camille, do you think the warning is against sabotage or just a failure of the system?"

"I'm not sure if it matters, but I think she meant something was going to happen, something caused by bad men. Not just a natural disaster."

"Nick, we need Angel's skills on the computer," Finn said.

"I'm on it."

"We've got to locate 1733, before we do anything else. We may have a shot at figuring out what we're up against based on its location," Norm said, "We haven't had a County Engineer, per se, since the Big Tide, but I've got some retired public works personnel living on the island. Some of them were out earlier checking the breakwater."

"Better contact them, see if any know where to locate the specs for the breakwater with regard to the numbers. Did anybody ask them about the presence of any serial numbers?" Finn asked.

"No, I don't think we did, we just did not realize at the time that 1733 was an ID for one of the breakwater segments," Norm responded.

"I think we're gonna need our rain gear again," Finn said.

"Most of the guys I referred to are at the EOC now," Norm told them, "I think we need to get to the EOC, and find the location of 1733 and check it out."

"I'll text Angel to meet us there," Nick said.

CHAPTER 15

The EOC was a study in controlled chaos. Phones rang non-stop, people texted furiously, Cheryl McIntosh was surrounded by ten of her officers all asking questions at once. Norm's presence, once noticed, quieted the room. He went to the small podium, stepped up to the mic, tapped it twice to make sure it was on and then gave people a moment to settle down.

Angel arrived with John Rocco and they gathered round Finn and Nick. Rick and Tara were talking to Big Dog but stopped and gave their attention to Norm.

"Ladies and gentlemen, once again our island is under attack, not just from Fiona, but from an international consortium that deals in stolen art, including jewelry, sculpting, whatever. We have reason to believe they will try to sabotage one of the breakwater segments. We know very little else. But right now, our priority is to locate one particular segment. It should carry the number 1733 on it somewhere. Are there any questions?"

Finn observed Norm with a faint grin. He envied his friend's ability to maintain his composure under duress, and to address a group of professionals with a confidence that registered with his listeners. It was why Norman James had the loyalty of everyone in the room. The fact that he was a Conch didn't hurt things either.

"I need the Public Works people to get with me in the map room. We have to locate segment 1733. Anyone with knowledge about the breakwater construction meet with us also. I've reached Paddy Kennedy and he's on his way."

The mention of Padraig Kennedy, the architect of the breakwater, created a buzz. Norm completed his comments with, "Everyone else, stand by. Cheryl is working on a duty roster. And remember, we've got a bit of wind and rain out there tonight, so pack your wet gear."

"Don't sugar coat it like that, LT," Joey said to mild laughter.

"Should we go to the map room?" Nick asked.

"Yes, I think we're on the guest list for this soiree," Finn said.

The map room was adjacent to the ops center and soon twenty-odd people were gathered round a large work station. Many of them had been out earlier in the day to ground truth the breakwater.

"Padraig will be here soon, but does anyone know if there is any order to the segments. In other words would 1732 be next to 1733?"

"Norm," an older man said, "I think there were three different types of segment pieces. The breakwater itself, the hydraulic stations, and the extension plates. But I don't know if they were numbered sequentially or not or if they were alike."

"Thanks, Bob. Where are the plans for the breakwater?"

"We should be able to access them on line," another man wearing an Aussie bush hat said.

"Trevor, get with Angel, he's the big guy standing next to Finn, start getting that info," Norm told him.

The room quieted down as the legend himself, Padraig Kennedy came through the door."

"Paddy, we're damn glad to see you," Norm said.

Kennedy was brought up to speed and quickly joined in, "We were working 24/7 for weeks to get the breakwater in place. I honestly can't tell you if the segments were arranged in any kind of order based on serial numbers or not. But I can tell you that I think segments from each consignment of them are together. In other words, 1733 is probably in a line of segments numbered 17-something, but the adjacent segments from a different consignment might be another series of numbers."

Finn spoke up, "Padraig, we think someone has already or is planning to sabotage that segment. We also think it is part of a plan to get off the island with stolen property worth several million dollars, without being discovered. Can you think of any areas of the breakwater that would facilitate something like that?"

"Let me think about that for a moment."

Kennedy studied the large plan view map of the structure.

"Norm, looks like Angel's got something," Finn said.

Angel strode toward the group of men, "LT, it's not much but we can verify there was a segment with that number, 1733. It's out there somewhere, in the breakwater."

"Thanks, Angel," Norm said.

"We're going to keep looking through the specs, see if we can find a clue where 1733 might be," Angel told him, and made his way back out of the map room.

"Can you explain to me more about what the purpose of sabotaging that segment would be?" Kennedy asked.

Norm explained succinctly what had transpired, the attack on Nigel, the possible presence of an international art thief, and the influence of Santos on the situation.

"Could they be planning to hijack a boat? But if they did, they wouldn't need to rupture the breakwater, they could use the lock."

"If we shut down the lock, they would be out of luck."

"True, so maybe they would need to attempt to breach the breakwater," Kennedy speculated.

"We're missing something," Finn said, "Norm, what kind of security is there at the museum during a heavy storm event?"

"Mel Fisher's museum?"

"Yes."

"Hard to say. I know they use one of the local private companies, for their surveillance cameras."

"Most people don't realize but between the items on display and the ones that are kept in the vault they are worth millions," Finn said.

"That might catch someone like Santos' eye," Norm said.

"Maybe it's one big smash and grab," Nick said, "the painting, the whiskey, and a few jewels from the Atocha."

"You know, that sounds more reasonable than you'd think," Norm said, "Especially after what we witnessed last night."

"What was that?" Kennedy asked.

"I'll tell you later, after a couple of pints of Guinness."

Kennedy picked up on Norm's reticence to elaborate, smiled and said, "I'll hold you to it."

"I'll give the museum a call and let them know I'm sending a couple of officers over there," Norm said.

"Might be a good idea," Finn said, "If they are willing to take a risk like this, there's got to be more involved than the whiskey and the painting. Nigel explained to me a bit of Santos' personality. He's the kind that would love to have relics from the Atocha on display in his private villa."

"Sounds like an asshole," Kennedy said, "And he wants to fuck with us."

"That about sums it up," Norm said.

"About your earlier question, Norm, I can't give you much of an answer. I recall that some of the segments were equipped with a ledge on the outer side for maintenance, and it seems like those segments were adjacent to the hydraulic stations on either side station walls."

"That's a start. How many hydraulic stations are there?"

"About fifty," one of the engineers answered.

"I still don't get it, a boat won't be able to get near the breakwater for several days," Norm said.

"No chopper is flying in these conditions," Finn said.

"We've got to find 1733 and prevent whatever they have planned," Norm said with intensity.

"I'll go see if Angel and Rick can identify the hydraulic stations," Finn said.

"Padraig, take a look at this photo, it's a freeze frame of the drone video. See the number? Do you think each segment was stenciled in the same place?"

"Norm, I wish I could tell you I knew. It just wasn't something I noticed," Kennedy said.

"We're going to have to get out there," Norm said.

Finn came back in and said, "There compiling a list of the hydraulic stations."

"I want everybody in the EOC in ten minutes. Right now, I need to talk with Cheryl and then get in touch with Commander Kenny at Boca Chica," Norm said.

Finn watched his friend leave, then he walked over to Kennedy who surprised him when he said, "Finn, haven't seen you since the Monkey Island craziness, good work."

"It was a team effort, Padraig."

"I heard your friend Nick and his buddy rescued the Peter Matthiessen too."

"We've been busy, these last few months. Nick and Angel, he works for John Rocco, have officially gained membership in the Conch Republic. They fit right in with our little band of nonconformists."

"I see."

"Padraig, is there a contingency plan for a breakwater failure?"

"It would depend on what kind of failure. I think we could contain things if one segment failed, or if several failed in different locations. But if a substantial section of multiple segments went down I don't know if we could survive that."

"Let's go see how Rick and Angel are doing with the hydraulic stations."

The EOC was subdued as people now realized the magnitude of the problem. They found Rick and Angel, along with two city engineers, poring over digital plans of the breakwater.

"How's it goin'" Finn asked.

"We're making progress," Rick answered.

"Angel," Finn said, "I want you to meet Padraig Kennedy."

Angel stopped his scrutiny of the plans, turned to Kennedy and said, "It's an honor sir, to finally meet you."

"Good work with the Peter Matthiessen."

"Thank you, couldn't have done it without my dawg Nick."

"We better focus on the task at hand," Kennedy said, "Glad we have you in the Conch Republic, Angel."

Angel turned his attention to the breakwater plans as Finn and Kennedy moved closer to the podium. They found Nick and Tara in conversation with Cheryl.

"Norm will be out here in a second," Cheryl told them.

"How are you Tara," Kennedy said to the girl with blue hair.

Finn showed mild surprise but realized Kennedy must have met Tara through Kate's work with Mote Marine and the Navy. Nick seemed a bit perplexed when Tara gave Padraig a hug.

Tara read the confusion on her friends' faces, "Padraig was one of the few people who listened to Kate when she tried to warn that the Big Tide was imminent."

"Dr. Sullivan's input was critical to my plan, had I not talked with her at length about sea level rise, I wouldn't have been nearly as prepared when it happened. That's when I met Tara, you had just joined the Doc as her grad assistant."

"Oh," was all Nick managed.

"Great work with the Peter Matthiessen, by the way. I spoke with Angel a moment ago. Glad to have you in the Conch Republic, Nick."

Finn saw that Nick fully realized the significance of that endorsement coming from a Conch legend. There was a slight uptick in the noise level as Norm appeared, then it quickly died as he mounted the podium. He looked out over the room full of people; his personnel, civilian volunteers, firemen and other first responders, retired Navy men and women. All here on a night no-one in their right minds would want to be out in.

"Let me say now, this is strictly a volunteer operation. I need five teams composed of five people to do a hands-on inspection of the hydraulic stations and the breakwater segments on either side. One of the five needs to be an engineer. I think we can count on round the clock duty until this thing gets by us. And I need to warn you that we anticipate some type of action from a well-equipped Euro syndicate as soon as conditions allow. Their plan may include sabotage of a portion of the breakwater system. Cheryl will coordinate the teams so get with her if you want to join us."

Finn knew Norm would not ask anyone to do something he wouldn't. If there was a manual for "leading-by-example," Norm wrote it.

He stepped down from the podium and walked over to speak with Finn and Padraig.

"I dispatched Big Dog, Joey, and Tina to Mel's museum."

"Have you heard back from them?"

"Not yet, I doubt they've had time to get there, given the conditions."

"If it's the same cats, they had no problem running an SUV through a restaurant window the other night," Nick reminded them.

"The museum has some security but they're not prepared for an assault by professionals," Finn added.

"You're making me more nervous by the minute guys," Norm said.

"We're here to volunteer," Finn said, "and we've even got our own engineer. Give us our locations and we'll get out there, but we'll go by the museum first, see what's happening."

"So, your team of five is you, Rick, Nick, Tara, and Angel?" Norm said with a small grin.

"That's why you get the big bucks," Finn said.

"I'll get your list."

"Something pinging your radar?" Rick asked.

"If you were planning to do a smash and grab at the museum, could you ask for a better night?" Finn said in a flat tone.

"I see your point."

Finn looked at his phone, the told the others, "Norm is texting the locations to me. I'll text them to each of you. There is weather gear in the cloakroom, if you need it. We'll leave in ten."

"Good luck, Finn," Kennedy said, "I'd kinda like to go with you but Norm has plans for me."

"Slainte," Finn told the legend.

Kennedy acknowledged the age-old Irish toast to health with a wicked grin and an impromptu jig.

CHAPTER 16

The wind pounded the SUV as sheets of rain shimmered in the glare of the headlights. Finn was at the wheel with Nick riding shotgun. Rick and Angel studied the locations they needed to inspect. Tara was texting but stopped suddenly and said, "We need to hurry. Tina was responding to my text and got cut off. It might be the weather but it might not be."

"We're five minutes away," Finn told her without taking his eyes off the road. Palm fronds cartwheeled down the street like tumbleweeds. Street signs shimmied in the gusting wind.

Rick and Angel stowed the electronics and checked their sidearms.

"Tara, would you reach in the back and grab my Stoner," Nick said.

She stopped assembling her slingshot and reached over the seat and grabbed the powerful rifle and handed it carefully to Nick.

"This will be a first. Never tried to shoot in weather like this," Nick said. To punctuate that statement, a plastic trash bin slammed into the side of the SUV causing everyone to flinch. Finn turned the corner off of Caroline Street onto Whitehead. They could make out flashing lights through the downpour.

Big Dog, Joey, and Tina were pinned down behind their police cruiser by gunfire that came from two large Toyota trucks. Two men advanced toward the unsuspecting trio to outflank them. Finn stopped and said, "Suggestions?"

"I'll take the two going toward them," Angel said.

"I think I can hit the gas tank on the nearer truck," Nick said.

"Give Angel a second then get their attention," Finn said.

Angel slipped out the door and disappeared into the silver rain that pelted down. Nick readied the Stoner, "Tara can you spread a tarp over my head for a few seconds?"

"Gotcha."

Nick stepped out and stayed low against the side of the SUV. Tara exited behind him and watched for his signal. He pulled a small monocular from his pocket and briefly looked through it. The wide brim of his bush hat helped keep the rain off.

Finn positioned the SUV to give Nick the most light on the target. The vehicle in question was thirty yards away, even on a clear day it would be a tough shot. Now, with winds approaching fifty miles an hour and rain falling in sheets, it would have been impossible for most people.

Nick Cassini's range scores remained unbeaten at Paris Island. His fame as a sniper was legendary throughout the Corps, but none of those shots came close to the degree of difficulty he now faced. But his friends were in danger and that filled him with a quiet resolve, that helped steady his nerves.

"You've got this," Tara said as she squeezed his right arm.

The Euros had not noticed the presence of their foes. Nick dropped to a knee as Tara spread a small tarp over his head then fought with the wind to keep it from flapping.

Two more men exited the vehicle Nick had targeted and moved toward the police car. A strong gust of wind caused the advancing men to stagger, as a third man joined them.

Nick composed himself, focused, slowed his breathing, and at the same moment time seemed to freeze and everything was crystal clear. He slowly squeezed the Stoner's trigger and sent a 5.56 x 45 mm cartridge screaming toward the hidden gas tank.

The explosion brought the rear axle off the ground and separated it from the chassis. A huge ball of flame erupted from the rear end of the truck. All the glass blew out sending shards everywhere including into the men headed for Big Dog and the others.

The three men who exited the truck were on the ground, knocked down by the explosive force. They struggled to regain their footing in the rain. Two of the men scrambled away from the approaching SUV, the third remained on the ground unmoving.

Finn began driving slowly toward the burning hulk as Nick and Tara walked behind for added protection. Tara had her H&K in hand as they withstood the downpour to go to the aid of their friends.

A body fell from the driver's side door as the vehicle continued to burn. Finn guided the SUV forward but suddenly the windshield was peppered with gun fire, the glass held.

"We'll have to let Norm know the bulletproof glass really is," Finn said.

"Did you see where that came from?" Rick asked.

"No."

Finn's phone, now set to walkie-talkie mode came alive with Nick's voice, "Shine the search light up on that second-story balcony to the right."

The bright light cut through the rain exposing a shooter on the balcony. Without hesitation, Tara sighted and fired two rounds. The man pitched backwards, then stumbled forward, he broke through the railing and fell to the rain-drenched street.

Gunfire erupted from the police cruiser and Finn saw Joey break toward the sidewalk. Big Dog and Tina laid down cover fire as Joey disappeared. The remaining truck began to back away but Nick ruined the front and rear tires with well-placed shots.

Angel moved stealthily, as he followed the two gunmen trying to outflank Big Dog and Tina. Through the driving rain he saw movement near a store front ahead. He paused and waited.

The two Euro-thugs moved on oblivious to Angel's presence behind them or Joey's ahead. He saw them draw even with Joey's position and walk on past. To Joey's credit, he played it straight. He emerged from his hiding place behind a banyan tree and yelled for them to drop their weapons.

A forceful gust of wind caused Joey to stumble as the two men turned and without hesitation tried to shoot Joey down. Angel, on the run, took them out with two rounds as Joey regained his footing."

"You OK," Angel asked as he reached his friend.

"Holy shit, where did you come from?"

"Thank Finn, he had a gut feeling you guys would need some backup."

"That must have been Cassini that blew the truck up," Joey said.

"Right."

Any men that remained alive from the assault force melted into the rain as the gunfire stopped. Finn brought the SUV up close to the police cruiser. Big Dog and Tina emerged from behind it. Angel and Joey appeared a moment later from the sidewalk.

"We owe you one," Big Dog told them.

"Was that the art thieves, Norm told us about?" Tina asked.

"Yes," Finn answered, "There's less of them now."

"Angel saved my Conch ass," Joey said, "thanks brother."

"Is there anyone inside the museum?" Finn asked.

"Yes, I think three people, one's a security guy and the other two are staff," Big Dog said.

"I've texted Norm, gave him a Sitrep, he'll be here ASAP," Finn said.

"Thanks, Finn."

"Are any of you hurt?"

"We're good," Tina said.

"We'll stay here until Norm arrives, then we've got some rounds to make," Finn told them.

"I'll go inside and let those people know what's going on," Tina said.

"Thanks, Tina."

"Let's get out of this damn rain," Nick said.

Everyone returned to their respective vehicles. The wind seemed to have lessened but the rain continued to pound. The streetlights created an eerie, ethereal feel to the sheets of rain. Finn knew they had not seen hurricane-force winds yet. He silently considered what winds speeds of one-fifty-five would do to some of the older buildings.

"What time do we expect Cat 1 winds?" Finn asked.

Rick checked his phone then said, "Not until after midnight."

"We need to check our five stations and get off the street," Finn told them.

"I think I see Norm," Nick said from the rear seat.

A matching SUV, to the one Finn drove pulled up next to them. The window lowered and Norm's face peered at them.

"Good call, Finn."

"Norm, I'll let Big Dog fill you in, we've got to check our parts of the breakwater."

"Good luck, keep me posted."

Finn backed up, turned around and headed northwest toward the first station.

"Rick, what are we looking for, exactly?" Nick asked.

"Any numbers and any signs of tampering with the hydraulic station."

"I'm scoping out the breakwater specs again, looking for a clue," Angel said as he perused a tablet.

Finn turned the SUV onto the short causeway that led to the breakwater maintenance path. The same one they'd been on earlier in the day.

Suddenly, the rain diminished to a drizzle. The quiet that filled the vehicle was noticeable. Finn drove onto the breakwater's vehicle path.

"That's just weird," Angel said.

"What's that?" Tara said.

"The rain stopping like that."

"It won't be for long," Tara told him.

"We're in a pocket of relative calm between larger bands that are moving in a counter-clockwise direction," Finn added.

Tara looked at Finn askance, "I didn't know you were a meteorologist too."

"In my former line of work, the weather was usually a critical factor in our operations. I've had some training in basic weather science but I'm no Jim Cantore. Not to mention living in Hurricane Alley all these years."

"If the eye goes over us, as predicted," Rick said, "You'll really see weird then."

"I can hardly wait," Angel replied.

Angel returned to studying his tablet as they neared the first of their stops. The breakwater lights, huge halogens that cast an amber glow to the hulking structure burned brightly. Finn slowed the SUV as they reached the first hydraulic station and its adjoining segments of breakwater.

"Nick, you and Tara look for numbers. Rick and I will check the electronics. Angel, keep an eye on things out here, if you would," Finn said.

"Ten four, Finn."

"Let's take advantage of the weather while we can."

The search revealed no numbers that were visible. Nothing had been tampered with inside the station. They moved on, the next station was about two thousand yards away.

"I wonder how Nigel's doing?" Finn asked.

"I can text Kate," Tara said.

"No, don't bother them. I'm sure he's OK or we would've heard something."

Angel spoke up from the rear seat, "I think there are three locations that might be attractive to saboteurs due to the relatively easy access due to causeway roads. One of those locations is number 4 in our series of five."

"Good work, Angel," Rick said.

"But, we are still missing something," Finn said, "How do they plan to get off the island, even if they blew-up part of the breakwater, the turbulence from the onslaught of water would kill them."

"I agree," Rick said, "We are missing something."

"Do you want to skip on down to number four?" Angel asked.

"Let's be methodical here. We don't want to overlook something. We'll keep our schedule, but Angel, could you text Norm that info?"

"Will do."

"At least they are down seven or eight men," Nick said.

"This Santos cat, I think has a pretty big organization according to Nigel," Finn said, "We could be looking at thirty or forty troops."

"The more the merrier," Nick said and added "Semper Fi" as he high-fived Angel in the rear seat.

Finn recognized the attempt to keep things light. Keep things loose. There was a lot at stake, but he knew he was surrounded by capable people that he trusted.

Oddly enough, for the first time in years, he felt as if he had a family. A concept he was fiercely protective of, especially in light of the situation in which they found themselves. Kate had made him consider feelings he'd not dealt with in years. He'd tried to fulfill a mentor's role in Nick's life without being intrusive. He viewed Nick as a younger brother. Rick, Sher, and Norman James were all deeply woven into the fabric of his life.

"Finn, we're here, stop," Nick's voice broke the reverie.

He instantly refocused and brought the SUV to a smooth stop.

They went through the same drill as they had performed at the first station. The results were the same and they moved on toward number three.

The skies continued to roil overhead even without rain. No glimmer of moonlight shown through the thick cloud cover. A night Poe would have felt uplifting, no doubt.

"I still can't find any info on where the 1700s would be located," Angel said.

"I wonder if the other crews are having any luck?" Rick mused aloud.

They pulled up in front of their third stop but before they could get out Angel excitedly said, "Rick, take a look at this, I didn't notice it before."

Rick took the tablet from Angel and focused on a place indicated by Angel's forefinger.

"Good eye, what the hell is that? I need to text Sammy, he's the engineer in charge of the breakwater. Give me a second."

"It looks like a hatchway, I wonder why you didn't see it at the other two stations?" Angel asked the group.

Finn responded, "I'd like to know that myself. I thought we were thorough."

Rick furiously texted as the others patiently waited. Drops of rain appeared on the windshield. The world outside the SUV looked dismal and bleak, the breakwater stood hard against the elements.

Tara gave Nick an exaggerated look and said, "Boy, you look like a drowned rat."

"Feel like one."

Finally, Rick gave his fingers a rest, turned to look at his friends and said, "There is an internal maintenance passage associated with the hydraulic stations, but not each station. Only one in five has access to the passages, that's why you didn't see anything."

"And we are just now finding this out?" Finn asked.

"Sammy didn't think it had any bearing on the problem, only a few of the Public Works' guys even know about it. I've texted Norm, we should be hearing from him shortly."

On cue, Finn's phone emanated the theme from "Jaws."

He put it on speaker and said, "Norm."

"Finn, it's just getting better all the time. Rick, what the hell is this maintenance passage?"

"Angel, feel free to jump in," Rick said, "Angel found a hatchway on the plans that is difficult to see because of its location. And it's not on each sheet, only every fifth hydraulic station."

"L.T.," Angel added, "It appears that the passage runs through the entire length of the breakwater."

"And no-one knew about this?"

"A couple of the Public Works' guys and that's about it. They didn't think it was relevant, they were looking for problems on the outside of the structure."

"By the way, Norm, Angel also noticed three places that might be easier to sabotage than others because of the proximity of the access causeways that bridge the gap between the island and the breakwater."

"Thanks, Angel. We're gonna have to put you on the payroll," Norm said.

"So, what's the plan?" Finn asked.

"We need to take a look at one of these passageways."

"We've got one after the one we're at now."

"Okay, let me know what you find when you get in there."

"Will do," Finn answered, "Over and out."

"Over and out," Norm said.

"Let's get this one done and go find our problem child."

They finished with no clues and no signs of any tampering. Rain fell steadily again, but the wind remained below tropical storm strength. Finn knew this would not be the case long and drove faster toward the fourth station.

"Angel, what are we looking for, inside the station?" Finn asked.

"A button, or a switch maybe that will open a hatch that is built into the wall. I would think we should look on the exterior wall for the hatch."

"Makes sense," Nick agreed.

"These passageways don't have much head room according to Sammy," Rick said.

"You better take Tara along then," Angel said.

"Are you saying I'm short?" Tara said with feigned indignation.

"No ma'am, just that you'll fit in there better than me."

"You can't argue with logic like that," Nick said in support of his fellow former-marine.

"Oh no, not logic, you know us girls just don't understand complicated stuff like logic."

"The slingshot's coming out next," Angel grinned.

"We don't have time," Finn said, "Angel take the point out here."

"Copy that."

Finn slowed to a stop in front of the fourth station. The dull walls glistened in the amber high-intensity lights as rain fell from an angry sky. No one was in sight as they exited the SUV and entered the station door.

Once inside, Rick got the lights on and they began to hunt for a mechanism that would open the hidden hatch. A cursory search revealed nothing.

"They really didn't make it easy to get into this thing," Nick said.

Tara sat down at one of the consoles that was equipped with a laptop and several camera feeds. She idly ran her right hand along the underside of the lip; her friends started when a portion of the inner wall slide open to reveal an access into the heart of the breakwater.

"What did you do," Nick asked.

"Found the switch, it looks like."

"Can you see anything in there?" Finn said.

"Let me shine a light in there," Rick said.

They crowded behind Rick to see what the light illuminated.

A narrow passage ran to the left and right away from the hatch. The walls were bare except for piping that ran along the wall at several levels. Tara snaked her way through the men and entered the passageway.

"Easy," Finn said.

"What's it look like?" Rick asked as he handed Tara the flashlight.

She beamed it down the passageway that ran back behind them until the sloping curve of the breakwater occluded sight. She kept the light on the ground as she swept it back the other way. Minimizing any chance of temporary night blindness caused by the flashlight's brilliance.

"I don't see a lot down either way," she said.

"Why don't you and Nick follow the passage that way," Finn pointed in the direction Tara had first shone her light. "And Rick and I will take the forward section."

The men crowded into the passageway with Tara. Everyone produced their own flashlight and each duo moved off down the tubular structure in opposite directions.

They could feel the vibration of waves hitting the breakwater. It was like a low-grade temblor as the ocean rhythmically pounded on the exterior of the breakwater.

"Are you claustrophobic?" Tara asked Nick.

"Didn't think so, but that vibration isn't helping any."

"Not a bit."

"What's that up ahead?"

They shined their lights toward what looked like the top of a swimming pool ladder. They found metal stairs leading down about six feet, then the passageway continued at that level.

Ten yards farther along they found a small table with several manuals stacked up on top. There was also a map rack with sheets of specs in a multitude of drawers.

Nick stopped and thumbed through the manuals while Tara examined the map rack and its contents. They quietly perused the material and hoped for a clue.

"Nick," Tara shouted, "Look at this," as she held up a large rectangular plan.

"Whatcha got?"

"Look, here."

"Holy shit," Nick said as he looked at a plan-view diagram of the central lock used for the cruise ships and large yachts. It was covered with numbers that began with 17. At one side was a panel labeled 1733.

"I'm texting Finn now," Tara told him.

"We should have thought about the lock area sooner," Nick said.

"Better late than never."

There were a couple of small locks built into the breakwater that accommodated pleasure craft, medium to large fishing boats, and most sailboats. They were found near Coupon Bight and the West Martello. Any boat traffic had to use the locks to traverse the breakwater to reach open water. The lock built to handle the cruise ships and transport vessels was the largest structure in the Conch Republic, dwarfing both Martello's and Ft. Zachary Taylor.

It operated as most hydraulic locks do; bringing a ship into the lock from a certain elevation and sending it out of the lock at a different elevation. In the case of the Conch Republic, ships at the current sea level needed to be lowered almost ten feet to the water level inside the breakwater.

Footsteps echoed down the metal passageway as Finn and Rick approached. The large map sheet was spread out on the table when they entered the alcove.

"Whatcha got?" Finn said as he and Rick drew near the table.

"Look here," Nick said as he pointed at the numbers on the segments of the lock that the map depicted.

"Good work," Finn said.

"It was Tara, I was looking through those manuals over there."

"There it is, 1733," Rick said.

"At least we're close to the lock," Finn said, "Rick, can you tell anything from where it's located as to what might be going to happen?"

"It's one of the side segments of the ship chamber, the compartment where they lower the ship by pumping out water," Rick replied.

"I'll let Norm know," he said and began to text.

"Nick, what else is in here, anything in those manuals?" Rick asked.

"Just standard operational info, what from I read."

"Tara, what about the other stuff in the rack?"

"Haven't looked at all of it. But, if we get through this storm, I'd have Norm make copies and put all this information in a safe place. In case we need it again."

"The hurricane night tour continues," Finn said as he looked at them, "We're meeting Norm on the lock in twenty minutes."

"Where's a Conch Tour Train when you need it?" Rick said.

CHAPTER 17

The rain felt like pellets of lead on any exposed body parts as wind whipped around the towering structure before them. The winds increased steadily, as the SUV pulled to a stop. The control tower rose in front of them, built to withstand winds of two-hundred miles-per-hour, the structure seemed to defy the storm. Finn hoped that in this case, technology would trump Mother Nature.

Adjacent to the control tower was the ship chamber within which segment number 1733 was located. The chamber, devoid of a ship, was an empty metal rectangle filled with water.

Finn led them through a door then up an enclosed stairwell to the lock's operation room. Behind heavy plies of storm-proof glass, the ops room overlooked the lock and any traffic that used it.

They found Norm talking with two of the engineers that manned the shift. Normally, there was round-the-clock personnel as the lock was used twenty-four seven. A storm event such as this had a protocol that required all human personnel to evacuate. This left the security and life-support controls in the hands of an AI program named the Emergency Management Mode Interactive Logarithmic Operational Unit (Emmi Lou).

"Over here," Norm called across the room.

Finn looked at the two men with Norm as he crossed the distance between them. He thought he recognized one of them, from a fishing tournament a couple of years ago. The other, he didn't know. Rick and Angel dropped behind to look at the bank of instrumentation that controlled the lock's operations. Nick and Tara had been drawn to the view outside the wide, plexiglass observation portal that ran the length of the compartment.

The storm in its elemental fury thrashed away at everything in its path. They stood transfixed at the windswept visage below them, surreal in the amber glow of the halogen lights.

"Finn, this is Eli Mann and Arch Peyton. They drew the short stick on the duty roster for hurricane duty. They'd normally let Emmi Lou take care of things but I explained the situation and they're willing to show us segment 1733 and get us down there to it."

"Is there anything special about that particular segment?" Finn asked.

"As a matter of fact, there is," Mann said, "There is a manual override switch in there that can bypass Emmi Lou."

Peyton added, "It's part of a maintenance passage that runs the length of the ships chamber. It has several access points to the chamber itself which we can completely expose by pumping all the water out."

"I see."

Suddenly a plastic trash bin, carried by the wind, slammed into the plexiglass causing Nick and Tara to jump away from it. The glass remained intact without a mark.

"That's the best stuff NASA has," Arch remarked.

Nick and Tara seemed less than convinced and retreated a few more feet away from the window.

"There isn't an override switch in here?" Norm asked.

"There is, but once the evac protocol is keyed in, you can't gain access until the protocol is cancelled. The switch in 1733 is accessible through manually operated hatches."

"Could we take a look at the one in 1733?" Finn asked.

"Follow me," Eli said.

"Rick, Angel, need you in the hole with us," Norm said, "Nick, Tara, keep an eye on things here, if you would."

Nick glanced at Finn, without moving his head. It was answered by an imperceptible nod from his mentor. A ghost of a smile appeared on Norm's face, but he showed no indication that he caught the silent communication between Finn and Nick.

"Are you expecting any real trouble in this weather?" Eli asked.

"Possibly," Norm tersely replied.

"Let's get moving," Finn urged.

They went down a series of metal staircases that reminded Finn of a Navy destroyer. At various levels they encountered intersecting metal catwalks and platforms.

"So, there is access to this internal maze from other than the control room?" Norm asked as they continued to walk.

"Yes, you can access this area from three other places," Arch replied.

Finn thought he could hear Norm's teeth grinding, after that answer. He distinctly heard a muttered, "It just gets better and better."

"And where would those places be?" Finn asked.

"We have two access tunnels running from the foot of Simonton Street underwater next to the western maintenance bridge and a final access that runs under the bridge."

They reached a broad grated platform along side of which ran segment 1733. It was a dull, dark color with several recesses built into a ten-foot long section of the wall. Arch led them over to one of the alcoves that housed the manual override switch for the AI program.

There was no real security other than a digital keypad that once entered, allowed the user to override Emmi Lou. Norm made a mental note to have public works upgrade the access security before the next catastrophic event occurred. Because he knew it would occur, of that he was certain.

"So, what would this allow the interloper to do exactly?" Norm asked.

"Well, you could fill or lower the water level in the chamber. But, there is an automatic cutoff when the lock is unoccupied that would prevent someone from trying to flood the island," Eli said.

"In a storm event like this, we lower the water level and use it as a containment pond," Arch added.

"So, the only result of overriding the system from this switch would be to raise or lower the water level, is that correct?" Norm asked.

"You could open the outer containment gate to allow something in or out," Eli said.

"I don't see what good that would do in these seas," Norm said.

"Something doesn't add up," Finn muttered.

"I'm going to have four men stay here through the night," Norm said. "I think you men should plan on staying also unless your families need you."

"We agree, given what you've told us," Peyton said.

"I'll have those men here in thirty minutes," Norm told them.

"Do you see any signs of tampering with anything near this area?" Fin asked.

"No, nothing yet, at least," Mann answered.

"The other access points you mentioned, can they be blocked off?" Norm asked.

A tremor ran through the structure and echoed in the open passageway. No one flinched.

"Things are picking up, we need to get back to the EOC," Norm said. "Can those other accesses be blocked off?"

"Not really because of the way they are constructed. Mostly open gangplanks and ramps."

"Great."

"You might want to make that six men," Finn said in a low voice.

Norm gave a slight nod of acknowledgment then said, "Eli, I want you and Arch to keep in touch by the hour. My men will help with any communication problems."

"Whatever we need to do," Mann replied.

"Good. Let's get back to the control room and we'll hammer out the details of a plan for the night."

Nick and Tara met them with news that wind speeds were approaching sixty sustained with gusts at eighty miles an hour. Speeds that could knock a vehicle of balance, and that were impossible for a human to withstand without being blown off their feet.

"My men are on the way," Norm told the engineers.

"Hope we don't see you again, tonight, Lieutenant," Arch said with a grim smile.

"I wouldn't bet on it," Angel said under his breath.

A maelstrom met them outside and they were drenched again by the time they got in the SUV. Norm was headed to the EOC while Finn guided the borrowed SUV back to the haven of the B and B.

CHAPTER 18

The storm had upped its punch a notch or three since they set out to inspect the stations. At the hurricane center in what remained of Miami, the radar scopes showed a small island engulfed in the middle of a swirling octopus with arms of wind and water. Protected by the stout breakwater that deflected the wave energy and displaced the wind's fierce onslaught, the island hunkered down and hoped for the best. The worst, however, was yet to come.

"Angel, looks like you'll have to bunk with us," Rick said.

"Have you been in touch with Red tonight?" Finn asked, referring to Angel's kinsman and boss, John Rocco.

"Yes, he says things are as prepared as they can be. He's in his office if you need to reach him."

Finn jumped the curb and got them as close to the porch as possible. They piled out and hurried to the cloak room to ditch their wet clothes.

Inside the B and B was buzzing with activity. Several of the CBees were on their phones. Two of the paying guests were helping out serving coffee and refreshments. Sher was everywhere with encouragement and a kind word for everyone.

"I really am the master of my domain," Rick said jokingly as Sher hurried over to give him a wet-willie.

"Why thank you, Nora," Rick ad libbed.

"Certainly, Nick, I just saw the thin man, he went that away," Sher said as she picked up on the riff.

"Coffee, I need coffee," Finn said in mock desperation, then in a more serious tone he asked, "How's our boy, James Bond?"

"Here's Kate, I'll let her tell you," Sher responded.

"How was your Tour de Breakwater?" Kate asked.

"We found 1733," Tara blurted out.

"Do tell," Kate said.

"It's complicated."

"Why in the world would I think it wouldn't be," Kate said with arched eyebrows that made Tara laugh.

"I need some coffee, myself," Kate said, "and I want to hear it all, complicated will not spare you."

"She who must be obeyed has spoken," Finn said.

"Who wants some Joe?" Sher said as she returned with a trolley packed with a large urn and all the accoutrements.

"Why don't we go in the big dining room and get out of the way in here," Rick suggested.

"Good idea," Finn said.

Rick took the trolley and pulled it into the adjoining room. The others followed him and soon everyone was sipping coffee as Tara recapped the evening.

"And so, we still don't know exactly how 1733 plays into things but we're making progress," Tara said in conclusion.

Camille Garnier had joined the group late, as she tended to Nigel during a periodic check-up.

"I still can't believe she reached us like that," Garner said, "There is something more to 1733, something as yet unseen."

"I tend to agree with Camille," Finn said, "Norm has posted six men in addition to the staff to guard the lock."

"Do you think it will be enough?" Kate asked.

"Hard to tell given our source is a woman who's been dead for a hundred and twenty years," Finn answered.

"I see your point."

"How's the patient?"

"I think he will make it," Camille answered. "He's awake."

"Could I speak to him for a few moments?"

"I think so, if Kate agrees."

"Make it short, that would have killed some people," Kate admonished.

Finn nodded and walked away. The others listened to Tara and Nick describe the view of the storm they had in the ops room of the lock.

"The raw power, it's just amazing," Tara said.

As if to accent that observation, the lights flickered briefly but stayed on. Time seems to slow down during a hurricane, minutes turn to hours, as the background noise of unrelenting wind roars like a never-ending freight train.

Finn detoured on his way to Nigel's room. When he opened the door, Nigel was making an attempt to sit up. When he saw Finn, his eyes lit up at the cup of tea in Finn's left hand.

"Thank Christ, a feckin' cup of tea," Nigel said, "Thanks, mate."

"No worries."

"How are things going?"

Finn concisely filled him in on the news about 1733 and the encounter at Mel Fisher's museum. Nigel listened attentively, sipped his tea, then finally said, "Bloody well tried to kill me, I won't forget that."

"Does all this have the feel of your guy Santos?" Finn asked.

"Very much so, I'd say."

'Nigel, we can't figure out what his play is about getting off the island. Any thoughts on that?"

"Let me consider that for a bit. I say, would it be too much to ask for another cuppa?"

"Not all all. I'll be back."

Finn stopped by the dining room, drew Kate aside and asked, "Will it hurt Nigel to have a second cup of tea?"

"I take it you have already given him one cup?"

Finn could see he was on shaky ground, he gave it his best Boy Scout explanation, "He likes his tea, it perked him right up."

"I see, well if the strychnine didn't kill him I doubt some Earl Grey will," Kate said with mock exasperation, "But if you grill him too long that might."

"Gotcha, Doc. I'll just take him the tea and leave him be to enjoy it."

"Just make sure you do. I know how you are when you are trying to solve a mystery like this," she said, then surprised him by kissing him on the lips.

He could taste the faint hint of green mountain coffee before she pulled back breaking the kiss. Finn held her close, felt her head on his chest and her arms around him.

They remained like that for several seconds until they both sensed the idyllic moment had to end and a return to reality, nightmarish as it was, was required.

"I won't stay long," Finn said and went in search of another cup of tea.

When he returned to Nigel's room, he found the Brit awake but not as pale as he'd been. Some color had returned to his face and the man seemed exuberant when Finn placed a second cup of hot tea on the night stand.

"Thanks, mate. You're a proper Godsend."

"I've been ordered by she who must be obeyed, to not stay long."

"What can I help you with?"

"Can you think of any angle we haven't covered that would explain how 1733 plays into this cluster?"

"One thing we've lost track of is that the real thief is out there as well as the fence."

"True, but whatever they do doesn't seem to be as threatening as Santos and his gang."

"Agreed, but don't forget they are most likely on your island too."

Finn nodded his head, then said, "Anything else about Santos?"

"Nothing that I can think of now. I must admit, I'm not feeling my best."

"That's understandable, I'll let you get some rest. Enjoy your tea."

Finn turned to leave the room and was almost to the door when Nigel said, "Finn, wait. I remember that there was a rumor, going round Barcelona and the Costa del Sol that he had a submarine."

"Who, Santos?"

"Yes, a sub to run drugs and whatever else."

"That's a game changer. I need to tell Norm. Nigel get some rest, I'll be back later if Kate gives the OK."

Finn texted as he walked. When he reached the dining room he remained standing and the others picked up on the vibe and the group quieted down.

"We may have a submarine involved," Finn told them.

"Say again," Rick mustered.

"A submarine."

"Holy shit," Nick said.

"Are they planning to torpedo the breakwater?"

"We don't know if there is a sub, much less if it is armed," Finn said in an attempt to steady the group.

"If they do, it is most likely a surplus diesel sub from the Russian fleet. Lot of them on the black market," Angel said.

"How many men would it take to operate a sub like that?" Rick asked.

"Have to research that one, but you would think at least thirty or forty men," Angel answered.

"So, what do you think their plan is?" Nick asked.

"Bring the sub into the lock and have their men get on it then leave? I'm just thinking off the top of my head," Finn told them.

"Does Norm know?" Rick asked.

"Yes, texted him immediately after Nigel told me he remembered hearing rumors of Santos and a sub."

"Could they get a sub into the lock?" Angel asked.

"I think so. One of the old diesel subs would fit into the lock, they're smaller than most of the cruise ships that use it," Rick said.

"Wouldn't they have picked it up on the Boca Chica sonar?" Nick asked.

"Maybe not, in this weather. It might appear as a biologic, with all the wave action and other background noise from the storm," Rick answered.

"All this and a Cat 5 hurricane to boot," Finn said with a smirk, "Hold on, I'm getting something from Norm." Conversation waned as everyone waited for Finn. After a few moments, Finn looked up and said, "Rick can you rig up a conference call and put it on the big screen in the sunroom?"

"Yes. Good thing we have a hard line connection with the EOC."

"My hero," Sher said and gave Rick an exaggerated hug.

"I knew it would pay off," Rick said referring to his project to connect the B and B with the EOC using fiber optic cable. Rick and Sher's work with the CBees made their place the "little EOC" during most emergencies.

"If Angel will give me a hand, I can have things ready in ten minutes."

"I'll let Norm know," Finn replied and texted something immediately.

The lights flickered again, but remained on. Finn was always uncomfortable when he couldn't see outside. Now, buttoned up tight, he felt like he was in the hold of an old tramp freighter, unable to see the storm that raged all around him. He felt Kate's hand on his arm, and immediately relaxed.

She looked in his eyes but said nothing. Another text alert pulsed on Finn's phone, he read it then told the others, "Norm will be having a meeting in thirty minutes. We should go to the sunroom when Rick is finished."

Kate's hand slipped down Finn's arm and her fingers interlaced with his. She felt Finn squeeze her hand, then release. But he held her hand as they walked back to the table.

"I need more coffee, some of Sher's special brand would hit the spot," Nick said.

"Yeah, it kept us going on our recent trip to Flamingo," Angel added.

Sher pointed at a second urn on one of the side boards, "Over there, help yourself."

"Thanks, Sher."

"Take that urn to the sunroom," Finn said, "We'll all need some of that before this night is over."

Some of the frenetic activity in the lobby had quieted down but the phones were busy as CBees answered questions and quelled rumors from frightened islanders. Sher explained to the others about the upcoming meeting and anyone that wanted to attend was welcome.

Finn's dive watch read 11:45. Dawn seemed like a hoped-for dream amidst a swirling maelstrom of uncertainty. Finn, by nature, was a lone wolf. He tolerated the pack, but didn't crave the need for others the way some did. It was one of the traits that made him well-suited to the job he held for nearly twenty years.

He would never be truly at ease in social situations, but his relationship with Nick had taught him that he could enjoy the company of others without sacrificing his individuality. Now Kate had taken a place in his life that no-one had previously occupied. It was the closest to a family that he'd ever experienced.

As the witching hour neared the group slowly moved into the sunroom. Rick and Angel were still making last-minute connections as people took seats.

Conversation was subdued as people settled into their chairs. The wall-mounted TV screen blinked to life and Norm's visage filled the screen. He was sitting in the EOC with the Conch Republic seal behind him on the wall. True to form, Norm wasted no time with pleasantries, he came right to the point.

"We are faced with another attempt to jeopardize our island's safety and the welfare of all islanders. Mayor Yearly is here to announce that martial law will be in effect until its repeal after the storm."

The camera shifted slightly to the left and a nervous but resolute Robert Yearly made the proclamation. A veteran of seven tours of duty as the mayor of Key West, he was no stranger to the vagaries of hurricanes but the current situation had left him shaken. He finished the short address and turned things back over to Norm.

"As you can see, we are totally fucked."

A gasp ran through the sunroom, the intake of breath in the EOC could be heard distinctly. Then, slowly, chuckles began to break out that was followed by crazy laughter. Finn marveled at his friend, he'd never seen him use that tactic. But when people are stressed out sometimes the most unexpected comment can break the ice and loosen things up. Finn smiled, at the effectiveness of Norm's out-of-character remark.

"Not that we haven't been in this situation before, like eight weeks ago," Norm continued. "But we are dealing with a hurricane of unprecedented force, that should the breakwater be compromised, we could be faced with deadly flooding. The next twenty-four hours will test us, test our resolve to protect our island and the way of life we enjoy here."

A voice on the EOC end said, "Whatever you need L.T."

Several other voices echoed that sentiment, leaving no doubt as to the mindset of everyone involved.

"I cannot believe he said that," Kate whispered to Finn, as she tried to stifle a giggle.

"It worked."

"Yes it did."

Norm outlined his plan to remain ready to deal with any hurricane-related issues and to pre-empt any attempts by outlanders to harm the breakwater. Even the announcement that the bad guys might have a submarine didn't dampen the positive vibe that Norm had created. The EOC barracks would be full to capacity tonight. The broadcast had reached Big Dog and the others at Mel's museum and the men deployed to the lock. Known only to Norm and Finn, the broadcast had also reached Commander George Kenny, Padraig's successor as base commander at Boca Chica.

Norm informed those who were viewing remotely that he would follow-up with individual calls to each group to detail some tasks. The live scene in the EOC was replaced by the Conch Republic seal, a manatee wearing a "Coral Reefer" T-shirt, holding a shaker of salt and a cheeseburger.

The sunroom erupted in a cacophony of voices. Finn remained seated as he felt his phone vibrate. He read the text, showed it to Kate. He waited until the room noise subsided then said, "Norm will be back with us in twenty minutes."

Coffee mugs were topped off, note pads were produced, and everyone made sure they had a pen. Finn noted, with a sense of pride, that everyone around him responded with a "can-do" attitude that characterized most islanders. There was no sense of panic or hopelessness, just a no-nonsense reaction to the problem at hand.

"A penny for your thoughts," Kate asked.

"Islanders, always amaze. You can't escape the reality you are on a small rock in a big ocean. More so now, than ever. It's a reality that fosters cooperation for the common good."

"Waxing philosophical, I see," Kate commented.

"I suppose. But it seems lacking on the mainland and has for years, even before the Big Tide."

"I agree, too much finger-pointing. Too much disparity between what is perceived as the 'public good' and what isn't."

"Nick showed me a video a while back. A guy named Tom McDonald. He's got it right in a song named 'Me vs. You.'"

"You'll have to let me listen to it."

"Let's get rid of Fiona and this asshole Santos and maybe we can find time to relax."

"And help me look for a house?"

"That too."

"I need to check on Nigel while we've got a few minutes."

"I'll come with you."

Kate walked over to speak with Camille for a moment then returned to Finn.

"Let's go."

Finn nodded at Nick, and said, "Back before Norm starts."

Nick gave a thumb's up as Tara gave a finger wave to Kate.

Nigel was sitting up but looked frustrated when they walked in his room. He perked up when he saw them.

"How are you feeling, Nigel?" Kate asked.

"Very annoyed that I am not helping solve the problem. After all, it's really my problem turned oh so very wrong."

"I wouldn't beat myself up, you followed your orders. Orders that were screwed to begin with."

"I could use one of those Mangrove Martinis I saw advertised all round town. What was it the 'bartenders convention?'"

"Yes, it's an annual thing down here," Kate explained.

"I guess a smoke would be out of the question?"

"Nigel, if you were to smoke in here, Sher would make the strychnine seem pleasant."

"On the other hand," Finn wryly said, "You could go on the porch but I doubt you could keep anything lit."

"Damn nicotine."

"I know it's tedious, but you need to stay put and let the fluids we're giving you flush any toxins out of your system that remain," Kate told him."

"What do you know about submarines?" Finn asked.

"I was a commander in the Royal Navy prior to my special assignments career."

"Write down everything I need to know about them. Kate, wouldn't it be better to have Nigel occupied in a positive task than sitting here fidgeting for a smoke?"

"Well, Finn, it's hard to argue with that logic."

"We'll get a notepad and pen to you and I'll be back after Norm's briefing," Finn told him.

Kate checked both IV's that were connected to Nigel's arms near the crook of his elbow. She carefully thumped one section of tubing but seemed satisfied that there was no problem.

"Your color is returning," she said as she checked his pulse at his left wrist. "Your still a little thready, but much better than five hours ago. You know, your buddy," she nodded at Finn, "narrowly survived a similar incident six months ago."

"I feel the bromance budding," Finn said.

"I say, did you?"

"Yes, she's right. She saved my butt too. Remember, Submarines for Dummies, I'll get someone to bring you what you need."

"I shall."

"We need to go."

Finn found one of the CBees, a young man named Evan Harrison who was manning an emergency line phone. Finn explained the situation and ask him to take Nigel a notepad and a couple of pens.

The sunroom was jammed with people. Nick had commandeered Finn and Kate's chairs before anyone else could grab them. They had a few minutes before the allotted time; Finn saw Kate with two re-nourished mugs of coffee in hand as he moved through the crowded room toward her.

"Nick, what's the latest on Fiona?" Finn asked.

"Looks like the worst of it will be between four in the morning and nine or ten o'clock in the morning. She's holding steady as a Cat 5."

"You would think they wouldn't be able to do anything for at least twelve hours after she rolls through. Maybe twenty-four," Finn mused out loud.

"So, maybe that gives us time to come up with a way to disrupt their plans," Nick said.

"Hopefully. Let's see what Norm has to say. Only a couple more minutes."

Conversation died as Norm appeared on the monitor.

"First, I want to thank the CBees and other volunteers working with Rick and Sharon Blount tonight. We appreciate your dedication to your jobs. I want you to know you make a difference. We anticipate the worst effects of Fiona to last for about twelve hours. She does appear to be picking up speed which may mean that time will be reduced. We just don't know conclusively if that will be the case.

Norm paused for a moment, then continued, "We don't expect any more activity from our Euro visitors at this point. Their attempt to do a smash and grab at Mel's museum was stopped with heavy casualties on their side. Any leads to where they might be staying should be sent to the EOC immediately. We'll be up and running all night. Are there any questions?"

The group did not waste time with superfluous questions or nervous inquiries. They were a veteran bunch of islanders who knew talk was cheap. They knew what had to be done. They were ready to do it.

"Alright then," Norm said, "We'll get through this, together. Over and out.

Once again the screen was filled with the salubrious manatee. People begin to leave, most steeling up for the long hours until daylight.

"What time is it?" Tara asked.

"A little after midnight," Nick told her.

"We should try to get some rest now, we've got a few hours before the worst," Kate said.

"I need to check back with Nigel on submarines. I won't keep him long, just get the list he's hopefully made, then leave. Scout's honor."

"I'm going to see if Sher needs any help," Kate told him.

"I think Tara and I will do a walk about and check the shutters, then try to get a nap."

"Thanks," Rick said, "I'm going to monitor the comm links and try to get forty winks.

"Yeah, I need a little rack time," Angel said.

Outside gusts pounded the B and B with blows that seemed to come from every direction. The low moan of the wind chilled the heart like a Banshee's scream.

CHAPTER 19

The seasoned Dade pine that was used in the construction of many old Key West structures and the superb carpentry work of 18th and 19th century craftsmen created work that defied the ravages of some of history's worst hurricanes. Old conchs swore that seasoned, Dade pine was as hard as concrete.

Finn sat with Kate in one of the small parlor rooms on the first floor. He couldn't help but think of the ironic contrast between the state-of-the-art structure in which he and Nick lived and the B and B, constructed at the turn of the last century.

"I'll give Nigel a little more time," Finn told Kate.

"I can't believe this guy has a submarine."

"He's not unique. I think it started with traffickers like Escobar and other South American drug lords. It's not that hard to get your hands on older, diesel driven subs, especially Russian ones."

"You're kidding?"

"Not kidding."

"How many people would it take to run one?"

"I'm hoping to find out from Nigel."

"Are you worried about the Mangrove Mansion?"

"More worried about our boats and equipment than the modules," Finn replied. "This will be the worst conditions its faced, but it was designed to withstand this and more."

"You sound confident."

"James Files was a brilliant engineer and he built a structure designed to run off the grid and withstand the worsening climate conditions, including stronger hurricanes due to increased water temperatures."

"I met his wife about fifteen years ago at a "Save the Manatee" seminar."

"Yes, Denise. She was involved in several conservation issues when they lived down here. She was a member of the Nature Conservancy also."

"You told me they are living in Georgia now?"

"Yes."

The lights went out without warning. This time they did not flicker back to life. Finn used his phone for light and got one of the oil-burning hurricane lamps on the table lit.

"Give Rick a couple of minutes to get the generators running," Finn said.

The old-fashion hurricane lamp cast a lambent light that flickered on the wall. For a brief moment Finn thought of the classic film, "Key Largo." How light and shadow are so artfully blended in a black-and-white movie to achieve an emotional reaction from the viewer. He looked at Kate in the subdued light and wondered if he had found his Bacall.

The lights blinked back on and stayed on. Finn slowly turned the lamp down, then completely off, "Best to save them."

"I'm going to find Camille, I'll track you down later," Kate told him.

"I'm off to question James Bond."

When Finn opened the door of Nigel's room, the Brit was sitting up, notepad in hand. He glanced up and smiled as Finn entered.

"Thank you for giving me something to occupy my time, I can't take just laying here doing nothing."

"Any progress with your notes?"

"Yes, I hope you'll be able to use the information to our advantage against them. I might add that you should contact your friend the base commander, he will be able to provide all you want to know, I would think."

"Excellent, Nigel. Do you feel up to just giving me some ballpark numbers?"

"Certainly."

"Roughly how many men would it take to operate a sub like you described to me, you said a diesel driven one, I think."

"I would think the least they could get by with would be forty, and that would be difficult. I think those old subs had a compliment of of at least fifty men and mostly likely sixty-five to seventy. A modern nuclear attack sub has a compliment of one-hundred-sixty sailors."

"I see. I wonder how many others might be in town? At least they are down five or six men after our encounter at the museum."

"What are you thinking?"

"Well," Finn hesitated, then said, "If they are planning to forcibly take over the lock, I don't see how they could. Especially now that Norm has reinforced security."

"That is a bit of an Agatha."

"A what?"

"A mystery."

"Oh," Finn said and then laughed. "But you see my point? If they can't take control of the lock themselves, there is no other way to get the sub into it. At least that I can see."

Nigel shook his head in agreement, "God, I could use a cigarette."

Finn smiled, "I empathize with you, my friend."

"Were you a smoker?"

"Not for a long time now."

"You're better off."

"I'm not so sure, sometimes."

"The women who saved me, Dr. Sullivan and Ms. Garnier, please give them my thanks. I've not had time to give them a proper 'thank you.'"

"I will, I'm sure they will be in to check on you through the night."

"Mate, this island, the people, you and your friends, quite unique, I must say. In the U.K. some places were hit much harder than others. The event you call the Big Tide brought us together as a nation more than anything since World War II. We are islanders too, you know. I see the camaraderie here, the willingness to pull together in the face of danger."

"We like to think that we can take care of most problems. Most times we can. This will be our first submarine."

"And my first Mangrove Martini, shaken not stirred."

"I need to get back, text me if you need me."

"Cheers for now."

Finn returned to the sunroom to find Rick and Angel poring over some blueprints.

"What's up? You guys give up on catching forty winks?"

"Impossible. Too much of Sher's coffee."

Angel added, "Yeah, I'm wired."

"We're looking at the lock specs, trying to find any possible entrance ways that could be blocked. Remember how, I think it was Eli, that told us that the passageways were mostly open ramps and stairs with metal gratings for floors," Rick said.

Angel added, "We're trying to find choke points that we could block and hopefully reduce anyone's chances of trying to break in from outside."

"Good idea. Where's Nick?"

"He and Tara are taking a look around, just to be safe."

"I have a bit of info from Nigel.'

"Whatcha got?" Angel asked.

"Hang on, getting a text from Norm," Finn said as he held up his index finger.

Rick and Angel sipped coffee while they waited for Finn. They both noticed the slight grin appear on Finn's face. He pushed an icon on the phone's screen, looked toward his friends and said, "We'll be getting a little help from the Navy."

"What's up?" Angel asked.

"Commander Kenny didn't like the notion of an unidentified submarine in his ocean, diesel or not. Royer will be here for the duration and it looks like they will be here within the hour. They are also bringing one of their amphibious troop carriers and two support vehicles."

"That'll help," Rick said.

"Are they going to be able to get across the causeway from Boca Chica?" Angel asked.

"Those vehicles are built to withstand a good amount of wind, it could be dicey though," Finn said.

"It will only get worse, they might as well do it now," Rick said.

"You're right about that," Angel said.

"They will be headed to the EOC, not sure what the plan is after that, but I'm sure Norm will let us know."

"What will Norm let us know?" Tara spoke from the door. Nick was beside her and they entered the sunroom but remained standing.

"Find anything that needs attention?" Rick asked them.

"Not yet, but the night is young," Nick said.

"Finn was going to tell us about submarines before he was interrupted," Angel said.

"Oh yeah,"

"Yeah, but first, our old buddy Commander Royer is headed to town with a detachment of Navy Seals."

"Good to hear, those dudes know their business," Nick said.

"So, what about submarines?" Tara said.

"Not much to tell, Nigel was filling me in on a few facts about the older diesel subs. I thought any info we have would be helpful."

"But, if we can keep them from taking control of the lock, they can't bring the sub in, right?" Angel asked.

"As far as we know," Finn replied.

"How many of their men do you think are on the island?" Rick asked.

"That, my friend, is a good question."

"There's less now, than there was," Nick said.

"True."

"Short of those Seals, I can't see anybody being out in this storm. Not even the bad guys," Rick said.

"So, I think, if there is a move to be made, they will try for within an hour or two of Fiona getting past us," Finn said.

"What's our best guess as to when that time window may occur?" Angel asked.

"I'm checking now," Rick said, as he looked at his tablet.

"What is it about our little island that draws all this craziness?" Finn asked.

"We do seem to attract a lot of bizarre bullshit," Nick added.

"Looks like late tomorrow afternoon, four or five," Rick said.

"We need to be ready," Finn said.

"If we survive the storm, you mean?" Nick said.

"Yeah, that too."

"You don't sound very positive," Tara said.

"My bad," Finn said, "There have been so many ridiculous end-of-the-world moments for us lately, I'm numb. What's one more catastrophe?"

"Remember when we had the T-shirts made that read, "Another weekend, another hurricane?" Rick asked.

"Yes, I do."

"So, you think we'll be OK?" Tara asked.

"Yeah, I think our team is better than their team, even with the sub," Finn said in a convincing tone.

"I bet we've got better coffee," Rick added.

"No doubt," Nick said, "It kept us going for Operation Flamingo."

"Yes it did," Angel said with a smile.

"Should the girl you rescued write a letter to the International Coffee Growers Association," Tara asked with a grin.

"Maybe just a text to the coffee brewer herself," Nick answered.

"Sher would get a kick," Rick said.

"So does everybody who drinks her coffee, especially the stuff with the plant-based stimulant in it," Nick said.

"You know, it's funny. Over the years we've seen the folks who's philosophy to get through a hurricane is to party 'til you puke, pass out, and wake up and the storm is gone."

"Of course, so is the electricity, the air conditioning, the ice, the beer," Rick added.

"The really fun part of hurricanes," Nick said.

"Is that sarcasm, I hear?" Tara jabbed.

"Finish your train of thought, Finn" Angel said.

"Well, at least they don't die from worry in the middle of the night with a heart attack."

"I would not want to be FUBAR for Fiona, and that's a fact, Jack," Angel said.

"Totally with you on that," Nick said.

"Did you find any easy access points on the spec map?" Finn asked.

"One place, so far. But, we haven't finished yet. And, until Fiona moves on, you couldn't get to it. The wind would make it impossible," Rick said.

"Make sure you get that to Norm, plus any more you find," Finn said.

Midnight approached on winds that relentlessly battered all in their path. The ocean was a grim masterpiece of power and turbulence, devoid of sunlight, a gray cauldron of nature's fury.

Inside the B and B, there was a quiet determination to meet the challenge. The phones were still ringing in the lobby where CBees answered all calls. Several people monitored Fiona's track, as they watched for the slightest change in her direction or intensity. A table with various snacks and beverages had been set up along one wall of the lobby.

Finn walked through the lobby and felt the energy of people responding to a crisis. It encouraged him that there were no panic-stricken sheep here. He was more a 'doer' than a 'thinker,' but there was allowance for each. Finn had received a classical education by today's standards. His intellectual prowess was unique, if not borderline bizarre. But, he was not a dreamer. A pragmatist was how he saw himself, dealing with reality, one day at a time. He smiled when he considered that the reality, as of late, of the Conch Republic had been anything but real.

"Finn, there you are," Kate's voice came from behind him.

"How's Nigel?"

"Remarkably resilient. He wants to talk to you, that's why I'm looking for you."

"Thanks."

"Looks like everyone is holding up well," Kate said.

"Yes, that's always encouraging."

"I need to ask Camille something, I'll see you later."

Finn watched Kate move through the crowded lobby in search of her friend. She had a languid motion when she walked that reminded Finn of a dolphin effortlessly gliding through the translucent waves of the open ocean.

He smiled, then headed for the pantry before going to Nigel's room. If Nigel couldn't smoke, Finn would surprise him with something else.

The Brit was perusing a tablet that Kate must have left with him. He smiled when Finn entered and said, "Handy little device this bit of tech is," as he held the tablet up.

Finn approached the bed and sat a tumbler filled with clear liquid down on the side table. Nigel eyed it with the expectant look of a feline perusing the catnip bag.

"G and T with a lime twist. Boodles and Schweppes," Finn said.

"You are indeed, a saint, Finn. And Boodles, God in heaven where did you come up with that?"

"An old friend used to drink it."

Nigel took a sip and a slight tremor ran through him as the gin and tonic worked its medicinal magic.

"Anything new?"

"Kate told me you wanted to see me?"

"Oh, yes. I remembered a name, a dummy company that Santos uses to guard his anonymity, El Jefe', Inc. Don't know if that will help but wanted to pass it on to you."

"The Chief, I'll keep it in mind."

Nigel continued to sip his gin and tonic with relish.

"To answer your question, nothing new," Finn said as he checked his dive watch. "But, the next six hours or so will be entertaining."

CHAPTER 20

The island hunkered down behind the curved walls of the breakwater. The darkness was broken only by street lights and the glimmer of neon that shone, glistening in the wind-whipped downpour. Duval Street, vacant and forlorn, stretched into the distance as water stood six inches deep in front of La Concha.

Street flooding and wind damage were everyday occurrences in the Southernmost town. A Cat 5 was not. In a place where there is no high ground on which to retreat, with the exception of Solares Hill at a mind-boggling 18 feet above pre-Big Tide sea level, flooding is always a threat.

Through the maelstrom a three-vehicle caravan shouldered its way along the streets of Old Town. The amphibious troop carrier, trailed by two military SUVs rolled toward the EOC. An airborne metal sign ripped from some store front slammed into the troop carrier then cartwheeled down the street. The caravan moved on, undeterred by the savage conditions.

"Hey commander, pretty messy out there," one of the Seals said.

"It could be worse, and it will be soon," Commander Hal Royer replied.

"Hey, is the Parrot open?"

"Shark bait, nothing's open," another Seal told him.

"OK, OK."

Another Seal said, "I'm getting thirsty, could use a cold one."

"We all could, Baldhead, but that ain't happenin.'"

"It's MREs or nothing with water. Or, if you don't like water, you can have the other water," the ensign Dom said.

"I thought this place was party central," Baldhead said.

"Fiona ain't giving' lap dances."

"Fiona, who the hell is that?"

"Fiona is the fucking storm, Baldhead. Watch the weather for a change instead of porn and you'd know that," Dom said.

"Settle down, guys," Royer said in a calm voice, "I'm sure we'll get a couple of dances in before the night's over."

Royer recognized his team was keeping loose. They were loud and profane but when things turned to shit, they were solid and then some. It was just hard to take them all out in public at the same time.

Inside the B and B, it might as well have been two in the afternoon. It seemed to Finn that no-one was sleeping. He understood. He'd never been one to sleep through something like Fiona.

He wandered back to the sunroom where Rick and Angel were going over blueprints.

"You guys still at it?"

"We're just looking for any points of entry into the lock that might need to be secured when Fiona gets out of here," Rick told him.

"We found some underground conduits and water mains that could be used if you knew how to access them," Angel added.

"We're keeping Norm apprised as we find things," Rick said.

"Mind if we check the latest on Fiona?"

"Sure, we've got access to a few weather channels and apps."

Finn took the remote and moments later the NOAA website appeared on the big screen. A look at the radar showed Fiona as the huge storm she was, her winds reaching as far as the Bahamas to the east, and the Texas coast to the west.

The Conch Republic lay square in her path. David facing Goliath, Jason taking on Medusa. Rocky and Bullwinkle versus Fearless Leader.

"Looks like she's picked up speed again," Finn commented.

"Yeah, it does."

"I think from three o'clock on, 'til around ten, we're gonna get pounded," Finn said.

"Norm has allowed me to hack into the public works cameras and keep an eye on the breakwater. As long as the cameras hold up," Rick explained.

"How many cameras are there?"

"About forty. Not counting the central lock, which has ten."

"I'm here for the duration," Angel said, "Thought I'd help Rick."

"Obviously we can't monitor everything, but if a segment is breached an alarm will go off and the nearest camera to it will cut into the screen and we can at least see what is wrong," Rick explained.

"So, there's the gin and tonic maker," Kate's voice said from the doorway.

"Guilty, as charged," Finn said, "It was medicinal."

"Medicinal?"

"I figured you'd yell at me less if I gave him that rather than a Marlboro."

Kate paused, tried not to laugh, then said, "It won't kill him."

"If the strychnine didn't, I figured he would survive some Boodles."

"Anything wrong?" Kate asked as she looked at the monitors that showed quick clips of various segments of the breakwater.

"No, we're helping Norm keep an eye out for any trouble using the Public Works' cameras that monitor the breakwater," Rick answered.

"We can also access some of the traffic cameras," Angel said, "Right now, there's the usual street flooding, but nothing extreme."

"We saw the Seals headed for the EOC a few minutes ago," Rick said.

"No kidding?" Nick said.

"They must have those carriers weighted with lead," Angel remarked."

"Wouldn't doubt it," Finn said.

"I wonder if our friends the whisky thieves are out and about?"

"You never know, but my guess is they are not out enjoying the Florida moonlight." Rick said with a smirk.

"Hopefully, not."

"If things get boring, we could always have another seance," Tara said.

The silence was deafening.

"Oops," Tara mumbled.

"Nick, take your girlfriend and go check the attic, would you?" Rick said.

"See, what you did," Nick said.

"Me," Tara said, "What makes you think I'm your girlfriend?"

"I'm guessing there is a ball bearing with my name on it if I get this wrong," Nick responded.

"There could be."

"Maybe we should discus this in the attic?" Nick said with a grin.

Tara hesitated, then said, "Maybe we should."

"And don't forget to check the freaking attic," Rick yelled behind them as they departed.

"And don't shoot anybody," Angel added.

"Call me crazy," Finn said, "Maybe another seance would help."

"You're certifiable," Rick retorted.

"I don't know if Camille would do it. That shook her up pretty bad," Kate said.

"Just ask her if she thinks there is a possibility we could learn anything else."

"I'll ask, but don't get your hopes up."

"Thank you."

The hundred-year-old structure creaked and moaned from the winds that buffeted it. Occasionally something was blown into the brick-like Dade pine with a loud thud. Finn thought of the old sailing ships, trying to stay afloat in this kind of storm. That must have made for some long nights.

Finn remembered weathering some hurricanes in structures far less stalwart than the B and B. He thought for a moment of the hapless W.W. I veterans, working on the Overseas Highway, on September 2, 1935. The Labor Day hurricane as it became known was the first recorded Category 5 storm to make landfall in the United States.

The rescue train, belatedly sent to take them back to the mainland was washed off the track and nearly three hundred men lost their lives. Fiona looked to be the equal of the Labor Day storm, unfortunately.

"I'm going to stretch my legs," Finn told them.

"Bring back some fresh Joe," Rick implored.

"No problemo."

"Get the good stuff," Angel said.

"Oh shit, there goes a camera," Rick said as he pointed at the small monitor on the table. The screen went blank for a moment then switched feeds to another location.

"I doubt that will be the only one," Finn said as he walked away.

Kate, Camille, and Sher were in the kitchen when Finn walked through the door. He quickly realized he was outnumbered.

"Lossy me," Camille said in an exaggerated Cajun accent, "Finn, you remind me of my Uncle. Now, Uncle Adolphus, he just wanted to know everything about everything. And even after a big ol' gator scared the bejeezus out of him, he still went out in the bayou to learn things. Well, one day he twern't so lucky, a gator got his right hand, took it clean off. After that he told us young'uns that he reckoned he'd learnt enough."

"I take it you're not a fan of another seance?" Finn said dryly.

"Whatever gave you that idea?" Camille replied coyly.

"Finn what do you hope to gain by putting Camille through that again?" Kate asked.

"I think I've underestimated the emotional effect of the seance on Camille," Finn said honestly.

"I have to admit having the spirit of a woman dead over a hundred years seemingly inhabit your mind and body is a bit disconcerting."

"I see your point," Finn told her.

"So, if you can give me a really good reason for an encore performance, I'll listen to your argument."

"Were you on the debate team at LSU?" Finn said with a grin.

"Captain," Camille answered.

"I think it is still hard to grasp what we experienced. And you definitely were the person who was most 'experienced.' So, I get it. Honestly, I don't know exactly what I'd be looking for, and for that reason alone I wouldn't want you to go through it again."

Kate broke in and said, "We've figured out 1733. We know the lock is probably a target, even if we don't know for exactly what. We also know our latest crazed psychopath has a submarine. What else could we possibly learn? From a ghost, no less."

"Two members of the debate team," Finn muttered, "Give women the vote, and what do you get? Lady scientists."

"You mean the lady scientists who saved your ass, those lady scientists?"

"Yes indeed, those lady scientists. I'm going to cut my losses here, and suggest that there is most likely nothing additional to learn from another seance."

"Maybe some day, but not tonight. Finn, I'm no bayou bumpkin, but that was the most unexplainable thing I've ever experienced. Felt like my Masters in Chemistry went right out the window."

"Camille, no worries. We are grateful for all you've done, we'd be completely unawares as to danger to the breakwater and the lock without you. Not to mention saving Nigel."

"That was a team effort," Camille replied.

"The boys in the sunroom need a caffeine fix, I told them I'd round some up."

"I'm getting ready to make three fresh pots," Sher told him.

"I'll stick around if you don't mind."

"As long as you don't have a ouija board with you, we'll let you stay," Kate said.

"Now, there's an idea."

"Don't you even start, Finn," Kate said.

"I'll bet you didn't know Finn used to be a Key West Ghost Tour guide," Sher said.

She might as well have thrown a grenade.

"Oh my God," Camille said.

"No way, our Finn?" Kate laughed.

"It was one summer."

"Finn, a ghost guide!" Camille snorted.

"I was in college."

"He was very good," Sher said and fanned the flame.

"Hurricanes bring out these kinds of stories, it's the stress" Finn said, "I owe you one Sher."

"Would like to have been a fly on the wall for that," Kate said with a grin.

"But I will say this," Finn said with a somber note in his voice, "That time, Norm and I saw Robert the Doll move, it was on one of the tours. If it'd been just me, or just Norm by himself, I wouldn't have believed it. But we both saw it. I've never had quite the same outlook on things since that happened. I mean, you really need to keep an open mind. I think that's why what happened at the seance intrigues me so much. It was unexplainable yet it happened."

"Finn, you're more open minded than most," Camille said, "But, you're right, some things just can't be explained by the laws of physics."

"What can be explained by the laws of physics is coffee," Sher said, "It's almost ready."

Finn was relieved the conversation was moving away from his ghost tour days twenty-five years ago. He was ready to get back to the relative safety of the sunroom. But not without an urn of Joe for his pals.

Outside, the wind was relentless, over one hundred miles an hour, with gusts to one thirty. Battering everything in its path. Finn was reminded of the old Conch who told him, "It's not that the wind blows a hundred and twenty, but that it blows one twenty for eight hours straight."

Finn knew how much work Rick had put into hurricane-proofing the old structure. Some newer buildings would not fare as well as the B an B did through this storm.

Sher's voice broke his reverie, "OK, hazel eyes, here's your coffee."

"Thanks, I know Rick and Angel will appreciate it."

"I'll walk halfway with you, I need to look in on Nigel," Kate said."

"Au revoir," Camille said.

As they walked, Kate said, "That house I wanted you to look at with me, I hope it makes it through this."

"We'll have to wait and see."

"Ever the pragmatist," Kate exclaimed.

"Well, we could get our rain gear and go take a look, you know."

"And a sense of humor from hell."

"Thank you, thank you very much," Finn answered in a dead-on imitation of Elvis.

"You better get that coffee to the guys," she said and kissed him lightly on the cheek.

Rick and Angel were engrossed watching the camera footage from around the breakwater when Finn entered.

"Got the mud."

"Finn, you've got to see this," Angel said without moving his head, as he continued to view the screen.

"It's Ma Nature at her scariest," Rick added.

Finn set the coffee urn down on a table mat and took the chair next to Rick. The wall-mounted monitor displayed a nightmarish ocean; a dark, frothy expanse churned into a relentless battering machine.

"We've been awestruck at the force," Rick said as he a rose and went to the coffee urn. He picked up Angel's mug on the way by him.

"Hopefully, the curvature of the plates will dissipate some of the force. But, looking at that, I don't know how much," Finn commented.

"I wonder if the Seals have made it to the EOC?" Angel said.

Finn understood his friends' fascination with the storm. He was mesmerized watching the sheer force and uncontrolled fury of Fiona. It was a sobering reminder that the cost of paradise was sometimes very steep. And dangerous.

"Maybe Finn can shoot Norm a text," Rick said.

"What?"

"I said, text Norm, see if the Seals made it," Rick said.

"Oh, my bad. I see what you mean about the spectacle," Finn said, "It's hard to turn away. But, yeah, I'll do that now."

A few minutes later, Finn told them, "They made it and are ready to kick ass."

"Those guys aren't bad for being Navy," Angel said.

"They're lucky to have Royer, the guy's going to med school after this hitch is up," Finn said.

"He definitely saved our ass on Monkey Island," Rick said in reference to events of several months ago.

"So far, the breakwater its doing its job," Angel said.

"A couple of cameras have gone down and some of the lights, but things are holding," Rick added.

"By the way," Finn said, "We won't be having another seance."

"Camille not up for it?" Rick asked.

"No, she's not. I underestimated the toll that experience took on our Madame Fontaine," Finn said using Camille's professional moniker as the Conch Republic's only voodoo priestess, tarot reader, and dispenser of holistic remedies.

"I'll be honest," Angel said, "It scared the pure dog piss out of me."

"No algorithms for what we saw," Finn said.

No nothing, for what we saw," Rick added.

"Except that we saw it. We all saw it," Finn stated.

"Copy that," Angel said nodding his head.

"Saw what?" Nick asked as he came into the sunroom, with Tara in tow.

"The apparition of Marie LeVeau," Finn answered.

"Yeah, we definitely saw it," Tara said.

"I'm with her," Nick said.

"How was the attic?" Rick asked.

"Tight and dry, so far. Man you could feel that wind up there," Nick said.

"Pretty spooky," Tara said.

"That seems to be the theme for the weekend," Finn said.

"You two need to look at some of this video from the breakwater. It's amazing," Angel told Nick and Tara.

"Yeah, grab some coffee. It's fresh," Rick said.

"Could use some of that million dollar stuff to liven up the Joe," Nick said.

"I think you'll find this lively enough. It's Sher's special stuff," Finn said.

They were drawn to the surreal view of the storm as it raged like Poseidon himself drove its fury. Spumes of wind-churned water rose high over the breakwater. The extension plates were activated to give added protection from the huge waves that crashed against the breakwater. The icy breath of reality struck them all; one small island protected from annihilation by a man-made wonder.

"Feeling fairly insignificant here," Rick said.

"Know what you mean," Angel answered.

"Are we waxing philosophical now?" Finn quipped.

"When you're on the brink of destruction I guess it makes you more reflective than usual," Rick said.

"It usually just makes me hungry," Angel said.

"Semper fi," Nick said.

"I need to speak with Kate," Tara said, "I'll be back in a while."

"Guess it's just us guys," Rick said as Tara departed.

"Break out the cards," Angel said.

"That was always the go-to way to kill time," Nick said.

"Even back in the day," Finn said with a grin.

"At least pre-Nintendo days," Rick said.

"I seem to recall the first mention of playing cards in Europe was in the fourteenth century. They came from the East," Finn said, "They've always been a favorite of the infantryman. Easy to carry, light weight, and hours of fun after a day of bloody conflict killing your neighbor."

"Is that a note of cynicism I hear?" Rick jabbed.

"When does truth become cynicism?" Finn countered.

"Don't get him started on one of those philosophy rants," Nick said.

"It's the storm, makes people contemplate their mortality," Rick commented.

"Sometimes it's best to see things in black and white rather than in color," Finn said, then went on, "I'll never forget years ago when I saw a colorized version of 'Key Largo' for the first time. I hated it. All the subtle play of sunlight and shadow captured in the original black and white version was lost in the colorized one."

"Thank you, Roger Ebert," Nick said.

"I see your point," Rick said, "So, you're saying that if the truth is cynical, we should recognize it as such."

"And vice versa," Finn replied.

"OK, OK, my brain hurts, stop it," Angel said.

"What, the marine whiz kid with a degree from M.I.T.?" Finn laughed.

"Yeah, syllogisms and logical constructs should be right up your binary brain," Rick said.

"I didn't know you were bi?" Nick said.

"Really, really guys." Angel said and threw up his hands.

"Have to tell Marilyn about this latest development," Nick continued to rag his buddy.

"Do so and die, Cassini."

"And we got here from playing cards?" Rick asked with flair.

"The vicissitudes of hurricane conversations," Finn said.

"At least we're not having to listen to a drunk gush about how much they love everybody 'cause they think they're going to die," Rick said.

"Been there, done that," Angel said, "Uh, not in a hurricane though."

"Remember that guy that passed out drunk in his water bed during Wilma and woke up floating down Key Deer Boulevard?" Rick asked.

"I was in the Caribbean when that happened," Finn replied.

"All we need is Quent singing 'Farewell Spanish Ladies,'" Rick said with a smile.

"And a bigger breakwater," Finn said picking up on the "Jaws" reference.

"You know, you may be right," Nick said.

"If these storms continue to escalate in terms of size and force, a reinforced breakwater may be needed," Rick said.

"Right now, we need to figure out the bad guys' next move," Finn said bringing things back in focus.

"You're right."

"It doesn't seem like there are many options," Angel said, "And all of them involve the big lock, am I wrong?"

"Not in the least," Finn said, "That's why, unless we hear something different from Norm, I think we need to be ready to go back to the lock when conditions permit. I know Norm will have some idea of how he wants to handle things overall. But, we need to be ready."

"So you think late-morning or thereabouts?" Rick asked.

"I think we need to stay on top of things. As soon as it is possible to move around outside, they'll make a move. At least that's how I see it."

"So, Defcon 5 at all times," Nick said.

"Probably D3 will do," Finn said, "But seriously, we don't want to get caught taking a piss.

"Copy that, Finn," Angel said.

"I'm thinking by noon we should be ready to move, regardless."

"I wonder if any other B and Bs offer this kind of hurricane experience package," Nick said.

"I doubt it, I think we're the only establishment that caters to people like you three rugged individualists," Rick laughed.

"We could do a podcast if the island wasn't staring imminent oblivion in the face," Nick said.

"We could still do it, oblivion or not," Angel said.

"Semper fi."

"Angel, take some of that nervous energy and do a quick scan of the hydraulic stations, if you would," Finn said.

"On it, it'll take a minute to switch the feeds."

"More coffee, anybody?" Nick asked.

"Thought you'd never ask," Finn answered with a grin.

CHAPTER 21

One thousand yards off the coast, just above the ocean floor, well below the effects of the storm raging above, a submarine waited. The diesel sub Mikhail Sholokov maintained radio silence. It ran on battery power as the crew tried to avoid detection.

The skipper, Sergei Belishnikov, was a renegade mercenary currently in the employ of Eduardo Santos. A former Captain in the Red Navy, the man was a crafty submariner and available to the highest bidder.

The Big Tide had increased options for people willing to work in the marginal trades. Trades such as forgers, counterfeiters, smugglers, and grifters in general. Mainland governments were strapped with housing shortages, unemployment, and infrastructure problems on an epic scale.

The prevailing thought in law enforcement was that if you were rich enough to own a Van Gogh or a Wyeth, then you damn well were rich enough to provide your own security. The rich had a lot less traction after the Big Tide. Especially if you were just rich for no good reason. A trust fund baby. Anybody named Kardashian.

Sergei Belishnikov was no trust fund baby. He was a seasoned sub commander and a man whose authority was rarely questioned. He didn't particularly like Santos, but he found the man's money irresistible. His fifty-man crew were veteran sailors, but they were nervous. This storm and the hastiness with which this voyage had been thrown together bothered some of the more experienced men.

Belishnikov's "first mate," Dmitri Smirnoff, another Russian, oversaw the daily operations and had apprised his captain that the crew was edgy.

"Keep the vodka locked up, Dmitri."

"Aye, Capitan."

"Give them some tramadol and tell them to be patient. We can do nothing until this Fiona is past us."

"Aye, Capitan."

Sergei pondered his situation. Santos sat safely in the Bahamas, where he had been dropped after his departure from Barcelona on the sub. Getting Santos' men with their loot off the island was on him and him alone. He preferred to work that way.

The old Russian saying that too many cooks ruined the borscht was true with smuggling ops also. The need for radio silence created a factor of uncertainty that Sergei did not like. There was always uncertainty in his line of work, but this bordered on the absurd.

He was playing footsie with a naval base that housed at least two nuclear subs, if they were in port now. They had a squadron of old Lockheed P3 Orion patrol aircraft that were designed for antisubmarine warfare but were effective against smugglers also.

Those were the deterrents that he knew about, what else they might have worried him. He slowly swirled the clear vodka in the tumbler he held. Stoli on the rocks, nothing like it to clear your head.

Sergei had a few tricks of his own. A black market device that distorted and disguised the diesel engines signature sonar return to sound like a biologic. He carried four conventional torpedos that he was not afraid to use.

He weighed all the factors as he stared into the clear vodka as if he gazed into a crystal ball. Patience was not a virtue Sergei practiced often, in this case there was nothing to do but wait.

His men were edgy and he didn't blame them. There was no assurance that this plan would work. The idea of slipping his two-hundred-fifty foot sub into the lock seemed doable on paper. The reality would be fraught with problems, even with diminished currents and wind speeds lowered, the actual positioning would require skill and luck. Sergei did not feel lucky at the moment. He sipped the vodka and cursed Santos.

Throughout the sub, the men did what sailors have done for centuries to pass the time. They gambled. Some played cards, some threw dice. Most of them cheated or tried to cheat, it was expected.

The pay was good but the risks were high. The lure of easy money has a very strong appeal as the late Glenn Frey told us. Most of the crew were eastern Europeans from Russia, Chechnya, Belarus and a few other former Soviet Socialist Republics.

There were electricians, radio men, welders, navigators, engineers, and sonar operators. Every man had a skill, or two. These modern "pirates of the Caribbean" were devoid of any connection to the romanticized version of sea dogs portrayed in book and film. No Johnny Depp's here. Only men making a dishonest living. They were more like your standard American politician than Captain Jack Sparrow.

Sergei knew the original plan was based on a surprise take-over of the lock controls, a quick in and out with the sub, pick up the men, then head for open water. He didn't see how that would be possible at this point. The radio silence prevented him from receiving any real-time information from Santos or the men on the island.

He would wait. He sipped the Stoli and turned up the volume on a version of Mussorgsky's "Pictures at an Exhibition."

CHAPTER 22

The storm scoured the empty streets like liquid sandpaper. Drops of water pushed by one-hundred-fifty miles per hour winds felt like lead weights. Hapless vehicles, overturned, were strewn through Old Town like Lego cars.

Chickens and feral cats huddled together under a white flag of mutual terror. The invasive Australian pines, brought into the Keys to serve as wind breaks, weren't doing their jobs. As evidenced by the numerous trees laying on the sand near Ft. Taylor.

Fiona would go down in Conch Republic history as a nasty bitch. Barometers were bottoming out near the mark set by the Labor Day storm. The breakwater withstood the assault of wind and wave, standing like a Shao Lin master, using the storms energy against itself.

Inside the B and B, Finn played a solitary game of mental chess against their opponent. He tried to follow through several scenarios to assess each one's viability.

"A penny for your thoughts?" Kate said.

Finn sat in one of the small alcoves that could be found on the first floor. He was in a favorite reading chair built before IKEA was born.

"I was thinking about the first time I saw a hurricane's track sped up on video. How 'alive' it looked, like some sentient being."

"Yes, I know what you mean."

"I wonder if our intervention at the museum will alter this guy Santos' plans?"

"Well, he won't be getting away with any of the Atocha treasure, at least," Kate said.

"Nor six or seven of his men."

"Hired mercenaries, weren't they?"

"Yes, replaceable parts for our Moriarty wannabe."

"So, what they've really got right now is a very expensive bottle of whiskey and a fake painting?"

"Exactly, Kate."

"Do you think they cut their losses and let the crew that's on the island fend for themselves?"

"Just what I've been thinking about, it would be logical. But, I'm not sure these men are, logical I mean. Maybe, there is still something we are missing . Something that would make it worth the risk to provide a submarine as a getaway car."

"What else on the island is worth that much?"

"That my dear is the question."

"Unless," Kate paused in mid-sentence.

"I know that tone," Finn said.

"Finn, what if it is all about the painting. Not just the fake one Nigel had, but others. The gallery and the fence, what if they had several stolen pieces. Expensive ones. Paintings that fetch upwards of a hundred million dollars at auction."

"That's a damn good hypothesis," Finn said, "And I think you need to explain that to Norm. Right now."

Finn quickly texted something, then placed the phone on the table. Forty-five seconds later the theme from "Jaws" emanated from the phone and Finn put it on speaker.

"Norm, listen to our favorite Lady Scientist."

Kate explained what she had outlined to Finn moments earlier. Norm listened without interruption until she finished then said, "Kate, that makes the most sense of anything I've heard recently."

"I think she's right. A million dollar bottle of whiskey isn't worth risking a sub for, but several hundred million might be."

"If that's the case, then we need to increase our presence at the lock as soon as we can get outside again," Norm said, "Let me confer with Commander Royer, I'll be back to you in a few," Norm said, then cut the call.

"Let's go to the sunroom while we wait. I want to see something on the map," Finn said.

"What are you thinking?"

"I want to see if we can minimize access to the lock."

They found Rick and Angel resting their eyes, engaged in a game of hangman.

"Kate's figured it out," Finn told them as they walked into the room.

"Figured what out?" Rick asked.

"What the bad guys are up to."

"Spit it out, we're all ears."

"I think they are trying to get off the island with upwards of three or four-hundred million dollars of stolen art."

"Whoa, say again," Angel exclaimed.

Kate ran through her theory and heard no dissenters.

"Do you think the art pieces are in the gallery?" Rick asked.

"They will have to transport them to the lock, where ever they are," Finn commented.

"If they are in the gallery, they won't have far to carry them, "Rick noted.

"It seems too obvious, that they'd be in the gallery."

"It does. Maybe that's what they were using the house for, to stash the paintings until time to go," Angel pointed out.

"Maybe the realtor stumbled onto something she wasn't supposed to see and they killed her," Finn added.

"So they may be riding the storm out in another house," Kate said.

Finn's phone sounded with the theme from Jaws.

"Norm, you're on speaker."

"Royer and his men want to do a remake of 'Singin' in the Rain,'" he says he'd rather be *'firstest with the mostest.'*"

"It's hard to argue with that strategy," Finn said.

"Who said that, anyway?" Angel asked.

"Nathan Bedford Forrest, I think," Finn said, then added, "The guy was a good tactician but his moral compass was a little skewed; he was the first head of the Klan."

"The KKK?" Angel asked.

"Yeah."

"So, the Seals want to go out and play?" Rick said.

"Looks that way."

"Finn, I don't think there is any reason for any of you to go back out in this right now. Let Royer and his team do what they do best. I may need you and the others for something else," Norm said.

"Works for us," Finn said. The others nodded in agreement.

"I'll give Royer your regards. Over and out."

"I need to talk to Nigel," Finn said, "Kate will you come with me?"

They found him and Camille talking about Cajun cooking when they walked into the room.

"We'll have to let you try some shrimp étouffée when you're feeling better."

"Nigel, excuse us, Camille. Nigel, are there any high value paintings notably missing or stolen. Pieces like Van Gogh's 'Sunflowers' or Monet's 'Waterlilies,' really up there?"

"As a matter of fact, six paintings such as you describe have been stolen from private collections in the last nine months."

Kate explained her theory as Nigel nodded his head in understanding and agreement.

"Yes, I think you've hit it. We should have raided the gallery. This has been a bugger-up from the start."

"Not to mention the leak that nearly got you killed," Finn reminded.

"Yes, I'll have to speak with someone about that," Nigel said in a tone that could have chilled the entire state of Arizona.

Finn knew whoever Nigel ended up 'speaking' with was in deep shit.

"I think Dr. Sullivan is correct; they could have close to half a billion euros in art work. That's a lot of shekels even for a man like Santos."

"Indeed."

"Do you think they will stick with their plan, to load everything on the sub and split?" Finn asked.

"I say, you know there's a good chance that they don't realize we're onto them," Nigel said.

"Really?" Kate questioned.

"Without our ghostly information we'd be way behind in figuring this out," Finn pointed out.

"True."

"Santos is an arrogant bastard. I doubt he thinks anyone on this little island can match wits with him," Nigel said.

"Believe it or not, per capita we're a brainy bunch."

"I don't doubt it, but Santos doesn't realize that," Nigel said.

"We need to play that to our advantage, then," Finn responded.

"In other words," Kate said, "don't let him know, they we know he doesn't know what we know."

"Jesus, Kate," Finn said as he tried to keep a straight face, "I would have sworn no-one short of a six-pack could possibly say that."

"By jove, I think she's right. Feint left on the pitch, but go right."

They stared at Nigel until he said, "Oh right, it's a football reference."

"Soccer?"

"Yes, football."

Finn steered the conversation past the vicious loop it was headed for and said, "So, it's another case of Key Westers playing dumb. No problem, there."

"Yes, right up our alley," Kate joined in.

"But, it seems to be working as of late."

"I'm going to have to come back to your charming island when someone's not trying to kill me," Nigel said.

"Nigel, we need to get back to Rick and Angel and see how they're doing on finding some choke holds to minimize access to the lock once the storm slacks off."

"Cheers for now," he said.

"We will check back with you," Kate told him.

When they were out of earshot Kate said, "He really should be in the Guinness book, you know. Sitting there nursing a gin and tonic less than twenty-four hours after being poisoned."

"Stiff upper lip, our friend, Nigel."

The lobby was eerily quiet when they walked in, punctuated by the harsh, abrasive sound of the relentless wind. A number of people caught a few z's in contorted positions half-sitting, half-lying down. They walked on through and out the archway that opened on the other side of the lobby. Kate led them down the hall to the left toward the kitchen.

"Let's see what's going on in here?" she said.

Sher and Camille were sitting at the counter going over a check list. Kate shared the latest developments with them.

"So, you really think they'll try to take over the lock?" Sher asked."

"It looks that way, right now."

"Why are people so fucking crazy?" Sher said in an exasperated tone of voice.

"Good question girlfriend," Camille said.

"Greed would be my guess," Finn said.

"Maybe the false belief that wealth justifies one's actions," Kate added.

"At least Machiavelli had some logic to underscore his 'ends justifies the means' philosophy," Finn said.

The lights flickered and stayed off. The generators kicked in and restored power. In the aftermath of the Big Tide, enterprising engineers developed a tidally-driven hydroelectric field. Large underwater blades, similar to those used in wind farms turned numerous turbines which in turn produced electricity. They also continually recharged the next-gen lithium battery array that filled an entire warehouse and powered much of the Conch Republic on a daily basis.

"Something must have happened at the warehouse," Finn said.

"Do you think it's sabotage?" Camille asked.

"Probably the storm, but I wouldn't completely rule out a little help from our Bulgarian friends," Finn said.

"It's hard to believe you could stand it outside now," Sher offered.

"Only if you're a Seal," Finn said, "I'll check with Norm about the warehouse."

A shudder ran through the building, which caused conversation to stop. Reinforced footers with tie-downs on joists anchored the venerable edifice solidly to the ground. If there's an Achilles' heel with regard to hurricanes, it's roofs. Rick made sure when they remodeled the B and B that the roof would provide no weak spots for the wind to attack. Camille muttered something in Creole, then said, "I hope my shop is going to be OK, I don't think its been through anything like this,"

"It's fairly well sheltered," Kate said optimistically.

"I hope that will keep it standing. I've got everything in water-proof containers, all my old papers, my books."

"What about your collections?" Kate asked.

"They're safe and sound, hopefully. You have no idea how hard it is to replace some things, take swamp witch hair, not easy. Not to mention a three-toed salamander's tongue."

Finn smiled as he listened to Camille, but he texted to someone at the same time. He patiently waited for an answer. Several minutes later he checked an incoming message, then told the others, "It looks like the eye will be passing over in about an hour. Norm is sending some recon teams out during the lull to check the warehouse, the lock, and a few other places. He's going to send one team by your shop, Camille."

"Tell him I appreciate it."

"No worries."

"I'm going to let Rick know the eye will be coming our way. He may want to do a quick recon on the building. See if anything needs bolstering," Finn said.

CHAPTER 23

Finn knew the hours of waiting weighed heavily on everyone. He smiled grimly as he recalled the effect of the hurricane on Edward G. Robinson's character, in Key Largo. You couldn't ask for a better bunch of seasoned veterans than the people he was with right now. No hurricane virgins, thank the tiki gods.

He tried not to think about how much could be lost should events turn out badly for the home team. That type of energy-sapping worry did no good. He focused on the present. He had never really contemplated that one person could change his life, until Kate Sullivan came along.

Nick's presence in his life was the result of a serendipitous encounter that brought the men together. The resulting bond was not expected but was mutually accepted in the manner of men. Finn took on the role of mentor to a young man just out of the marines, trying to get his bearings in a rapidly changing world.

When he entered the sunroom, Nick and Tara sat with Rick and Angel watching the monitors. Rick noticed him and said, "We've only lost four cameras, so far."

"Norm says the eye will be here in about an hour. Wanted you to know in case you want to do a quick look around outside."

"Thanks. We better take a little walk. We should have what, thirty-five to forty-five minutes?" Rick said.

"I'm game," Nick said, "I need to move around."

"I'm in," Angel added.

"I'll tag along," Finn said, "I wouldn't mind stretching my legs."

"How 'bout you, Tara?" Rick asked.

"I better go, the four of you unsupervised in the eye of a hurricane might not be a good thing."

"We did pretty good at Flamingo," Nick reminded.

"True. Well, if I'm going with you, I better go to the little girl's room. See you in a few."

When she was out of earshot, Angel said, "I've got twenty that says she comes back with at least two pistols and a slingshot."

"No takers there," Rick said, "We know our girl with blue hair. At least two and the slingshot."

"Speaking of getting ready," Finn said, "I need to get a few things myself."

"Me too," Nick added.

"Let's meet in the cloak room, in thirty minutes," Rick told them.

"My gear is in the spare room," Angel said, "I'm going to hang with Rick a little while, we're still looking at access to the lock complex. Trying to find ones that might not be obvious."

"See you in a few," Finn said and walked out of the sunroom.

They gathered in the cloak room, as Rick called it. A typical utility room for hoteliers. For a group of civilians, they looked menacing. They all carried registered firearms. But these weren't liquored-up thrill seekers, these were four former Eagle Scouts and a girl with blue hair who believed in being prepared.

"You know Finn, the fact that this is not the first time you have been in the eye of a storm doesn't surprise me," Angel said, "Weird, but not surprising."

The eye of a hurricane usually ranges from twenty to forty miles in diameter. Fiona's was almost forty-five miles, the towering wall of thunderstorms surrounding it rose high over the Straits of Florida. Finn glanced at his dive watch and noted it was a few minutes after four-thirty.

Rick cracked the heavy storm door and looked out into the darkness. The rain was reduced to a drizzle and the wind seemed to have magically disappeared. An eerie quietness hung heavy in the air, as Rick drew the door open and they walked outside.

"Man oh man, that's just gash," Nick said, as he looked around at the grounds illuminated by headlights they all wore attached to their headgear.

Limbs of all shapes and sizes covered the ground. Scattered litter was everywhere. Street signs separated from their poles, had embedded themselves in trees. One that read PEDX was sticking in one of the porch columns. The stillness in contrast to what they witnessed was chilling. They shuck off the vibe and began an inspection of the buildings.

"Watch your step, there's a lot of crap on the ground," Rick said.

"Copy that," Nick replied.

"Angel, could you come with me, let's check the generators."

"Sure, Rick."

"We've got about forty minutes. There won't be a lot of warning when the other side comes round," Finn reminded them.

They began an earnest inspection of the exterior of the building while Angel and Rick inspected the building that housed the two large generators they used.

Finn made his way around to the side yard where the gazebo was looking like a little worse for the wear. Some of the lattice work had been blown off, and a large limb had damaged the roof but it stood upright.

He continued walking while he surveyed the hurricane shutters on the rear wall of the inn. He side-stepped a metal garbage can, dented and battered, with Jerk-Fusion stenciled on it. He noticed the lack of prowling feral cats, usually very active at this time of morning. No chickens either. The animals knew it wasn't over yet. He checked his watch, about twenty-five more minutes.

Nick and Tara caught up to him as he rounded the side and headed toward the street front.

"Find anything that needs attention?"

"No, not yet. Rick did a helluva good job when he remodeled the old place," Nick answered.

"Look, down there," Finn said as he pointed down Whitehead Street. Several blocks away headlights from a vehicle could be seen coming toward them.

"Follow me," he said as he quickly headed for the shelter of the borrowed SUV parked in front of the inn.

"Let's see who this is," he told them as they settled in behind the hood.

The crouched patiently in the dark as the headlights moved slowly in their direction. The attenuated stillness was eerie. The sound of Tara assembling her slingshot punctuated the need for caution. The air was heavy with salt, saturated to one hundred percent humidity, it felt like wearing your worst Christmas sweater soaked in egg nog. They were all sweating.

The lone vehicle continued to move closer, the glare of its lights prevented any recognition of it. Nick gave a furtive peek over the hood but merely shook his head when he crouched back down.

The headlights cast an ethereal, X-Files pall down the length of the empty street littered with debris scattered from curb to curb. It seemed to move with intent toward the inn. A spot light flicked on and swept the area in front of the inn.

Finn held his hand up for patience, as Nick and Tara readied themselves to shoot. Suddenly, a familiar voice shouted, "Anybody home?"

"Jesus, it's Big Dog," Nick exclaimed.

The ghostly vehicle pulled up next to the curb about ten feet from the spot where they hid.

All three emerged, to find their NBA-sized friend along with his fellow LEO Joey, in the driver's seat of an SUV similar to the one Norm had loaned them.

"We're headed back to the EOC," Big Dog told them, "Norm told us to let Ms. Garnier know her shop is holding up so far."

"Did you see anybody suspicious out and about?" Finn asked.

"Like our Euro friends?" Joey replied.

"The very same."

"If they were, we didn't see them, but we were only covering a specific grid area. Another team had the grid with the lock, haven't heard anything from them."

"What are you guys doing?" Joey asked.

"Quick recon on the buildings and grounds," Finn answered, then looked at his watch.

"We better keep moving," Big Dog said.

"We'll pass the word to Madame Fontaine," Finn told him.

"Watch your ass," Nick said as he fist bumped Big Dog.

The SUV drove away down the street as Rick and Angel appeared from the side yard.

"Who was that" Rick asked.

"Big Dog and Joey out making rounds."

"Anything happening?" Angel inquired.

"Nothing involving our Euro friends, at least in the grid they were assigned to search.

A sudden breeze reminded them their window of time was about to close. A few drops of rain splattered loudly on the wet pavement.

"Any problems in the generator shed?" Finn asked.

"Everything's Jake, nice and dry."

"We better wrap things up out here," Finn suggested.

"The old homestead is holding up, so far, knock on wood," Rick said.

Nick nudged Angel, and pointed down the street away from the direction Big Dog and Joey took when they departed. Angel looked in time to see two vehicles cross Whitehead Street moving west.

"Got a couple of bogies here," Nick informed the others.

Everyone turned to see the second vehicle as it disappeared out of sight. Finn checked his watch, time was short.

"We've got time to check that out," Finn said, "I've got the keys, who wants to go for a ride?"

Less than a minute later, they were all in the SUV headed for the intersection where they observed the vehicles. Finn guided them through the debris that littered the street. He slowed even more as he approached the turn, then stopped.

"Nick, take a peek around the corner," Finn told his friend.

Nick smoothly exited the SUV and walked slowly to the corner of the building that fronted on Whitehead. He cautiously moved into the deep shadow of a banyan tree and looked down the crossing street.

Three minutes later, he returned to the SUV, "Good call, Finn. They are about two hundred yards down the street but something is blocking the road. They're trying to move it."

"I'll let Norm know," Finn said and picked up his phone.

"Are you sure it's the Euros?" Rick asked.

"I'd bet my Slayer collection on it."

"That's good for me."

"What's the plan, Stan?" Tara asked.

"Why do I feel like we need to apply for membership in Vigilantes R Us?" Finn mused.

"Concerned citizens, that's us," Rick said.

"Norm wants us to keep an eye on them, but don't engage unless forced to do so. We've got about ten minutes until conditions will deteriorate."

"Do you think they've got the art with them?" Tara asked.

"They could be going to get it," Angel pointed out.

"Nick, you and Angel have the most experience with this type situation. Get as close as you can, see what they're up to. Norm's putting a response team together. They'll be here as fast as they can."

The two men moved with stealth, their movements seemingly choreographed. They faded into the dark like whitetail bucks disappearing into the high grass of the Everglades.

"Rick find some real-time data on when this balmy weather turns to crap."

"On it."

"How 'bout me," Tara asked from the back seat.

"Sit tight, for now. Keep an eye out."

"OK, we've got about ten minutes until things get worse again," Rick told them.

Nick and Angel moved cautiously down the sidewalk toward the knot of men and vehicles. There was not much cover, but they hugged the deeper shadows along the store fronts. They squatted behind a long planter box and surveyed the situation. Nick pointed out a lone man who seemed to be acting as lookout. The others, nine or ten men, wrestled with a large marquee that was blocking the intersection.

"What's the play?" Angel whispered.

Nick raised his finger, then rapidly texted something on his phone. A few seconds later he said, "Stay put, for now. We've got ten minutes 'til things get bad."

The men were yelling in a language neither Nick nor Angel understood. The lead vehicle, some kind of truck with a crew cab, edged up to the marquee and began to push it out of the intersection. Metal twisted and shrieked as the marquee slowly buckled and moved backward.

Down the street, in the direction they were headed, blue lights blossomed in the night like neon strobes. Rain began to fall as large drops splattered around Nick and Angel onto the sidewalk.

The truck and its companion, an SUV, both backed up moving toward where Nick and Angel hid. Suddenly, from the direction they had come, another set of blue lights erupted in the intersection. Multiple red lasers cut through the night and fell on the vehicles as they tried to flee.

Suddenly, the lead truck barreled down the side street and the other vehicle followed. Nick and Angel stepped into the street as Finn eased up beside them in the SUV. From the other direction, two police trucks pulled up and stopped.

Norm got out of the lead truck and walked toward Finn and the others.

"We don't have much time, what did you see?"

Nick spoke up, "Two vehicles, ten men, don't know if they had any art with them or not."

"I've got to put you two on the payroll," Norm said.

"We've got a few minutes, do you want to follow?" Finn asked.

"Yes, at a distance, let's see if we can figure out where they're headed."

Nick and Angel jumped in and Finn turned onto the side street with the two police trucks behind him.

"Nice work with the light show," Nick said.

"Yeah, how'd you do that," Angel asked.

"The blue lights come standard with this model," Finn said, "But Rick and Tara came up with the laser finders."

"It's just some range finders we found in a utility box. Pretty effective though."

"Our Euro friends hauled ass," Angel said.

"They're headed away from the lock," Finn observed.

"They are, you think it's misdirection?" Rick asked.

"No, I think they saw a quick way out and hauled ass."

"How long do you want to stay with the tail? We've got nine minutes and counting," Nick said.

"Hey, what's that?" Tara said.

Ahead, the tail lights of one of the vehicles shown brightly and illuminated two silhouettes standing in the middle of the street.

Finn didn't hesitate as he shouted, "Incoming" over the linked com channel to the other vehicles and jerked the SUV hard to the left. He saw the following vehicles take evasive action from the corner of his eye as a projectile from a grenade launcher whizzed by them and continued down the street until it skittered onto the pavement and exploded.

Nick and Angel exited each side of the SUV and laid down a burst of rounds in the direction from which the grenade originated.

"Good eye, Tara."

Norms voice came over the com, "Good instincts up there. I see no point in dodging another one of those. Let's wrap it up."

"Yeah, there's nothing to be learned from the second kick of a mule," Finn said.

"Who said that?" Angel wanted to know.

"Who else, Mark Twain," Finn said with a smile.

"I agree, let's get out of this before we can't" Norm said.

CHAPTER 24

Fiona churned north into the Gulf of Mexico with a projected path straight for the Houston metroplex. Her backside winds began to pummel the Conch Republic as Finn parked the SUV as close to the inn as he could manage. Daylight was still two hours away as the rain returned driven by increasing winds.

In the cloakroom, they shook off their wet gear and boots.

"Wonder where our friends were headed?" Finn mused aloud.

"And where did they end up?" Rick seconded.

"Maybe they'll get caught in the backside. They may not have a clue that they're getting ready to see the second half of Fiona's act," Tara said.

"Not many hurricanes in Bulgaria, for sure" Angel said and grinned.

"We do know that there are at least ten of them, probably more," Finn noted.

"I could use some Joe," Nick said.

"Me too," Tara echoed.

"Me three," Rick followed.

To their surprise, they found Nigel sitting with Kate, Sher, and Camille at the kitchen table. They crowded in and surrounded the four at the table.

"Cheers, mate" Nigel told Finn.

"He's on probation," Camille said with mock severity.

Finn didn't wonder that the man who had cheated death preferred the company of others during the deep, darkness of the empty hours of the night. The time of night fishermen and bread men know intimately, the time of night when bodies are dumped. The time of night when the hollowness of lies told by your lover resonates in your soul.

Nigel and his nursing crew listened wide-eyed to Finn's account of their foray into the eye of the storm.

"A rocket propelled grenade, you say!" Nigel exclaimed.

"Never a dull moment with Finn and associates," Kate said.

"'Finn and associates,' sounds like a law firm," Rick said.

"Or a loan shark operation," Nick quipped.

Tara ferreted out a nearly full urn of hot coffee and began to collect mugs to fill.

"I say, Sher's coffee is quite interesting," Nigel said.

"He must have tried the good stuff," Rick said with a knowing look.

Finn gratefully accepted a full mug from Nick who was helping Tara.

"I guess there's nothing to do now but wait?" Angel sighed.

"It's too bad you chaps didn't get a look in those vehicles," Nigel said, "I'm more convinced than ever that Dr. Sullivan is spot on in her assessment of the situation."

"And she's handy with a hypodermic too!" Finn remarked.

"Nigel, what kind of containers would they use for the art pieces?" Finn asked.

"Assuming the pieces are all paintings, they would probably use hermetically sealed museum cases."

"How much space would they take up"?

"There are some standard sizes, but also some that are designed for special dimensions, especially large paintings. Like Monet's Waterlilies."

"So, what type of vehicle would you need to haul them around?" Nick asked picking up on Finn's drift.

"Some type of lorry, I would think. Truck, for you Yanks."

"That narrows it down," Rick deadpanned.

"If we have an idea of what kind of vehicle they will use to get to the lock area with the paintings, we'll have a better chance of spotting it." Finn explained.

Nigel reacted with understanding, "We don't know how many pieces they have, but as Dr. Sullivan has surmised it may well be ten or more. We know, that six well-known pieces have been stolen in the past year. So, my guess is probably twice that many. Many owners of historically documented pieces are reluctant to report theft, because they acquired the piece through questionable circumstances."

"You mean, their stolen art got stolen," Angel said.

"Quite right," Nigel said, "I would think a lorry the size of one of your moving vans, or something similar."

"That's a start, any other features that might give us a clue."

"I would think a lift on the back, would be needed," Nigel answered.

"How 'bout refrigeration?"

"Not necessarily."

"I doubt there will be many vehicles out there when these people will be trying to get to the lock. They won't wait for Fiona to completely clear out. They'll go as soon as the winds get down under forty-five or so. It seems like they will have to have at least four vehicles, with one that will be able to clear the debris out of the way," Finn said.

"So, in other words, these A-holes will be pretty easy to spot," Nick said.

"Like Macy's parade," Rick said.

"Who is Macy?" Nigel asked.

"A department store in New York City," Kate told him.

"Oh, well that explains it," Nigel said.

"They throw a big parade at Thanksgiving every year," Finn added.

"And, …"

"And, they will stand out like Macy's parade to anybody watching," Kate finished the metaphor.

"Blimey, I'm slow. Must be the strychnine," Nigel said as he got the picture.

"Couldn't be the boodles?" Finn said with a smile.

"Certainly not."

"So, we need to be ready to go when?" Angel said.

"That's my cue," Rick said as he scrolled his phone.

"Is there any other place they could try to leave the island?" Finn asked them.

No one spoke for several moments. Finn patiently waited as he gave them plenty of time to contemplate their answers.

"I can't think of any, the only passage through the breakwater is at the central lock" Rick said, "But, to answer your other question, I'd say by nine we should be ready to go."

"Four hours, give or take," Kate said.

"Thinking ahead," Sher said, "We've got a whole bunch of mouths to feed some breakfast to and as chief cook and bottle washer I'm dishing out chores, so see me."

"That's my gal," Rick said with a grin, "Always on top of things,"

"I'll leave that one alone, honeybuns."

Kate stifled a laugh in Finn's arm. It appeared everyone would leave that one alone. A red-faced Rick chose discretion over stupidity and remained silent.

"Moving on …"

"You white folks sho no how to put y'all's foot in y'all's mouth," Camille drawled.

"Breakfast at six," Sher said, we'll face things better on a full stomach."

"Who said that?" Angel asked.

"Either Patton or Junior Samples," Finn answered.

"We need to keep an eye on things, Fiona is picking up more speed and our window may increase by thirty or forty-five minutes," Rick said.

"Duly noted," Finn said.

The inn showed signs of life as groggy volunteers stirred, stretched, and surveyed the world through squinted eyes. People slowly remembered where they were as reality crowded in on those first waking moments.

Despite the stress of the moment, and the tedious hours of withstanding Fiona's might, everyone did their best to rise to the occasion. *These were veteran campers*, Finn thought to himself as he walked through the lobby.

His small room on the second floor, adjacent to a similar one where Nick bunked when they stayed with Rick and Sher, was neat and orderly. The bed was made and the small work table was uncluttered with only a laptop and a Carl Hiaasen book on it.

Finn walked in and shut the door. He took a deep breath and slowly exhaled. He sensed the durable strength in the old Inn's wooden framework. He felt a fleeting vision of old forests, their ability to withstand the elements and flourish.

He sat on the edge of the bed and let the events of the past two days run through his mind. The stillness of being alone is more than many can tolerate. Finn embraced it, he found solace in the lack of distractions. He wondered if Kate would understand this need for personal space. She was certainly a distraction, but the kind a man would have to be crazy to ignore.

Finn's mind wandered. He entered that quasi-twilight zone place between sleep and consciousness. Sometimes it did him more good than sleep. He relaxed, and his breathing slowed. The hurricane lamp on the table cast flickering shadows on the wall. The room seemed to take on the appearance of a nineteenth-century parlor as Finn's eyes grew heavy.

He was never certain, later on when he thought about it, if he dreamed what happened next. In a plush, red velvet chair, Marie LeVeau sat staring at him with dark, piercing eyes.

"Egout," she spoke in French.

When Finn regained consciousness, Kate and Camille stood in front of him, looking at him with concern.

"Finn, what happened?" Kate asked.

Camille added, "We came to tell you breakfast is ready, and we found you unresponsive on the bed."

"What time is it?"

"Nearly six-thirty."

"Seven? That can't be, I only dozed off a few moments."

"It's been over an hour since we saw you last," Kate told him.

Finn tried to focus, everything was fuzzy.

"Did you find him?" Tara's voice said from somewhere outside the room.

"In here," Kate replied.

Nick followed Tara into the room, "You okay?"

"What's all the fuss?" Finn asked.

"We've been looking for you when you didn't show up downstairs for over an hour," Nick replied with concern.

"I saw her," Finn said as he tried to convince himself as much as tell the others what happened.

"Who?" Tara asked.

He took a mug of coffee that Kate offered to him and sipped at it before he replied.

"Camille, what does *egout*, I think it was, mean?"

"Egout? It means sewer in French, why?"

"Earlier, I saw Marie. She was in a red chair. In a room that looked like it was a hundred years old."

"Finn, did you bump your head again on something?" Nick said.

"You are sounding pretty whacky, even for a ghost tour guide," Tara said.

"No doubt, I barely believe it myself, but nonetheless, I need to let Norm know. The sewers, somehow they are planning to use the sewers," Finn said and started to stand up but swayed and sat back on the bed.

"See what I mean," Camille said, "It really takes it out of you."

"I'll never doubt it again," Finn said.

"You're telling us you saw Marie LeVeau?" Nick asked.

"Yes."

"Right here, in this room?"

"Yes, but it somehow changed. Seemed like a different place. Then she said that one word 'egout,' and that's all I remember."

"I'm contacting Norm now," Rick said.

Finn drank more coffee and tried to clear his head.

"Rick, what's up" Norm's voice came through the speaker.

"Got you on speaker here, Norm. You need to hear what Finn has to say."

Finn gave a concise and accurate account of his experience with Marie LeVeau.

"So we're back to the sewers," Norm said, "seems like we're spending a lot of time there lately. Rick, didn't you and Angel take a look at that?"

"We did, but we only focused on the conduits inside the lock."

Angel added, "Ask the Public Works guys to identify all the direct lines that the lock empties into, Rick and I could backtrack from that info any places that look vulnerable."

"I'll have Cheryl get that info ASAP."

"Are they using the sewer as a way to gain access to the lock or are they trying to sabotage it?" Kate asked.

"That, Dr. Sullivan is a very good question," Norm said.

"I'll get my crew here at the EOC on it. Rick, I'll get you the info Angel asked for. I haven't heard from Royer in the last thirty minutes or so, but no problems, yet. I'll let him know the latest development. I'll be back in touch. We should be able to get outside by nine or a little after. Oh, one last thing. Finn, don't forget to renew your old business license."

"What?"

"In case you want to start up the ghost tours again, over and out," Norman disconnected before Finn could speak.

No one spoke, then Nigel's very British voice broke through the silence, "Are they giving bloody ghost tours now?"

CHAPTER 25

Day dawned on the Conch Republic, grey and sullen, as Fiona barreled farther into the Gulf of Mexico. Following seas began to subside. Winds gusted to gale-force strength but were sporadic and lessened through the morning. The calling cards of a Cat 5 storm were everywhere.

Tangled limbs and palm fronds covered the ground. Some streets were impassable where large trees blocked the road from curb to curb. Sheets of poorly attached plywood were strewn helter-skelter.

It would take months, if not longer, to recover from Fiona's onslaught. Some buildings were destroyed, unable to withstand one hundred-fifty mile-an-hour winds. Most of the houseboats at the Margaritaville Marina, where Toby Ireland's "Emerald Isle" was berthed, rode out the storm without mishap. Others were not as lucky, and had sustained major damage. Many were not seaworthy and needed repairs. In the Conch Republic, boats were a primary transportation for may people.

Finn fought off all attempts to convince him to remain at the inn due to his unexplained encounter.

"I'm fine," he told Kate, "Besides I'm the wheelman."

"You're Pat Sajak?" Tara asked.

"He's the driver," Nick explained.

"Oh."

Finn didn't feel like running a marathon, but he kept that to himself. He gathered his personal gear, including his Desert Eagle, and his dive knife. He found the others in the cloak room sorting through supplies.

"Norm wants us to drive a grid pattern toward the lock. Take our time, look for anything unusual."

"Normal unusual, or humongous Cat 5 unusual?" Nick said.

"Both."

The inner door of the cloak room suddenly opened and a person entered and quickly shut the door.

"Nigel, what the hell are you doing here?" Finn asked.

"If I don't smoke a cigarette I'm going to kill some innocent bystander, I have to get outside," The British agent said with a raspy voice.

"There'll be hell to pay," Finn said in a bad imitation of the Duke.

"Get some rain gear off that rack," Rick said, "where did you get those khakis?"

"Your lovely wife."

"I thought they looked familiar."

"Take a quick look around the building, for Rick's sake, then we'll start our grid pattern," Finn said.

The morning was heavy, saturated with moisture from Fiona. Everyone immediately began to sweat. The breeze did little to cool them as they split up and walked around the grounds from different directions.

The air was immediately filled with the distinct aroma of tobacco as Nigel lit a Dunhill. There was no significant structural damage visible to the naked eye, although the gazebo looked pretty bad. The yard was spackled with limbs and flower petals that covered the ground like a carpet.

"All the work really paid off, Rick," Finn told his friend.

"Good to know we can withstand something like Fiona" he replied.

"We better get moving," Finn said.

Rick rode shot gun. Tara sat between Nick and Angel in the back seat. Nigel squeezed into the jump seat behind them. Finn eased the SUV across the yard so as not to leave deep ruts in the soggy ground. Once on the street, Finn drove south on Whitehead. Few others were out and about yet. The morning was a most peculiar grey, the sun hidden by the massive cloud bank spawned by Fiona. Rain was sporadic, sometimes pelting down for several minutes, then subsiding to a drizzle.

Finn slowly wove the SUV through the debris on the street. The farther into Old Town they drove, the extent of the damage was more apparent. Many roofs were torn completely off the taller, two-story buildings that lined the road. Some storefront windows were shattered where plywood had come loose and left the glass exposed.

Finn took a left on Petronia Street, then three blocks later, took another left on Elizabeth Street and reversed their direction. They were now driving toward Key West Bight. Suddenly Tara yelled, "Stop," then she crawled over Nick and opened door and jumped out.

Finn barely had time to brake before she was out on the street. Nick followed, on instinct, but he had no idea where Tara was going. She stopped at a small, dark, bedraggled dog and stooped down. Nick caught up to her and took a scan around the immediate vicinity.

She picked the puppy up, a pit bull. It was alive, but needed attention.

"Good eye, Tara," Nick said in support, "Better bring it, uh, her along, we need to keep moving."

They quickly returned to the SUV. Tara gave the pup some water which she gulped down. Then she snuggled into the crook of Tara's arm, wet and dirty. She smiled and softly stroked her head.

"No sign of the bad guys," Rick pronounced.

"I've got an idea," Finn said, "Next manhole we see, I want to try something."

"Are we gonna play Jean Valjean?" Rick asked.

"Who the hell is that?" Angel wanted to know.

"The guy from Les Miserable," Finn said, then added, "he was being chased through the Paris sewers by a merciless cop who's credo was 'the law is the law,' with no regard to context."

"How do you know this stuff?" Angel asked incredulously.

"Quirky memory," Finn answered with a shrug of his shoulders.

"So, we're gonna take to the sewers?" Nick asked.

"Maybe not," Finn told him, "Let me try something first."

"There, ahead on the right," Rick said and pointed his finger in the direction of the next intersection.

Finn pulled as close to the curb as he could get, about ten yards from the manhole. It's cover remained on in spite of the outflow that was bubbling up from it's vent holes.

Finn placed the SUV in park and jumped out. He took a few steps, inspected the effluent coming up from the sewers and saw what he suspected.

"Rick, can you and Angel pull of the sewer plans and tell me if this one is a secondary conduit or on a main line"

"On it," Angel replied.

Rick said, "There's no way they could be using this sewer without dive equipment, not to mention the valuable art."

"Exactly, we need to find a manhole that is not overflowing, if there is one,"Finn answered, "I'm texting Norm."

"Their only other option is to move above ground, in the open," Nick said.

"Maybe they're planning to use a balloon," Tara said.

Nick looked sideways at her, with a WTF-expression on his face.

Tara grinned and said, "I read Mysterious Island not too long ago."

"Still, it's not out of the realm of the possible," Finn said, "Lately, nothing around the old rock is impossible."

"So it would seem," Rick said in support of his friend.

"This one is a tertiary conduit, which may explain its overflow," Angel told them.

"Can you locate the main sewer lines that drain from the lock?" Finn asked.

"Give us a few minutes," Rick replied.

"Getting something from Norm," Finn said.

A gust of wind rocked the vehicle but subsided a few moments later. Skies swirled with heavy, cumulus clouds that trailed Fiona's central core.

"No sign of trouble at the lock," Finn told them.

"Where the hell are these guys?" Nick said.

"Okay, we've located three main conduits that drain from the lock area," Rick said.

"Where's the nearest?" Finn asked.

Rick held up his tablet for Finn to see and said, "Right there."

Finn recognized the location highlighted with a red circle and started the SUV moving toward it.

"What are you thinking Finn?" Rick asked.

"Need to take a look in one of those sewer mains."

Another hard downpour rattled off the windshield and roof. The SUV rolled on as Finn avoided the worst of the debris in the street. There was no break in the swirling cloud-cover, the street scene before them looked like an eerie charcoal drawing.

"Finn, what are you looking for?" Nick asked.

"Just a hunch, I want to see if our friends have tampered with anything?"

"Sabotage? But, won't that hurt them as much as us?" Rick asked.

"I don't see the angle either, Rick. What you said makes sense to me, but let's go take a look."

Five minutes later they were at the intersection marked on the tablet. Finn slowed the vehicle and stopped a good twenty feet from the manhole. Nick and Angel followed Finn out of the SUV. No water was bubbling up through the vent holes. Angel hefted the crowbar he carried in his right hand.

"Let's get the cover off," Finn said.

They wrestled it up and rolled it onto the pavement with a heavy thud. A ladder descended into the shaft, where the three men could see water as it rushed below in the large main. They also noticed a backpack-size apparatus attached to the ladder about halfway down.

"Good hunch, Finn" Nick said.

"Angel, is it on a timer or set to a remote frequency detonation?" Finn asked.

"I need to get closer." Angel replied.

"Bro, you sure you wanna do that?" Nick asked his friend.

"I need you two to hold my legs, I'm gonna take a look," he said as he knelt down and went headfirst into the hole using the ladder for stability. Finn and Nick grabbed a leg apiece and held on tight.

Out of nowhere, a large Monitor lizard came scurrying down the street. It seemed disoriented, but it spotted Finn and Nick and ran toward them. Tara yelled a warning, as the carnivorous creature closed the distance to her friends. In rapid succession, three metal balls struck the lizard in the head, launched from Tara's slingshot. The impact knocked the lizard down, and three more slammed into its head, rendering the reptile unconscious.

Angel, still head down, did not realize the danger his friends were in, or how close he was to being dropped.

"OK, I've got what we need, pull me up." Angel yelled.

He was hoisted up as fast as they could pull him. Tara walked toward them as Angel regained his feet.

"Holy shit, what is that," he said and pointed to the lizard.

"Monitor lizard, probably illegal, somebody's 'pet' no doubt," Finn said.

"Nice slingin' there," Nick said.

"And thank you both for not dropping me. Beers on me for the rest of the week," Angel said.

"The week ends tomorrow," Nick pointed out.

"OK, OK, given you were fighting off the velociraptor there, make it next week too."

"Semper Fi," Nick said.

"What did you find?" Finn asked.

"It's on a timer. Set for two hours from now. I can disarm it, but that would alert them to the fact we've found it. They might detonate the others. Figured you'd want to discuss this with Norm before we do anything."

Good job, Angel. I've texted Norm. Let's get back to the SUV."

They replaced the manhole cover

"What about Godzilla, there?" Nick asked.

"I don't think it needs to be running around," Tara said.

"Did you kill it?" Finn asked her.

"Don't know."

"I'll take care of it," Nick said and walked over and dispatched the potential threat with one round from his sidearm.

"That thing could've killed a kid, maybe an adult," Tara said, "Wonder where it came from?"

"Miami is still the capital of the exotic animal trade, probably some idiot picked it up there," Finn answered.

In the vehicle they explained to Rick and Nigel what they found.

"But, what are they trying to do?"

"Good question, friend," Finn replied as his phone sounded the theme from "Jaws."

"Must be Norm," Nick said.

"Nope," Finn said as he eyed the phone as if it were a sea snake, he punched an icon and waited.

"Finn, is Nigel with you," the very pissed-off voice of Dr. Kate Sullivan said.

"Safe and sound."

"Dr. Sullivan, my apologies," Nigel spoke from the jump seat, "I had to get some air?"

"Would that air have smelled like a Dunhill?"

"Caught like a school boy," Nigel answered.

"Kate, I'll take full blame," Finn said, "But right this minute we're a little pre-occupied. We found some explosives out here, timed to go off in a couple of hours."

"Oh."

"Gotta go, we'll see you later."

"Just make sure you do, Finn. You can't get out of house hunting that easy."

"Damn," Finn replied.

"We'll be waiting. With a blood pressure cuff for Nigel. Over and out."

"That went well," Rick smirked as he spoke.

The bass tones of "Jaws" signaled Norm's return call.

"Tell me what you've got."

Finn summarized what they'd found, then let Angel explain the details of the explosive package.

"LT," Angel said, using Norm's nickname, "It's nothin' fancy. Garden variety. They can be defused. But, if one is disturbed, it will show up somewhere. They're probably using a laptop to control the packages with a shared timing device."

"We're really going to have to start paying you."

"No worries, LT."

"Any ideas how many of these we might be dealing with?"

"Not a clue," Finn answered, "We're not even sure what they think they will accomplish."

"I could see it if we were dealing with Al Qaeda or a similar group, but these Euros don't strike me as the suicidal type."

"No argument there."

"I have already got as many boots on the street as possible, they're inspecting every access point. They will only observe and mark the location for now."

"Man, there's no rest for the weary," Rick said.

Finn asked, "Norm, what's the latest from Royer at the lock?"

"Still quiet."

"These guys don't seem like finesse types, nothing complex," Finn said, "Maybe they're planning a diversion, to draw us away from the lock."

"But, they don't know that we know, what we know," Rick said.

"That's right, I think," Norm said sounding slightly confused.

"We're one up on them there," Finn added.

"Still, there's something missing. There's more to the play than some diversionary explosions," Norm said.

"They have a submarine," Tara said.

Long moments limped by as her statement sunk in to the others.

"We'll put you on the payroll too," Norm said.

"We've only been thinking of it as an escape vehicle," Finn said.

"And not an offensive weapon," Nick said to complete the thought.

"That's a game changer," Norm said with a sigh.

"What about Boca Chica?" Tara asked.

"They moved the two that are based there out of Fiona's path," Norm answered.

"A fucking submarine," Angel muttered.

"I'm betting my bead collection the real target is the desal plant. That would hurt us the most without jeopardizing their crew," Finn said.

"But, isn't the plant inside the breakwater?" Tara asked.

"Yes, but its intake tunnels and electrical conduits from the wind farm are outside the breakwater," Rick explained.

"Finn, I think you're right, it makes the most sense from a tactical perspective," Norm said.

"You better let Royer know ," Finn answered.

"Doing that now."

"How much time before those explosives go boom?" Angel asked.

"Ninety minutes," Rick answered.

"I have a feeling we'll hear something from our European friends in the next hour and a half," Finn said.

Norm voice broke back in, "Royer's been alerted, he's briefing Commander Kenny and Padraig on the situation."

"Do you want us to continue the search for explosives?" Finn asked.

"Would appreciate it. Looks like you are in a grid that is unassigned to any team."

"Can do."

"Have we considered these gift packages may not be restricted to sewers?" Rick said.

"I wouldn't doubt it, but how much time have they had to plant them? I mean, I don't think there can be a whole lot of them given the fact it would still have been dangerous to be out here two hours ago," Finn said.

"Norm, if you can send us the locations where your teams find any more packages, Angel and I maybe able to estimate a source area," Rick said.

"So far, they've found only two in addition to the one you found. You'd need more data than that, wouldn't you?" Norm responded.

"Yeah, a couple more would help, but that's like wishing for a sharper guillotine," Rick said.

"But, Rick and I can try one of my algorithms on the three we have, we might get lucky," Angel said.

"You can use the onboard computer in the SUV and link to our to our database and servers."

"Thanks, Norm."

"I need to take this call from Commander Kenny at Boca Chica. I'll send you the data. Talk to you in twenty minutes, see what we've got."

"Ten four, over and out from the hole-in-the-wall gang," Finn said.

"What?" Tara said.

"Butch and the Kid," Rick added.

"Butch and the Kid?"

"You never saw Butch Cassidy and the Sundance Kid?" Rick asked.

"No."

"Youth," Finn said.

"I say, I've even seen that one," Nigel said from the back.

"Careful, Nigel, you haven't seen what she can do with a slingshot," Nick said with a grin.

"Oh, I saw her knock that beastie on its arse," Nigel said, "You're quite the shot, my dear."

"Why thank you, Nigel," Tara said with a demure smile.

Nick and Angel exchanged glances, but said nothing.

"We better get moving," Finn told them.

"Where to?" Nick asked.

"Finn, why don't we make for the next manhole conduit that we identified earlier as a primary one, and we'll keep an eye out along the way," Rick suggested.

"It's at the intersection of William and Caroline streets," Angel said.

Finn turned on Windsor Lane and angled toward the historic Key West Cemetery. The grounds were covered with limbs and wind-blown debris. There was an eerie look to the place reputed to be haunted by locals. Finn turned left on William Street and drove toward Caroline Street.

A large, battered roof lay partially across the road ahead of them. Finn slowed and ran up over the curb causing the pup in Tara's arm to give a tiny snort. They passed the hulking roof and continued to toward Caroline Street.

"How much time?" Nick asked.

Rick looked at his tablet and said, "One hour, twelve minutes."

"No pressure there," Nick said.

"Absolutely not," Tara echoed.

By the way," Rick said, "There's a couple of thermoses in my backpack with some of Sher's special blend. It's back there with Nigel."

"Find those thermi, Nigel" Finn said.

"Where's a Mangrove Martini when you need it," Angel groused.

"Hey, keep an eye out for the million-dollar bottle of whiskey. That's floating around here somewhere," Nick reminded.

"True," Angel said with a wistful sigh.

"I'd be happy with some Joe," Finn said.

"Coming up, lads, and lass," Nigel replied from the back.

"There should be some plastic cups back there too," Rick said.

"Righto."

"I've got one," Finn said, as he held up a mug with a large alligator on the side that read "Okefenokee and Satilla Expeditions."

"What's that word? Okefenokee?" Angel asked.

Tara answered before Finn could, "It's the largest wetland wilderness in the United States. It means 'trembling earth' from the Creek tribe."

"Where did you come by that? Nick asked.

"One of my old friends from work, he's retired, and works with his wife as swamp guides. They sent me the mug several years ago."

"Where is it?"

"It's in Southeast Georgia, about 650 square miles in size, if memory serves," Finn replied.

"See, it's not just grad students in biology that know about the place," Tara said with a small pout.

"We love grad students," Nick said, "But, we love Lizzie Borden with a slingshot more."

"Your lucky I've got this puppy in my arms, buster."

"You got a name for that thing yet?" Angel wanted to know.

Tara gave the pup a quick inspection then said,

"Well, she's definitely a 'sheila,' I'll have to think a bit for a name.

"What about Fiona?" Finn mused aloud.

"That's it, Finn. I like it. Fiona."

"Now that that's settled, let's go find some explosives," Rick said with an eye roll.

The SUV rolled on down William Street as the wind scattered light-weight debris this way and that. The smaller, compact houses along the street showed minor damage, but for the most part had survived the intensity of the storm.

"Remember, these guys are hiding out somewhere and I doubt they are very far from the lock," Finn pointed out.

"Finn, the more I think about it, I don't believe they could have placed many of those, there just wasn't enough time," Rick said.

"I hope you're right."

Norm's voice seemingly came from thin air, everyone jumped.

"Can you read me?"

"He's coming through the vehicle com link," Finn said with a grin. "Loud and clear, Norm."

"I'm going to give the order to disarm the explosives we know about fifteen minutes prior to detonation. We'll see if these guys show themselves prior to that time, or if they stay quiet until after the prescribed time."

"We're headed toward a possible location now," Finn said.

"I see you're on William moving toward Caroline," Norm said.

"Yes."

"After you check your target, meet me at the lock?"

"Will do."

"Over and out."

They arrived at the location without incident. People were beginning to dig out and survey the scene firsthand. The streets remained devoid of traffic as Finn slowed to a stop next to the sewer conduit. Nick and Angel casually exited the SUV and sauntered toward the cover.

Tara followed and scanned the vicinity around them. Suddenly three trail bikes broke from a side alley toward the trio. Before Finn could react, Nigel was out of the SUV and fired several rounds from his Walther PPK that sent the lead bike crashing to the pavement. Tara took one shot and the second biker flew off his wheels and remained unmoving on the wet ground. The third biker veered away, but another volley from Nigel knocked the rider off and into a telephone pole.

Finn and Rick joined them, "You were not outside the vehicle" Finn said as Nigel looked perplexed but slowly got the drift.

"Absolutely not," the Brit responded.

"What the hell was that?" Angel asked.

"A stupid move? Nick answered.

"Better check that access, we need to keep going. Nigel, back to the vehicle," Finn said.

Minutes later, Angel gave a "nothing here" sign and they replaced the heavy cover. They returned to the SUV and headed for the maintenance bridge that led to the Control Center.

"I've let Norm know we need clean-up on aisle 3," Finn said.

"I'm beginning to think our Euro-friends are a little overconfident," Rick said.

"I doubt they were expecting to run into people with our credentials," Finn said with a stony expression of intensity.

"Probably haven't seen a voodoo priestess in Bulgaria lately," Rick mused.

"Or an Olympic silver medalist in shooting," Nick said as he looked at Tara.

"Maybe there is a lack of control over the men that are here. Sitting through a storm like Fiona can mess with your head," Finn said, "That might explain the attack, maybe they are loosing their discipline. That could be an advantage for us."

"How much time?" Angel asked.

"Thirty-five minutes."

Finn drove onto the western maintenance bridge as a few gulls began to appear, they swooped and darted with raucous caws that carried on the wind. They observed one of the houseboats that usually berthed at the Margaritaville Marina had broken free of its moorings and rested on a sand bar to their right. Several dinghies were aground or floated loose in the water.

"Looks like the houseboats did better than some of the houses we passed," Rick said.

Finn found a parking place along the maintenance road that ran adjacent to the control center. They noticed the Seals' wheels snugged up to the inner wall of the structure. Several police vehicles were present also.

Big Dog met them outside, along with two Seals

They followed Finn up the stairwell to the operations room. Norm was huddled up with Commander Hal Royer, leader of the Seal detachment.

"Finn, over here," Norm said as he motioned for them to join him.

"Commander Royer, we've got to stop meeting like this."

"Finn, seen any mutants lately?"

"Only on Duval Street."

"We found five, including the first one you discovered," Norm said, "I've got teams standing by to disarm on my command."

Royer added, "We thought they might communicate with us, but nothing yet."

"We'll still go with the fifteen minute margin. I've issued a stay-off-the-streets order in case there are some we missed," Norm said.

"Commander," Finn said, "Do you concur that the desalinization plant is the most likely target of any sub attack?"

"The lieutenant and I were discussing that very subject a moment ago. I would have to agree."

"What are your orders Commander?" Norm asked.

"To follow your orders."

Finn smiled, but said nothing.

"I'd rather these assholes not get off our little chunk of paradise," Norm said in a rare break of professionalism, "But I think we've got to play it by ear. We need to stay flexible."

"Agreed," Royer said.

"What's the time?" Finn asked.

"Nineteen minutes," Norm said, "I'll give the order now to disarm them."

"Will they know?"

"Yes, that's why we'll synch all the locations, to disarm at the same moment," Norm explained.

"Hope they didn't have those locations under observation," Angel said.

"We had a broad perimeter and my men saw no-one, did you happen to see anyone at the locations you stopped at?' Norm said.

"Only our three stooges on the trail bikes, but they won't be making a report," Finn answered.

Suddenly, the open police band crackled to life on the control center speakers. They heard a deep voice, "My name is Aleksandar Andonov, Lt. James, and I'm ordering you to prepare the lock for an incoming ship."

"You're in the Conch Republic, Mister Andonov, where nobody likes anybody giving orders," Norm answered.

"You have fifteen minutes to comply."

The radio went silent and Finn held up his finger until they were certain it was off.

"Guess that answers that question," Nick said.

"Let's hope, there's not five or six packages that were missed," Finn said.

"They're not going to be happy campers," Tara said, "When they realize."

"Fuck'em if they can't take a joke," Angel said.

"Don't sugarcoat it like that," Nick told his friend.

Royer spoke up, "When nothing goes boom, I'm guessing their next move will be the sub."

"Is it possible to locate that signal?" Finn asked.

"Cheryl is working on it as we speak," Norm answered.

"LT, we've confirmed all the packages are disarmed," Joey said as he joined the group.

"Lieutenant," Royer said, "We need to stall for time. Can you manufacture a story that the lock can't be opened immediately?"

"I can think of three off the top of my head," Rick said.

"What he said," Norm held back a laugh.

"Commander, what's your plan?" Finn asked.

"We need an hour, maybe a little more. In the mean time, stay loose and ready for anything."

"Sounds like Duval Street on a Saturday night," Nick said.

Once again the open channel barked to life, "You have only made things worse for yourself, Lieutenant James," the surly voice of Andonov spat.

"Why would that be?" Norm said innocently.

"You discovered our little surprises."

"We'll be only too happy to open the lock but here's my chief engineer to explain why we can't right now," Norm said.

Rick picked it up with out missing a beat, "One of the intake conduits is jammed with debris. Divers will have to go in and remove the flotsam. Until then, the lock is frozen in place."

"You could be lying."

"Why don't you come on out and we'll show you first hand," Norm responded.

A pause hung heavy in the air, "You have one hour," Andonov snarled. The radio went quiet as Royer gave a thumb's up.

"This guy's been watching too many Tarantino movies. He thinks he's a tough guy," Finn said with a sour look on his face.

"Uh oh," Nick said, "I've seen that look."

"What's the call, Norm?" Finn asked.

"I think it's time we gave them a dose of Conch hospitality. If we can get a lock on their location from those broadcasts, I say we take it to them, sub or not."

Royer shook his head in silent agreement and Nick and Angel burst out with a loud "Oo Rah."

The room buzzed with electric excitement. The harrowing night of a Cat 5 gave way to the feeling that they were finished with waiting. They'd endured enough and were ready to act. Islanders were doers, not thinkers. Pragmatic and not prone to flights of fancy, they knew there was no free ride in Paradise. Everything was earned, nothing was given to them. Now their existence was threatened by another group of men driven by greed and a thirst for power.

"They have no idea how pissed off we are," Tara said.

"No, I don't think they do," Finn said in a tone colder than a mausoleum at midnight.

Royer spoke to his expanded team, he assigned most of them to move out but told several to stay put and keep an eye on things at the control center.

"I'm not so worried about an attack on the center, and we don't know how many players are on the other team."

"I'm getting something from Cheryl now," Norm said, as the control room grew silently as people stopped their preparations to listen.

192

Norm read silently for several moments, then said, "They're still working to narrow the area but they've got a rough idea. Give us a minute and I'll get it on the big screen."

Subdued conversation rippled through the knots of people standing in the room. The staff of engineers and techs were not use to the level of intensity that emanated from the Seals and the girl with blue hair and her friends.

The big screen showed a rough rectangle bounded by White Street, Eaton Street, Elizabeth, and Truman streets. The area encompassed the historic Key West cemetery.

"Cheryl should have it reduced soon, but there's no need to wait. I want that area sealed off."

"We've got forty-five minutes," Royer said, "Teams One and Two, with me. Team Three remain and defend this facility."

"I'll leave four of my men here but I need the rest on the street. Joey, you're in charge here when we leave. I'll take Big Dog with us," Norm said to the former Key West high school football star turned cop.

"Copy that, LT."

"Let's set up a command center at the foot of the maintenance bridge. We can use the public parking lots along Front Street," Norm said.

People began to gather their gear and prepared to embark. The Seals led the way, taking the stairwell to the ground exit. Finn and the others followed.

The rain was a drizzle but the skies churned above them. Billowing, dark cumulus legions scudded across the rooftops of Old Town.

"Did they not consider we might be able to locate them from their transmissions?"" Rick asked as they drove across the bridge.

"I think they have made an amateur's mistake," Finn said, "They are simply too overconfident."

"I can see where having a submarine on your side might lend itself to that," Rick retorted.

"Nonetheless, I think it is our biggest advantage," Finn said.

"What's Royer got up his sleeve?" Nick asked.

"Not sure, I didn't have a chance to ask him why we needed the hour. Somebody give me a jolt of Joe, please," Finn said as he held up his mug and passed it to the backseat.

In the rear view mirror Finn spotted Norm's SUV as it trailed them across the bridge. Ahead, Royer's caravan of vehicles turned off the bridge and onto Front Street.

The others followed the Seals into the parking lot near the Schooner Wharf bar. They parked in a defensive circle leaving enough room for everyone to gather in the interior space.

More squad cars, some firetrucks, and other public works vehicles arrived and spread throughout the series of linked parking lots. A portable command center was set up within the protected area of the encircled vehicles.

Norm discussed his plan with the fire chief, Caleb Jernigan, and Commander Royer. Jernigan smoked a Lucky Strike much to Norm's surprise. Jernigan caught the expression and said, "I know, I know, I quit five years ago. Etoilier, my wife, was nagging me to death. But, this damn hurricane has stretched my nerves to the breaking point."

"Smoke your ass off, Caleb. I maybe having one myself before this is over," Norm told his friend.

"I need you to block as many of the intersections along this rectangle with your heavy equipment as you can."

"We've got about thirty minutes left of our hour," Finn said.

"Commander Royer, anything yet?"

"Need a little more time," Royer said but with a confident tone in his voice.

"Caleb, we need to block the access to the western maintenance bridge also. We don't want these guys to make it out to the lock."

"Ten four, LT" the veteran fireman said.

Jernigan departed to organize his firemen. Finn noticed former British SAS officer Richard Lancaster and several of his cronies had arrived. Lancaster was a stout guy in a fight, Finn had first-hand knowledge of that fact. Lancaster spotted Finn and Norm and walked toward them.

"The lads and I thought we'd pitch in, if you need us," Lancaster said referring to the dozen or so ex-pat Brits with him.

"Glad to see you Sergeant-Major," Norman said, "Yes, very glad to see you."

"We've picked up one of your countrymen it seems," Finn said.

"Oh, I say."

"Let me introduce you," Finn said and motioned for Lancaster to follow him.

They found Nigel as he studied the street plan on a tablet he held in his right hand. He brandished a Lucky in his left hand as he saw Finn coming toward him. When he saw Lancaster with Finn his eyes widened. When they arrived, he snapped to an erect posture and gave a crisp salute and said, 'Sir, Sergeant-Major Sir."

"You two know each other?" Finn asked somewhat surprised.

"Nigel, is that you lad?"

"Yes, sir, Sergeant-Major."

"Relax, lad, relax. Finn, Nigel was one of my best students some twenty-five years ago."

Finn noticed Nigel managed to hang onto the Lucky, then said, "I see you met our fire chief."

"Yes, indeed. Pleasant chap."

"Nigel's had a rough stay in our little burg, someone tried to kill him yesterday morning."

"Bloody uncivilized of them," the Sergeant-Major replied.

"Indeed," Nigel concurred.

"Strychnine, no less," Finn added.

"I say, that's a bit extreme."

"Sergeant-Major, would you mind keeping an eye on Nigel for me?" Finn asked, "If he doesn't make it through the festivities this morning in one piece, my ass is in hot water with his doctor."

"I say, can't have that. Come along, lad, I'll introduce you to me mates."

"Would there be any chance of a hot cup of tea?" Nigel asked.

"We've brought the portable tea pot with us," Lancaster said, "Never leave home without it."

Finn smiled as the two Brits trundled off toward a group of men talking with a couple of the Seals. He knew Lancaster would keep a close eye on his former student. He spotted Norm across the parking lot.

"What's the plan?" Finn asked his old friend.

"I think I'll go with a bluff, first. Ask for thirty more minutes."

"If that's a wash?"

"Tell him it will take thirty minutes to arrange a clear path to the lock. If that's where he's trying to get to."

"Either way, you're gonna get your thirty minutes."

"That's the plan. Give us time to close a perimeter on the location they are sending from too," Norm said.

Work continued on blocking off the intersections that would impede travel for anyone attempting to leave the rectangle. Finn saw the unique nature of islanders who normally didn't like to be told what to do, as they worked seamlessly with the Seals, and Norm's people to respond to the crisis. He knew they were running on empty at this point. The last four days had been fraught with tension in the face of the preparation for a storm the magnitude of Fiona.

"What's on your mind?" Norm's voice broke into the reverie.

"You don't want to know."

"LT," Big Dog spoke through the open channel of Norm's walkie-talkie.

"What's up, Big Dog?"

"We've got the bridge entrance blocked off."

"Ten four, good work. Over.

"Everything's quiet here, LT."

"Copy that, over and out."

"So, is this the result of that "Be Assertive" seminar you went to last year, dictating the terms?" Finn asked with a smirk.

"That's it, exactly," Norm smiled at Finn's tactic to keep it loose.

Royer returned from briefing his men and said, "We're ready to move in, whenever you give the word."

"Good, let's do our civic duty and welcome these gentlemen to the Southernmost place you don't want to be when you have pissed off the residents."

CHAPTER 26

The neighborhoods encompassed by the rectangle were a mix of residential and commercial uses. Now, waterlogged and weary, they stood eerily devoid of people as locals were taking the shelter-in-place order seriously. Limbs of various sizes were everywhere.

The Seals, with their armored vehicles led the way into the rectangle. They entered at the southwest end of it along Elizabeth Street. There was no sign of movement.

Finn glanced at his dive watch, twenty minutes remained of the hour. Ahead of them, Royer had stopped. The com link came alive with Royer's voice.

"Let's huddle up. Over."

"Copy that, over and out."

Finn and the others met Royer along the curb of the street.

"Ms. McIntosh," Royer said, referring to Cheryl McIntosh, Norm's second-in-command, "has notified me they are going to narrow the search area in a couple of minutes. Thought we should wait."

"Good move," Finn agreed.

"I hope Norm's bid for thirty more minutes works," Royer said.

"How much time?"

"Fourteen minutes."

"Getting something here," Royer said as he read a text.

"From Cheryl?" Rick asked.

Royer nodded, but continued to read. Finally, he said, "OK, it looks like we need to move northeast, toward Southard Street and the cemetery."

"We spend too much time around that cemetery lately," Nick said.

"We'll proceed cautiously, Norm doesn't want us to engage them until the hour expires."

They returned to the vehicles and waited for the Seals to roll.

The day grew lighter as the heavy cloud cover slowly dissipated. The air was still thick as a brick and the streets were soaked and dotted with large pools of standing water. The Seals moved ahead three blocks, then stopped at a pre-arranged intersection. They would wait here until the next communication from Andonov occurred.

Finn stopped the SUV ten yards from the Seals and put it in park. The minutes moved by slowly like a ditch digger in July. He could feel the tension, the uncertainty of the moment worked on everyone. The pup remained asleep in Tara's lap, but she was the only one not feeling the strain.

Suddenly Rick said, "You know, this reminds me of when my cousin got caught tupping a sheep."

"Tumping a sheep?" Tara asked.

"No, not tumping, tupping."

"What the hell is 'tupping'?" Angel wanted to know.

To everyone's surprise, Nigel spoke, "I think the OED, the Oxford English Dictionary, defines it as having intercourse with a sheep."

"Jesus Rick, your cousin was fucking a sheep?" Angel said.

"He'd eaten some shrooms, so we cut him some slack. It was back in north Florida when I was a kid."

"Would you be so kind as to reminds us of how that reminds you of this?" Finn said.

"Oh, I have a feeling our Euro-friends are fixin' to get tupped."

"Thanks for clearing that up," Finn said as he held up his right hand for silence. He pointed to his watch.

A few seconds later the gravelly voice of Andonov barked over the com channel.

"Your hour is up."

"Yes, it is, Mr. Andonov and we need thirty more minutes to finish the clean-up. We'll be happy to escort you to the lock at that time."

A long silence ensued. Finn wondered if Norm's direct approach would work.

Norm's voice broke the pause, "Thirty more minutes, if you harm any part of the desal plant, you'll have to fight your way to the lock, Mr. Andonov."

"Thirty minutes, Lieutenant."

Finn spotted Royer as he walked back toward them with a confident stride. He leaned in the driver's side window and said, "Norm must be a poker player, 'cause that was a helluva bluff."

"He said he'd get those extra thirty minutes," Finn said, "Now what?"

"We need to pinpoint their location. Then contain them."

"What about the sub?" Rick asked.

"That's the X factor, isn't it?" Royer said, then added, "I'm sending in a couple of recon teams on foot while we wait to get an electronic fix on them. We've got thirty minutes to find them."

Royer returned to his men. Finn sat with the others in the SUV with the A/C cranked up. As he looked over his companions he couldn't help but smile at the idea of this bunch as "concerned citizens." He smiled because of the irony that made it such in the time of the Big Tide. If you weren't concerned you were probably dead.

Participation, the cornerstone of democracy, was required in every aspect of life these days. Not just politics. The everyday challenges of living in Paradise these days required participation, there were no spectators. Only the tourists, who pretended they were locals, but knew their time in the Southernmost den of iniquity was limited, got a pass. Everyone else was working on a plan to separate the tourist from his money. Life revolved around creative ways to extract the tourist dollar from said tourist.

"I say, I hope your Commander Royer knows what he is doing," Nigel said, "These men are remorseless."

"My money is on the Commander," Finn said without hesitation.

"Must be the strychnine, I'm not usually this much of a nervous Nellie. Think I'll have a smoke," he said as he opened the rear tailgate door and stepped out.

"I can tell you I didn't feel that spry after I got poisoned," Finn said with a grin.

"I wonder if he's licensed to kill?" Rick mused.

"I would say that's a fact," Nick said, "He didn't blink when the idiots on the trail bikes showed up."

"The man needs to quit smoking," Tara said.

Finn read a text then said, "They've narrowed it down to a six block stretch along Grinnell Street."

"How's the time?" Nick asked.

"Fifteen minutes," Rick answered.

"They want us to follow the Seals," Finn told them.

"Then what?" Nick said.

"We follow the carefully orchestrated plan," Finn said with a straight face.

"We're playing this by ear," Nick surmised.

"Flexible response capability," Rick offered.

"We're playing this by ear," Nick repeated himself.

Nigel crawled back in the vehicle as the motorcade slowly moved forward again. One block from their destination the Seals again halted. Royer exited the lead truck and motioned for Finn and the others to join him.

"We've got about seven minutes to go. Whatever happens, we'll stand ready to respond the best we can," Royer told them.

Finn looked at the people in front of him. None of them had to be here. They chose to participate. To be a part of their time, not just a spectator of life, viewed from the safety of a gated community. These islanders, his people, his friends, would not be bullied, threatened, or intimidated. They waited grimly, but defiantly for the time to elapse.

"Your time is up, Lieutenant," a new voice spoke over the channel.

"To whom do I have the honor?" Norman responded cooly.

"It does not matter who I am. You have five minutes to reconsider or I will fire a torpedo into your desalinization plant's intake apparatus."

There was a long, hard silence that stuck in the air like a wad of phlegm in a coal miner's lung.

Suddenly a voice boomed through the speakers, "Unknown submarine, this is Captain Allen Smith of the United States Navy submarine Intrepid and I have two fish locked and loaded on your ass. Stand down and get the hell out of my waters."

In the parking lot, a subdued sound, turned into a roar as the men and women responded to the unexpected turn of events. Inside the rectangle, the Seals and other deployed personnel readied for the next move.

Norm's voice broke onto the open channel, "Mr. Andonov, I suggest you put your weapons down and surrender. Your submarine will be delayed."

Royer was using hand signals to indicate his men were to "saddle up" and get ready to roll. He had flour men still out on recon. Finn and the others followed suit and jumped back in their vehicle.

Norm's voice continued to buy time for the noose to be tightened around Antonov's location.

"There is no way off the island. I suggest you surrender."

"Surely, you don't think your pathetic little police force can stop me and my men?" Andonov replied.

"We've done pretty good so far," Norm said.

"We'll see, Lieutenant, we'll see."

The open channel went silent. Finn kept pace with the vehicle in front of him. They moved down the middle of the street toward the target ahead of them.

Finn could feel a renewed confidence among his friends, even the pup was awake and alert. Three blocks away, Finn could see a small industrial complex that of three buildings. The Seals slowed, then came to a halt in the middle of the street.

Royer was out of the vehicle before it completely stopped and coordinated the placement of the trucks and the troop carrier that completely blocked the road. He motioned for Finn to pull in close behind the truck nearest to them.

"Stalemate right now. They're in that complex of three buildings ahead on the left."

There was an eerie sense of a moment out of space and time, not your ordinary Saturday in the Conch Republic. Finn considered the enormous swing of events, and thanked St. Elmo for his patronage.

They all stood next to Finn as Royer described the situation, "We've got the roads blocked. Unless they can get by us or the hook and ladder truck at the other end of the street, they're not going anywhere."

"Remember, they've got at least one RPG," Nick reminded them.

"We've got snipers in place," Royer responded.

"Looks like Mr. Bulgaria has got himself in some deep shit," Angel said.

A Seal came running up to Royer and reported, "Sir, we think they're getting ready to make a break for it."

"Copy that, Sharkbait."

Suddenly gun fire and an explosion rocked the street. A second explosion sent some type of chemical fire thirty feet into the air. Three heavy-duty non-military hummers barreled out of the closest building to the street.

One peeled off and went toward the firetruck. The other two came directly toward the Seals. Everyone took cover behind the vehicles. Nick was sighting his Stoner over the hood of one of the Seals' trucks.

The Euro-thugs sped toward the barricade of vehicles. Automatic weapons fire burst from the windows of the advancing trucks. Nick sent one round through the driver's side windshield. The truck veered crazily as the driver slumped dead behind the wheel. Someone tried to snatch the wheel back, but overcorrected and the truck tilted, then righted itself and slammed into a light pole.

Several men were trying to extricate themselves from the truck. Finn watched as a burly man with Slavic features emerged from the disabled carrier. He shouted orders at the men around him. A man struggled out of the truck and fell on the ground by the man who Finn assumed was Andonov. He raised his hand for help, but the Bulgar pulled his sidearm and shot the man in the head.

Finn burned with an intensity most men never felt. The intensity of a man fed up. Fed up with greed, and senseless violence. Fed up with assholes who didn't want to live and let live. He'd had enough.

Nick nudged Angel and nodded toward Finn, "Keep an eye on him, I've never seen him like this before."

The skirmish raged on as the Seals blocked any line of escape. The Euros began to fall back, seeking the shelter of some of the houses on the residential side of the street.

Finn never lost sight of Andonov. Nick and Angel never lost sight of Finn. More back up arrived but sporadic gunfire ripped through the air.

Finn followed Andonov down a line of frangipani trees between two bungalow-style houses. From ten feet away, Finn could see Andonov was about six feet, four, nearly Angel's size. But much beefier. A thick, muscled guy with no fat.

Finn, at a shade over six feet, seemed at a noticeable disadvantage in a hand-to-hand situation with this mercenary. But his daily training regimen in the Krav Maga fighting technique was demanding and kept him in shape.

The Bulgar was attempting to communicate with someone on his phone, he did not hear Finn approach.

"Mr. Andonov, I presume," Finn said with a flat voice.

"Who the fuck are you," he said as he eyed the Desert Eagle in Finn's left hand.

There was no answer from the man, only a stare that would have chilled Leatherface. Andonov suddenly threw the phone at Finn and raised his gun to shoot but Finn fired a shot slightly to the right of the large man's head.

"Put the gun down. I'll do the same."

The mercenary grinned and said, "Whatever you say, bossman."

He slowly dropped the gun.

"Step away."

The man complied and Finn holstered his Desert Eagle.

The big man charged like a rhino, Finn flexed his knees and crouched in anticipation of the attack. As the man neared, Finn shifted his weight and caught the Bulgar with an elbow strike to the temple. The blow would have knocked most men unconscious, but the burly man shook his head and cursed in pain.

He regained his balance and sized up the smaller man in front of him. Finn remained still, Andonov pulled a knife from a sheath on his leg. Several feet away, Nick and Angel stood behind a banyan tree watching the drama in front of them.

"I'm going to help," Angel told his friend. Nick grabbed his arm and held him, "Not yet."

Andonov moved warily to his left, but closer to Finn. The knife in his hand, moving in a sinuous manner as he tried to mesmerize Finn's focus. Gunfire erupted close by but Finn remained undistracted.

The big man lunged forward, timing it with a slashing downward motion of his arm that held the knife. Finn grabbed the man's arm as he brought it down and used the man's momentum to pitch him forward. The mercenary lost his footing and stumbled to one knee.

Finn waited. His opponent scrambled to his feet, sensing the man in front of him was not some drunk parrothead. Gunfire continued in the distance. The Bulgar moved closer, waving the knife in a slow arc in front of him.

Suddenly Finn moved like a moray eel, slipping inside the arc of the knife, he snap-kicked the man's right knee and the sound of cartilage tearing was heard as he screamed in pain.

Finn stared at his opponent, hobbled on one leg.

The Bulgar flipped the knife in the air, grabbed it as it came down and threw it at Finn. The blade flashed by inches from Finn's face as he remained steady and dodged the thrown weapon with a minimal expenditure of energy.

"Mr. Andonov, you should not have come here," Finn said in a tone that would have pleased Hannibal Lecter.

"Fuck you, asshole. What are you going to do, one of those American citizen's arrest pieces of bullshit?"

"No, nothing like that," Finn said.

Andonov pulled a small pistol from his boot, but Finn reacted in a blur; he kicked the pistol from the man's grip and in the same motion circled behind him placing the Bulgar in a full Nelson as he drove him to one knee.

Finn's grip was like steel. He slowly began to twist the man's head. The mercenary struggled, in vain.

"You've caused us a lot of problems, Mr. Andonov. You killed innocent people," Finn said as he twisted the thick neck harder.

"I know you're bluffing, asshole. You don't have the balls to kill me."

Finn applied a steady, relentless torque until Nick and Angel standing twenty feet away heard the sickening snap of the man's neck. They rushed toward Finn who responded with a defensive posture until he realized who was coming toward him.

"Finn, are you OK?" Nick asked as he looked at his friend with concern.

"Holy shit, that guy's huge," Angel said, "And very dead."

Finn's gaze was distant, directed at some faraway thought or place. Nick offered his friend some water from a canteen, "Here, man, drink some of this."

Finn grasped the canteen and slowly he saw the face of his friend come into focus before him. He blinked, then seemed to remember where he was.

"That was krav maga, wasn't it?" Angel asked.

Finn silently nodded.

More emergency vehicles arrived as Antonov's men began to surrender under the withering assault of the Seals and Norm's island personnel.

Nick could see his mentor was trying to come back from the place he had been moments ago. As a former marine sniper, Nick knew the feeling of detachment needed to complete an unsavory task. Finn's head wound had re-opened and blood trickled down the side of his face. He absently brushed his fingers across the dripping blood and stared at it in his hand.

"Finn, talk to us," Angel said in a gentle voice.

"Is everyone Jake?" Finn managed weakly.

"We left Rick and Tara with the Seals. I've sent Norm a text," Nick said, "let him know their leader is down for the count."

"Can you believe that sub got here in time?" Angel said.

"Better to be lucky, than good, sometimes," Finn said.

"Let's get back to the wheels," Angel said, "You need to put a new dressing on your scalp wound, Finn."

When they arrived, Nigel was going through some carrying cases. He saw them and motioned them his way. They found Royer and some of his men pulling similar cases from one of the abandoned vehicles the Euro-gang used in their getaway attempt.

"I say, Finn, we've found the art work. Your Dr. Sullivan was right.'

"We found something else, too," Norm said as he walked into view from around another truck.

"What's that, L.T.?" Nick asked.

"The fence. And two of his accomplices. There in the first building. All dead. It looks like Santos decided to cut out the middle man completely."

"That would explain why we couldn't find him," Nigel said, "Leftenant, I think we should be judicious in reporting the situation. This may be just the thing to ferret out our mole. If we play our cards right."

"Agreed," Norm said.

People began to appear on the street as Conch Radio gave the "all-clear" to leave their homes. Some appeared shell-shocked n the aftermath of Fiona and the threat of a breach to the breakwater.

Nick pulled Angel to the side, out of earshot from the others, "No need to mention that to anyone. If Finn wants to talk about it, that's up to him."

Angel gave a silent nod of agreement then said, "Semper fi" as he fist bumped Nick.

CHAPTER 27

They arrived at the inn several hours later after the art work was secured in a vault in John Rocco's office building. Casualties had been light for the home team; mostly non-fatal wounds but two feral chickens had been caught in a crossfire and were destined for the early-bird island kebab at the Caribbean jerk shack in Bahama Village.

Kate checked out Nigel first with a professional eye, her eye brows raised when she took his blood pressure. She stared at him, "Your pressure reads like a man half your age, one that doesn't smoke," Kate said in a tone of exasperation.

"I'm sure it's the lovely ambience of your fair island, my dear."

Kate faltered for a moment as she looked at James Bond, then she smiled, and said, "now, let's take a look at you," as she gently turned Finn's head in her hand to look at the makeshift dressing that had been applied to the re-opened wound.

"Tara did that in the field," Finn told her.

"Good job, Tara," Kate told her grad assistant and best friend.

"Thanks."

Kate sensed Finn was preoccupied with something. She conveniently suggested he come with her to "take his blood pressure" away from the hubbub of the crowded lobby. He followed her to one of the parlor rooms and they sat down on one of the settees.

"Finn, what's wrong?"

He slowly took her hand, felt the strength there. He looked in her eyes and saw the resolve and perseverance of a good soul.

"I'm not good with words."

"You don't have to be. Your actions speak eloquently enough, believe me."

"There's a fine line between a terrorist and a freedom fighter," he said, "Kate, in my past life, I killed for my country. But, truth be told, there is not much difference between me and a guy like Andonov."

"Oh Finn, that's not true."

"It is, Kate. And I need for you to understand that before we go house hunting."

Kate saw the unguarded eyes of the man she admired and thought she loved. She felt the turmoil and angst of a man's honesty, in his self-examination.

"Finn, I understand that you are the least co-dependent person I have ever known. I understand you hear a different drummer. But you are not a raving psychopath and if I'm not mistaken Tara's rescue pup seems to like you. Dogs are hard to fool, Finn."

"There's a ringing endorsement."

Sunday morning featured the sun that had not been seen in nearly four days. Work on the gazebo was in full swing along with a Sunday brunch on the grounds at the B and B. Hogfish nuggets, grits, Caribbean omelets, sliced fruit were laid out on picnic tables not far from the gazebo.

"I still can't get my head around the last few days," Rick said as he hammered a new strut into place.

"Key West weird, for sure," Nick agreed.

"The only thing that didn't happen was Robert the Doll going for a stroll during the storm," Tara said.

"When will you be starting up the new ghost ours, Finn?" Norm wanted to know.

Vonda James, laughed and said, "Oh my God, I remember those, Finn you were a teenager."

"Just about."

Tara helped Nick replace some of the damaged lattice work as Finn sat at the picnic table next to Kate. The morning heat was not uncomfortable and a stiff breeze from the west helped to dry out the waterlogged town.

Camille Garnier's shop had survived Fiona's wrath. She meted out bowls of her Bayou Teche' gumbo for all who wanted it as she stood by the table talking to Sher.

John Rocco and Angel, walked around the corner carrying several sheets of plywood for the gazebo.

"Really appreciate the help with the gazebo," Rick said.

"We really appreciate a place to stay during the bad-ass storm," Tara shot back.

"Indeed," Nigel added. He drank a steaming cup of tea but didn't push his luck with a smoke.

"Nigel, you'll have to come back sometime, when someone's not trying to kill you," Finn said.

"Did they find the whiskey?" Angel called from the gazebo."

"Yes, in with the art," Nigel told them.

"The home team pulls through," Finn said.

"You're a lucky man, mate," Nigel said to Finn. "I don't know what more you could want."

Finn realized the likable Brit was keenly correct. The threat of losing that intangible thing called family, had galvanized him into extreme action. Action he would take again, if confronted with the same threats.

The focus for the next weeks would be recovering from Fiona and the assault on the island by the Euro-thugs. Norm would co-ordinate a task force to improve security at the central lock and upgrade portions of the breakwater as needed. The others would slowly return to their everyday tasks as inn keepers, marine biologists, entrepreneurs, and thugs, as Kate referred to Finn and Nick. Likable thugs.

One thug would be house hunting while the other would be assisting the assistant with collecting some post-storm samples. Not very thugly in Finn's mind, but times were changing. Hell, Snoop Dog was family-friendly these days and Death Row Records had a deal with Taylor Swift. Go figure.

Hurricane season was not over, far from it. Two more months of trying to reason … The Weather Channel folks quickly moved out headed for the next disaster leaving the island to deal with the massive clean up. Conch Radio was on 24/7 with helpful directions and "boil water" announcements.

There had not been a problem with looting in the Conch Republic since the early days of the Big Tide. Three trap poachers were caught red-handed up on Big Pine Key. Finn had been there that day and remembered what happened.

Times were hard, in the first months after the water rose to the current level. People were struggling, kids didn't have enough to eat. These three, showed no remorse for their action. Taking food that wasn't theirs, with no regard to who might be going hungry.

The crowd that gathered that day at the intersection of what had been US1 and Key Deer Boulevard were all long-time Piners. A small armada of personal water craft from fishing boats to jet skis bobbed in the water under the traffic light.

The three poachers were handcuffed but defiant. Finn watched from his work boat. The locals were a surly crowd that day. Poaching was a serious offense in the new seascape of the Big Tide.

A kangaroo court of sorts found the trio guilty of poaching. When they began to throw ropes over the crossbar that held the traffic signal the poachers began to struggle. They were clubbed to the deck of the boat with gaffs, then hoisted into the air.

The bodies were left to rot and to remind it was not a good idea to steal from your neighbor. Finn doubted there would be a problem after Fiona.

Finn remembered those difficult days as he watched his friends carry on with the task of rebuilding the gazebo. The laughter, the banter that flowed easily among people who knew each other well, made Finn smile. Even the pup, Fiona, sensed no immediate threats as she gamboled on the grass next to Tara.

"Instead of mimosas this morning, I've mixed up a batch of Mangrove Martinis," Sher said, "If anyone is interested."

"No offense," Finn said, "But, I think I'll stick with the coffee."

The End – *For Now*

THE BIG TIDE CHRONICLES IV
A SMUGGLER'S MOON

The November sun glistened on the bay that stretch into the Straits of Florida from New Havana on the northern coast of Cuba. The Big Tide had reshaped the islands of the Caribbean with its rising waters. It reduced their land mass and caused the relocation of thousands of people to higher ground.

Most of the islands, were themselves the top sections of numerous submarine mountains that stretched across the reef infested waters of the Caribbean Sea. New Havana maintained its stately ambience through a mix of the surviving Spanish architecture built on high ground and the blend of people who came to Havana for various reasons.

A weather-worn sloop rode on the hook in a small inlet just north of the city. The water lapped gently against the sloop as two men casually fished over the side. They wore shorts and tank tops. Ball caps shaded their faces, but each wore a pair of polarized sunglasses to reduce the incessant glare and to be able to read the water in the unrelenting sun.

The younger of the two men wore his hair in a single braided pony tail that reached to his waist. The older man had close-cropped dark hair in a casual military cut. The Cuban patrol boat had stopped by earlier. Their papers were in order; the Policia didn't search hard enough to find the hidden compartment built into the faux wall of the front cabin.

"They'll be back," Finn said when they were gone.

"We'll be ready," Nick answered and cast a shiny baitfish into the clear, calm water.

"It's the 'politics of contraband, it's the smuggler's blues,'" Finn said with a smirk.

Visit circulartides.com for more information

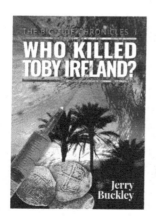 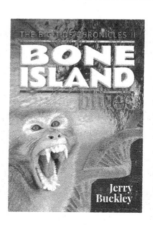 

home of: THE BIG TIDE CHRONICLES